the
BOOKWRM
box

Helping the community, one book at a time

BECAUSE YOU'RE MINE

NEW YORK TIMES BESTSELLING AUTHOR

CLAIRE CONTRERAS

CLAIRE CONTRERAS

BECAUSE
YOU'RE
mine

NEW YORK TIMES BESTSELLING AUTHOR
CLAIRE CONTRERAS

Copyright © 2018 by Claire Contreras

Cover Design: By Hang Le

Editor: Mara White

ISBN: **978-0999584460**

ONE

CATALINA

"I HAVE A HUGE FAVOR TO ASK."

I look up from the floor, where I'm stretching my feet, and raise an eyebrow at my sister. "Last time you asked for a huge favor, it ended with me moving to another continent."

"This is nothing like that." Her cheeks flush as she sits down in front of me and starts stretching her own legs.

I take in her attire—yoga pants and a loose fitting t-shirt. Her dark red hair is up in a high ponytail. Growing up, people always confused us for twins. Being nineteen months apart and having the same light skin and red hair will do that, I guess. She got the lighter eyes, though, which I'm eternally jealous of. We're similar in a lot of ways, from our build to our fighting spirit, but Emma is much more outgoing than I am. At a party, I'm the wallflower, while she's the center of attention. Around men, she's smiley and flirty. I'm more reserved.

The only place I let myself stand out is on center stage. The moment I step off, I keep my head down. That's one reason why I hesitate every time my sister asks me for a favor. I was living in London a couple of years ago when Emma called begging me to come back home. There had been a late night special on people with ties to organized crime and lo and behold, most of the men in our family were featured in it. It's not like I didn't know about it. I'm not stupid, but I never in a million years thought it would ever come out so publicly. I mean, everyone is supposed to look at the mafia in a romantic light. They don't want to see people gunned down or businesses burned to the ground. They don't want to feel unsafe in their own neighborhoods. Why couldn't the news just let people have their false sense of reality and leave our family out of it? Maybe if it hadn't affected our lives as much as it did I wouldn't care. It's not like I had a solid relationship with my father before all of that, but Mom packed her bags up and virtually vanished from our lives because she didn't want to deal with the aftermath of it all.

Out of the three of us, it affected my sister the most. It devastated her, not only because it attracted attention to us based on our family name alone, but also because she'd made a career of exposing criminals and wrongdoers, gaining millions of followers on social media for her "woke mentality." All things that would be gone in an instant if anyone caught wind that she was Joseph Masseria's daughter.

My sister though . . . the news devastated her, not only because it brought too much attention on our family, but because she'd made a career out of pulling the veil back on criminals and wrongdoers. To make matters worse, she felt the need to break up with her boyfriend and move away. It was too much, she'd said. Thankfully, the documentary left us out of it, but it wasn't enough. When she called crying, saying she needed me here, I came. I left The Royal Ballet where I'd been dancing and auditioned for the New York City Ballet, thankfully landing a job there, which made my move a lot more enticing.

I start applying ointment to my feet and massaging it in. My sister's doing barre stretches when she meets my eyes again. She's been quiet this whole time, which scares me a little.

2

"I was offered an opportunity to write an article about some people who are cheating the system so to speak. I'd have to go to Chicago and Boston," she says, rushing to reassure me that she's not going back home for good. "I'd only be gone three weeks—tops."

"But what about school?" School is the reason Emma moved to New York a few years back. She's been attending Columbia and working on getting her journalism degree.

"That's the favor."

I stop rubbing my feet and gape at her. "You're joking."

"It's only one class. I'm three credits away from graduation and this class is perfect for what I'm currently working on," she says, her eyes lighting up. "And it's only twice a week. You'll be in and out, I swear."

"You can't take it online?"

"Not this one." She gives me this look like she's going to cry if I say no. "Please? I'll give you my firstborn."

I laugh. "What makes you think I'd want your firstborn? If it's anything like you, it would be snippy and inquisitive and never shut the fuck up."

"Hey." She leans in and pinches my inner thigh. I yelp and slap her hand away.

"Dammit, Emmaline."

She smiles at me. "Please? It's only two days a week."

I sigh heavily, rubbing the area she pinched. Bitch. "What days?"

"Tuesdays and Thursdays."

"Time?"

"Ten thirty to eleven thirty."

My jaw drops. "Emma."

"I know, I know." She cringes. "It will be tight with rehearsals."

"Tight is a hell of an optimistic term. I was thinking impossible. Did you already register?"

3

"I just did the other day, but it's full so I'm in the top ten on the wait-list."

I stand up and *battement* to loosen my hips. "Are you going to yoga?"

"Yeah. Wanna come?"

I think it over. I'm sore as hell, but that's nothing new. Maybe yoga would help loosen my muscles a little more tonight. "Yeah. I'll go."

Emma links her arm through mine as we head down to the lobby and walk from our apartment building to the yoga studio we frequent down the block.

"So?" she asks.

"I'll do it," I say. "But no more favors for at least two years."

"Deal." She smiles wide.

"And you owe me like three protein shakes when you get back from Chicago."

"Deal."

"And some new leotards."

"Deal." She laughs, opening the door to the studio and pulling me in. "What ever happened to the dancewear line that asked to sponsor you?"

"I haven't had time to go over the contract yet." I sigh heavily. I haven't had time for much lately. Not that I normally have much time, but still, between performances and rehearsals I've barely had a chance to breathe.

"You should really let Dad give you money for your own dancewear line, Cat. He's dying to help you out."

"No." My voice is definitive. "I'm not taking blood money. I can't believe you'd even suggest that."

"I know he's done messed up things in the past, but he's not a bad man," she says quietly. I shoot her a look. She cringes. "Not a terrible man. He loves us you know."

"I'm too exhausted to argue with you right now."

"Seriously, Cat. I get that what happened was heartbreaking

for you, traumatizing, even, but dad always had the best intentions in mind," she says. "Think about it. Look at everything you've accomplished. You've lost, you've mourned, it's time for you to live a little."

She's not wrong. I do need to live a little. I've had ten years to heal from the losses and I have, I'm fine, but every so often something happens—I'll see an expecting mother or a happy couple—and a wave of emotion comes crashing down on me. I focus on yoga and clear my mind. It's why I've done so well for myself in the dance world, focusing on movement and stacking up performances helps me clear my mind, or maybe it just keeps me so occupied that I don't have to think about anything else – not the dead ex-fiancé, not the missing mother, and definitely not my future which is what frightens me most. After yoga, when my sister and I are on our way home, I ask her about the class again.

"You realize if it's a math class, I'll fail." She already knows this, but I feel it bears repeating.

Emma laughs. "I would never ask you to take a math class. I want to keep my almost perfect grade-point average."

"So, what class is it?"

"The Evolution of Organized Crime in America."

I stumble over my own feet. "You're joking."

Emma grabs my arm. "Oh, come on."

"What if they start talking about Dad or Gio or Frankie or Wallace?" I whisper-shout.

"We use mom's last name for a reason," she reminds me.

I scoff. "Yeah, because mom's side of the family is so much better."

"Well, at least they're not spotlighted on CNN specials."

"Not yet," I mutter, my stomach roils with the thought. "I can't believe you signed up for this course. As if you need any more knowledge on organized crime. Didn't we do enough Googling? I'm pretty sure we're experts by now."

She snorts. "I want to see if there's anything interesting. I'm pretty sure the professor is a former FBI agent, so that'll be a cool take on our family history."

"Oh yeah. So interesting." I shake my head, upset with the fact that I'm the one who has to sit through it. "Does Gio know about this?"

"No, but what's he going to say?"

"I don't know, that siblings aren't supposed to turn against siblings?"

"If he really felt that way, he'd already be pissed off at me for my blog." She shrugs. "Besides, I bet they don't even cover up to our generation."

I hope not. I don't want to give my sister the reputation of the girl who puked all over the classroom.

TWO

LORENZO

I RARELY SLEEP. As far as I'm concerned, it's a waste of time. Time I could be using to make money or figure out ways to make it. So when the phone rings in the middle of the night, I'm not surprised. People know they can call me any time and more likely than not, I'll answer if they're worth my time, and looking at my friend Ben's name on the screen I know this will definitely be worth my time.

"Tell me you have good news," I say by way of greeting.

"I have good news."

I smile. "You found her."

"Sort of. Her sister registered for the class I'm teaching this semester."

"That is good news." I grin. If I track the sister, I'll get to the girl. "What class? Some FBI shit?"

"A class on organized crime."

I blink in the darkness. "You're joking."

"Not joking."

"That's a class?"

He chuckles. "Believe it or not, people are actually paying thousands of dollars to take it."

"You're an idiot. Why not teach it on your own and pocket the money?"

"Because there's a thing called tenure and I'm trying to get it," he says. "Besides, I like teaching at a college level. If I open my doors to everyone, I'll have assholes like you coming in and rebutting everything I say."

"So you're admitting your teaching is shit? Is that what's happening right now? Should I call the dean of the school and report this?"

He laughs. "Asshole."

"Are you in town or still down in Miami?"

"Still down here."

"When are you heading up?"

He's quiet for a beat. "Why are you asking? You thinking about coming down?"

I yawn. "Shit, why not? I can work on my tan and check out a few things."

"I'm sure you'll be working down here," he says with an amused chuckle. "Let me know when you land."

I hang up the phone and call my friend who pilots private jets. Sometimes he's flying empty planes back and forth to and from Miami to park them or pick up his clients. If I'm lucky, I can get on one of those flights and head down. The sooner the better.

THREE

CATALINA

IT'S REALLY NOT unusual for my sister to chase stories for different newspapers she freelances for, so having her gone isn't really that crazy. It's the fact that she asked me for this massive favor because she knew there was no chance of me saying no. I'm not much of a no person. Obviously. I take a deep breath as I step into the auditorium. I'm ten minutes early, so I'm hoping to snag a seat in the front. Instead, I find myself with my back pressed up against the side of the room, shoulder to shoulder with two other students with the same intentions. I'm baffled by this. In all my years, I've never seen anything like it. It almost makes me want to scream and tell them to find another interest to sink their teeth into. Surely they don't need to know about crime.

"This is only his second semester teaching here and I heard the first semester the class was even more crowded than this one," one student whispers to another.

"I'm only taking this class because I heard he's so hot," another student whispers back.

I feel my eyes bulge out of my face. They can't be serious.

My sister needs this class for real and these idiots are in here for kicks? I say this aloud and both heads turn toward me.

"Why do you care?" one of them asks. She's a blonde, uppity type I know well because I've been surrounded by them my whole life.

"I care because I'm on a waiting list and I need this class for reasons other than gawking at the stupid professor."

"Well, you should've registered sooner." She purses her lips and rolls her eyes, looking back at the front of the room.

"Unless James Dean is teaching the damn class, there's no need for this foolishness and last time I checked he died over sixty years ago," I say, feeling like the only reasonable human being in a room full of teeny-boppers. Even though this is an upper level course, I'm sure, at the most, I'm only a year older than the others. It's not like college has an age restriction.

The doors open again and this time the room fills with gasps and whispers. I turn in anticipation, but the row of people standing in front blocks the view of the door. It feels like an eternity before I get a glimpse of something, and even then it's only a hand swinging a matte black motorcycle helmet as the professor walks toward the desk in the center of the room. I snort. *Can this get any more cliché?* He puts it down on the corner of the desk with a thump and sets a messenger bag in the middle with another thump. He glances around the room, taking off his leather jacket as he does and tossing it over the chair behind him. It lands perfectly folded over the back without him even turning. I roll my eyes. Now he's just putting on a show, but I get the appeal. He's what my friends would call *panty-dropping-gorgeous*, with a well-defined jaw and dark brown hair that stands in every direction, probably from the helmet. Whatever the case, it makes you want to run your fingers through it in an attempt to tame it. His mouth is full and sinful and when it moves into a ghost of a smile, my heart trips. *So, I get it. I get it.* I glance back at the blonde repeat student from before and she smirks at me like she's proved a point. I roll my eyes just because.

"We have a full house here," the professor says, his deep voice matching his over-the-top-sex appeal. "I can't have you standing on the stairs. It's a fire hazard. You'll either have to sit up here on the floor in front of my desk or come visit me during office hours."

We all rush to sit on the floor and take a seat crisscross-apple-sauce in front of his desk like we're in grade school. A part of me is disgusted with myself because for starters, I practically ran to the front of the room and secondly, I'm looking up impatiently, like a damn dog wagging its tail as it waits for a treat. What the hell is wrong with me? I'm acting like a groupie. *It's the hair*. No. It's those muscled forearms. At least that's what I tell myself, but then I get a glimpse of his eyes and I don't even know what color they are because they bounced away from me so quickly, but *Holy Moses,* they're enchanting. A sign-in sheet is handed out on a clipboard and I sign my name at number eight. If there are eight people ahead of me, I'm never going to get in this class. *Fuckers.*

"Let's kick this off by talking about Italian immigration and the origin of small-time crime in America," the professor starts, pacing the room in front of us.

He's wearing jeans, black Converse, and a plaid button down with the sleeves rolled up. He rolls them some more, exposing more of those thick tanned forearms. Did he tan recently and if so, where? Because New York has been rainy and definitely not tan-friendly lately. Or maybe he's naturally that olive color? Inquiring minds want to know.

"Some of you probably think of organized crime and relate it to *The Godfather*," he says, smiling a bit as he looks around the room. "Am I right?"

Everyone starts chattering, mostly in agreement. He ignores them and continues.

"A lot of these people came from Sicily and other parts of Italy, where organized crime was already established. It wasn't like *The Godfather*, by the way. Italian-Americans wanted those ideals over here. If it does so well in Italy, why not bring them?"

"Did they report back to the people in Sicily and all the other places?" someone asks.

"They did. In fact, the orders came from Italy."

"Why not just start over?" another asks. Someone else asks, "Did they have to share a portion of their income?"

"To answer the easier of the questions, yes they did share their income. It works sort of like a pyramid, but not a pyramid scheme," he says with a chuckle. Most of the class laughs along. "To answer the first question, starting over is difficult. If you already have everything laid out for you, why not use that as a stepping stone?"

"Because you have your own ideals and want to be independent," I surprise myself by saying aloud.

It takes every ounce of me not to slap my hand over my mouth. I'm not supposed to be calling attention to myself for any reason, dammit. The black Converse shoes stop directly in front of me. I swallow and force myself to drag my eyes up the dark jeans, past the button down that presses onto him so completely, the unbuttoned collar up top, the jawline, the light beard, the straight nose, and finally his eyes, which are an intense light brown hue that's almost golden and make me forget my name for a moment.

"You're assuming they have different standards." He puts his hands in his pockets as he looms over me.

"It's not an assumption. If they were on board with the way things were run, they would have kept a capo di tutti capi and let things be, but they didn't."

He opens his mouth, closes it, and frowns at me. "What's your name?"

"Emmaline."

"Emmaline," he repeats and I get this strange sensation with the way he says it that makes me want to reach into his mouth and take out my sister's name and replace it with mine. What the hell? He speaks before I have a chance to fully process what just transpired. "You Italian, Emmaline?"

"Half." I fight the urge to glance away or look down and let my hair curtain over my face as he scrutinizes me. Thankfully, he only does it for a beat before going back to his lecture.

"So, let's assume they didn't want to be under the rule of one boss," he says, pacing again. "What do you do? Even criminals follow an order. You don't want things to get out of hand, right?"

"You create a gang," one guy calls out. Another laughs.

"Not a gang. The mob," another one says.

"The mob is a gang," a girl says.

"Obviously," another adds.

I grit my teeth and drop my attention to the floor. I hate that they associate organized crime with gangs. They're not entirely wrong of course, but still. It's like how you feel entitled to make fun of your friends and family but no one else can. The tips of the Converse shoes come into view again, stopping directly in front of me.

"Is it fair to call the mob a gang?" he asks, and because I feel he's talking to me, my gaze snaps to his once more. My pulse quickens when I find him looking directly at me.

"I mean . . ." I start and stop speaking, my brows pulling in slightly as I start again, "A gang is by definition a group of criminals, but the way modern society thinks of gangs is like Bloods and Crypts and people who go around shooting up rival gang members."

"Isn't that what the mob does?" a girl behind me argues. "They go around killing people for no reason whatsoever."

"That's a misconception." I look over my shoulder trying to

place who said it, but can't because the auditorium is beyond capacity.

My answer, of course, is something I tell myself to help me sleep at night. I hope like hell they don't just go around taking people's lives. In truth, I don't know what the heck they do. It's not like we talked about any of that at the dinner table. I just know my father is a very highly respected business man in Chicago and if you ever say my last name—his last name—there, people treat you like royalty. It doesn't change the fact that I don't plan on going back any time soon. That last name has burned me on more than one occasion.

"And you would know this how?" blondie up top asks. "You in the mob?"

"No." I shut my mouth and scowl before responding, "I'm just saying, organized crime rings weren't formed with the intent to commit violence. Were they doing illegal things? Yes, but they weren't killers."

"You like to differentiate your criminals, Emmaline? Treat some a little better than others?" the professor asks.

I glance up at him again, feeling a blush creep up on my neck, from the amusement sparking in his eyes as he watches me. Yeah, I definitely see the appeal to this man.

"I'm just stating that not all criminals are killers."

The guy beside me shakes his head. I hear chatter behind me that tells me they disagree. I cross my arms because I really don't give a shit what their opinion is. As far as I'm concerned, they don't have a right to opine unless they're directly affected by it anyway.

"Has anyone started reading the text?" the professor asks. "What did you find?"

"They created The Commission to bring about order," a girl behind me says. "Obviously that was a stupid idea."

I bite my lip and look at the floor in front of me, wishing

my brother could be a fly on the wall. I feel myself smile as I picture what his reaction would be to these people's questions.

"Who's heard of Charles Luciano?" the professor asks. I look up quickly and our eyes collide once again. "Emmaline?"

"He formed The Commission so that the families who came from different parts of Italy could organize."

"Hmm." The way that *hmm* vibrates in his throat makes my pulse quicken. I lick my lips and look at the tips of his shoes again. "You must have watched more than a few mafia movies."

"You could say that."

"Well, let me be the first to say that it's nothing like in the movies."

"And you would know." I raise an eyebrow.

"Evidentially, since I'm the one teaching the course."

The class laughs at that.

"Is that why you teach under an alias?" I taunt, knowing damn well I'm poking the bear and clearly not giving a shit how hard the bite will be. "You're trying to conceal your identity from the big bad wolves?"

He chuckles as he paces to the other side of the room, but it sounds forced like he's trying to rein in his anger. "Whether I choose to use my legal name or SpongeBob Square Pants is none of your concern."

The class laughs again. I shrug because he's right. One point for hot professor guy. What the hell do I care what name he uses? He continues his lecture and thankfully doesn't call on me anymore. After class, he asks those of us sitting on the floor to come check in with him, so we all form a single-file line. I'm standing behind two friends who keep whining about which of them will make it and which won't and how the one who does can just take sneaky pictures for the other. Annoyance sears through me once more. My sister is going to be bummed but I definitely won't be able to get into this class. There's no way. I start texting her to let her know while listening to the girl in

15

front of me flirt and giggle and even invite the professor to a party. I catch the tail-end of that conversation and bring my phone up to semi-hide my face.

"I don't attend student parties," he says in a bored tone as if he can't be bothered with a twenty-something hitting on him.

"Oh. Well, we can do coffee or whatever," she says.

"I don't do coffee *or whatever* with students either."

"Oh. Okay. Maybe after the semester is over," she says.

"Probably not," he says with a finality in his tone that has her scurrying off without saying another word.

That's gotta be embarrassing. I almost feel bad for the girl. I lower my phone and stand in front of his desk. He starts marking things and switching from one page to the other and from my vantage point I can't really see what's what, but I do think it's funny that his notebook has graph paper, which I haven't seen since high school.

"Little Red," he says, still marking up the notebook in front of him. I frown, unsure of whether or not he's talking to me. I do have red hair, though, so *maybe?*

"Excuse me?"

He glances up. "I take it your mother is the Italian half?"

"Father."

"With the last name Álvarez?"

"Oh. That's my mom's." I wave in dismissal. "Long story."

"Hmm." His eyes scan my face and I swear they glow, feeling like the stroke of a match against my skin with every inch he takes in. I'm pretty sure my face turns at least twenty different shades of red.

"Excuse me, but I need to get to my next class," the guy behind me says.

"Sorry. I'll be quick." I glance at him and back at the professor. "What do I need to do?"

"Come by my office on Thursday."

"Will I be able to get into the class?"

"Thursday at three o'clock is the final drop day, so I should know by then."

I sigh. "No one is going to drop this class."

"You'd be surprised."

"There are like twenty people on this list alone," I argue. "And most of them are only here to gawk at you, which makes this really unfair."

His eyes glitter in amusement. "And you?"

"What about me?"

"What are you here for? Not to gawk?"

"Obviously not." I roll my eyes. "It's my last semester and I need this class."

"What's your major?"

"I really need to get to my next class," the guy says again.

I sigh again, but this time I make an annoyed sound and signal him to go ahead. The professor looks over at the guy and hands him the sign-up sheet to add his email address. The guy gives it back and exits the classroom, leaving me and the professor by ourselves.

"So, do you think I can get in?" I ask again.

"I don't think you need this class." He stands up, and only then do I really notice how tall he actually is.

I'm wearing sneaker wedges today, but still. He must be at least six-three. And those hands. I'm a hands girl. They look like they're well-used. I watch as he unrolls his shirt and buttons each sleeve, then puts his jacket back on before picking up his helmet and messenger bag. It all happens in a fluid motion that probably only takes a few seconds, but my throat is parched from experiencing the show all over again, because *damn* he is hot and maybe I would sign up just to gawk like those groupies after all.

He must be between thirty-five and forty, I gather, then shake the thought away because it really doesn't matter. I'm trying to become a student in his class and he doesn't do *things* with students. And even if he did, I've vowed off men and if he is FBI like Emma thinks, I definitely cannot get involved with this one. Not even as a friend. Not even as an acquaintance. Gio wouldn't approve and Dad . . . the thought alone makes me shiver.

"I just told you that I need the credits," I say, returning to the task at hand.

"What's your major?"

"Journalism."

"Shouldn't you be taking an English course?" He signals me to start walking toward the door. I do. He falls into step beside me. He even smells good, this guy.

"Already did."

He stops walking when we get to the end of the building. There's a group of guys wearing purple fraternity shirts tossing around a football nearby and some other people scattered around the lawn. I take it all in and think I could've totally come to school here. Not that I regret studying abroad, but still, this seems fun.

"I'm only in my office on Thursday from eleven-thirty to twelve-thirty," he says suddenly.

My eyes snap to his. "I can't make it at that time."

I wasn't even going to come to class that day. I figured I'd befriend someone and copy their notes. Thursday is a full dress rehearsal and those always take longer.

"You either make it, or you don't." He shrugs. "How bad do you want this?"

Not at all, I want to say, but don't because my sister would kill me if I lost this opportunity. On the other hand, I can't jeopardize my own career and job for a stupid class.

"I really can't make it at that time."

"I'm going to be honest with you, Emmaline." He tilts his head, his eyes scanning my face. "I don't want you in my class at all, so I'll be glad if you don't go."

I blink and blink again. "That's rude to say."

"It's the truth. Take it or leave it." He walks away.

I gape, watching him retreat. It takes my brain a second too long to kick my feet in motion, but as soon as it does I'm scrambling after him.

"But why?"

"I only teach one course a year and I do it because I enjoy it. I don't enjoy people calling me out in front of an auditorium and asking me about my name. I enjoy teaching because people are hungry to learn, not because I like to be challenged about how much I know or how I know it."

"Do you work for the FBI?"

He lets out a surprised laugh. "I'm not answering your nosey questions."

"We're not in the classroom," I point out.

He raises an eyebrow. "And you're not my student."

"Yet."

"Not ever if I have my say."

My eyes narrow. His glint with mischief. "With all due respect, *Professor*, you're a bit of an asshole."

"That is the most disrespectful thing a student has ever said to me."

"I'm not your student. Remember?"

With that, I walk away. I don't expect him to follow me, and he doesn't. I know my sister's going to be upset, but I'll have to make her see the logic in all of this. I have rehearsals on Thursdays and can't make it to his office. And besides, I don't think I could survive a semester of him.

FOUR

LORENZO

"YOU FOUND HER?"

"Oh, I found her all right."

"And?"

I glance up at my friend Mike and shrug. His eyes narrow slightly. He's known me way too long to not read into my expression, as passive as I may try to keep it. We're at his tailor shop in Queens, a little place that looks beat down from the outside but is actually crazy dope on the inside. His grandfather opened it when he got here from Jamaica, then passed it down to Mike Senior, and now Mike has been the face and head of it for a few years while his parents travel the world. It's the best tailoring and custom work you can ask for when it comes to suits and tuxedos. It also holds one of the biggest basement vaults in the north east, the type no man, regardless of how skilled he is, can break into. Therefore, most of us keep our prized possessions here. Masseria has a vault in Little Italy, but I don't trust them the way I trust Jamaican Mike. After a moment, Mike stops hemming the dress pants in his hand and sits down on the couch across from me.

"What are you not saying?" he asks.

Dominic makes an amused sound beside me. I glare at him. "Don't you have places to be?"

"My car's at the shop. I have nowhere to be," Dom says.

Mike looks at him. "What's he not saying?"

"I don't know what you're talking about," I respond.

"I'd rather not comment," Dom says.

Mike chuckles, eyebrow raised. "Smart man."

"So, you found Catalina," Mike repeats.

I nod.

"Have you told Silvio?"

I press my lips together. "He knows."

"You don't look happy about that." He frowns, then gapes at me, at Dom and back at me. "You caught feelings for her?"

"No. Fuck no." I scowl. "She's just a mystery, that's all."

"A mystery." He gives me a *shut the fuck up* look.

"Yeah, you know. Someone I can't figure out."

"First time in thirty years I've heard you refer to a woman as a mystery," Mike says. He glances over at Dom. "You ever heard him call a woman a mystery?"

"I've never heard him call women anything at all," Dom responds.

I grit my teeth together and focus on my newly buffed brown shoes. I do it every time I come in here. It's not really much to look at but I'm not in the mood to have this conversation with these idiots. Dominic has only been working for me for a few months and the kid still hasn't figured out whether or not I'm liable to shoot his ass. I am, but I wouldn't. His dad's too important to our family and the only reason I gave Dominic a job to begin with. Even though Dom is young and a hot head at times, he's a good kid and I don't ask him to do anything too crazy. I love to make money, but I don't want anyone dying on my watch. As long as he lays low and knows I'm the boss, we'll be all right. Mike's a different story. We don't owe each other shit, but our loyalty has stood the test of time nonetheless. I've known him most of my life, and because of that, he knows he can say whatever he wants to me and I won't get mad. Not really anyway.

"You sure you're not doing this for revenge?" Mike asks, expression serious again.

I stay quiet because I don't know the damn answer to that question. Mike takes my silence as confirmation. He knows me too well. He knows I don't do anything without reason, and yeah, a lot of us are keeping tabs on these girls, but none closer than I am. Maybe it is revenge I want.

FIVE

CATALINA

I'VE BEEN PERFORMING SO LONG that I haven't had much time for a life that doesn't revolve around the stage. I rehearse twelve hour days and would never think of complaining about it because I know how fortunate I am to have this. And yet, my sister's words of advice ring true. I know I need to cut back. I promised myself I would a couple of years back, but I can't seem to stop. I'm addicted to staying busy.

Emma keeps telling me to go back to school and get a degree, but it seems like a difficult task seeing that I don't even know if I can make it to something as simple as office hours. Besides, whenever I spend too much time dwelling on hanging up my pointe shoes, I feel panicky. Dance, for me, is like breathing. I need it to live and I'm not sure I can without it, but I've seen so many of my peers go on to expand their horizons and do different things and I don't want to rule out that possibility for myself. A lot of people in the company have gone on to be featured on Broadway now, which means there are more opportunities for us out there, yet when I think about doing something else, it's usually outside of the limelight.

Maybe I'll teach. Maybe I will dive into the dancewear business and see where that goes.

"Mademoiselle Álvarez, I see you still prefer to do your warm up ten minutes before curtain call."

At the sound of Madam Costello's voice, I startle and look up from my spot on the floor, smiling so wide, my bottom lip cracks.

"You missed our earlier warm up," I say to her, standing up. I don't bother mentioning that the only reason I'm doing this again is because I think I pulled a muscle the other night. Instead, I throw my arms around her. "I didn't know you'd be here."

"Ah, I couldn't miss my favorite pupil's final week of performances, could I?"

My smile falters a tad. "I wish you'd have let me know. I could've given you my family tickets."

It's not like they ever use them, I want to say, but don't. I don't have to. She reads the anguish all over my face even if I am trying not to let it show. I let go of her and take a step back to admire the beautiful gold dress she's wearing. She's a tiny thing. Tiny, but powerful. Her body toned from years of ballet. Though she quit dancing professionally in her prime, she's been teaching a handful of students for decades. It's nearly impossible to get a spot in her class regardless of what kind of connections you have, which is why I count training with her for as long as I did as one of my biggest accomplishments. She taught me during a time when I needed a teacher, a friend, and a maternal-figure and she was all three to me.

"I'm so glad you're here," I breathe.

She pinches my chin and examines my face. "We're not having a breakdown, are we?"

"No breakdown." My smile is shaky. She lets go of my chin and places her hand flat on the center of my chest.

"All of these emotions, you channel them," she says. "Anger, fear, sadness—those are your most valuable tools. Use them out there."

"I will." I smile wide.

"Good. Now, please show this theatre what a principal dancer looks like." She leans in, drops a kiss on my forehead, and pivots gracefully. I smile as I watch her walk away, with her head held high and her back perfectly poised.

"Was that Madam Costello?"

"The one and only." I turn to Justin.

"No pressure," he says, exhaling as he rotates his neck. "No pressure at all."

"I bet there's a famous basketball player or politician in the audience tonight." I wink, laughing at the way his expression morphs from pure horror to amusement. We currently perform a pas de deux together three nights a week and twice a day on the weekend.

He holds his head high and offers me his arm. "Let's give them our best show."

"Let's." I look around at the rest of our company, my dancer sisters and brothers whom I've spent more time with than my own blood siblings.

"Curtains in two," one of the stagehands announces, and just like that the butterflies begin to swarm my stomach.

It only happens when I'm less than five minutes from taking stage. Once I'm out there, my nerves melt into adrenaline and my movements just fall into place. Dance is like water to me. I've been doing it so long that I don't think about the steps, I just do them. At the first strums of the violin, I take a deep breath and walk onto the stage. There are a few claps from the crowd that I take in as I begin my performance. I use the melancholy of the music to drive my movements, the tempo of the violin makes me think of my father and in turn, makes me want to weep for our failed relationship. The harp reminds me of my mother and the selfless love she gave us before she left, which sometimes I wonder if that was also a form of selflessness, and again, I want to weep. I think of my sisters, of my brother who never stood a chance against our name, and fall into the emotion that stirs in me. By the time Justin meets me on stage, my chest is heavy. His hands on my ribcage as he lifts me, give me comfort. The way he yearns to catch me and keep me after my *tour jeté* and holds me during a *pas de chat* that I use to try to get away, feeds the fury inside of me. Throughout the performance we play a game of cat and mouse, him chasing, me running, soaring until I finally get away from him only to realize how much I enjoyed the feel of the chase and the way he tried to shield me from the world around us.

In the end, I *grand jeté* back to him in a show of faith – *"please still want me,"* the gesture says, and his secure catch responds, *"always."* My heart explodes along with the audience, all of my emotions bursting with their cheers, tears pouring out with exhaustion and sweat as I curtsy, clutching Justin's hand tightly as he bows.

"Nice work," he says so that only we can hear.

"Ditto," I respond, because his performance is always equally if not better than mine.

The rest of the company comes out and takes their final bow with us, then Justin and I take our curtain call before we all leave. The audience continues to clap and Justin chuckles backstage.

"You know you have to go back out again."

I grin as he walks back out one more time, taking a bow before he calls me over. I bow and walk out one more time, taking a deep curtsy. A massive bouquet of white flowers catches my eye as I straighten. I smile as the bouquet of white hydrangeas nears, knowing that Madam Costello is behind the gesture. Few people know my favorite flower, and she's one of them. I can't see much of the audience with the spotlight beaming on me, but as the man holding the flowers nears I notice his large hands, and when he hands the flowers over to me, his fingers brush up against mine, jolting me. Literally. One of us has static that zaps us both. I open my mouth to joke about it but freeze when the flowers lower and I see it's the very professor who kicked me out of his classroom yesterday.

In my completely-caught-off-guard-haze, I realize that he looks amused before he turns around and walks away, one hand in the pocket of his dress pants, the other swinging casually. Somehow I manage to get a grip and smile at the crowd once more before heading to the spot where Justin's standing. The curtains drop and Justin puts a hand around my waist.

"You look pale. What happened?" he asks. "Is it the flowers?"

I hug the flowers to my chest. "No. I just . . . I'm fine. It's been a long week. "

What is the professor doing here and why would *he* hand me flowers? How did he even know I liked them? How was he allowed to bring them up to me? Surely there must be an explanation as to why he's here. He doesn't seem like the type of man who would be interested in the ballet, but he must have a connection to be here, let alone be allowed to hand off flowers to a principal.

"Cat," Justin says, pulling me from my thoughts.

"Yeah, no. It's nothing." I push the thoughts aside and smile brightly for him. I calculate the time it'll take us to go home and get ready versus showering here, which we rarely do, and decide it's the only way we'd make it to dinner right away. "I guess we'll have to shower here for once."

Justin laughs as he walks away. I head into shower, while the girls are all talking in the dressing room about tonight's performance. Normally, I'd be listening and contributing to the conversation, but my mind is elsewhere. For a moment, as I dress, I wonder if I imagined him here. I shake the thought away quickly. It was him. His large hands, that sure-of-himself look on his face. But *why?* It's *that* question that makes me dress faster. I need to find Madam Costello because I'm sure the flowers are from her. How does she know him and what is he even doing here?

SIX

CATALINA

I ADJUST the dip of my low-cut spring maxi before closing my coat. The weather is unsure of whether it wants to side with spring or stay in winter a while longer and the nights are chilly. I step out of the room and find Justin, who's changed into jeans, a white t-shirt, and a corduroy navy blazer, and Madam Costello talking in the hallway. She smiles when she sees me.

"That was your best performance to date."

"I had to step my game up since you're here." I kiss both of her cheeks and look into her deep green eyes. "Thank you for the flowers. I assume they're from you because you're the only one who knows those are my favorite."

"Are you surprised I remembered?"

"Not really. You've always known more about me than my own mother."

Her smile falters as she wraps an arm around my shoulder and pulls me close. "I was just telling Justin that I want to take you out to dinner with my family and I won't take no for an answer. It's long overdue."

"Oh, but I can't intrude," I say. I met her daughter, who was much younger than me, a few times when I was a teenager, but even then it's not like we all hung out. Family dinner sounds . . . formal.

"I've already invited Justin as well."

I look at Justin, who shoots me a look that says *you better not ruin this moment for me*. "Fine, but only for a little while."

"You'll stay the whole meal," she says, grabbing my hand and Justin's and leading us down the corridor. When we reach the door, Justin opens it for us and we walk out. Off to the side, I see the professor on the phone. He looks like he's arguing, but when he faces us, our gazes clash, and he stops talking altogether. He shoves the phone in his pocket as he walks over to us. My heart is hammering and I'm about to ask Madam why he gave me the flowers when he stops directly in front of us and she lets go of my hand and turns to me.

"Catalina, this is my nephew, Lorenzo," she says with a proud smile. "Loren, this is a former pupil of mine, Catalina."

"Catalina." The professor, Lorenzo or *Loren*, repeats. It's a deep murmur that makes my pulse quicken. He offers to take my hand and I give it, squeezing instinctively as he raises it to his mouth, his hazel eyes intent on mine. "It's a pleasure to meet you."

I swallow because I can't seem to find words, but manage to smile politely at him as he lowers my hand slowly, his thumb brushing over it in a way that makes my toes curl. So, his name is Lorenzo Costello? Madam introduces him to Justin who stands beside me. A part of me wonders why he didn't call me out on my lie. Why he didn't say we'd met just yesterday when he'd been disagreeable about letting me into his class. Then again, I'm not going to be the one to bring it up either.

A heavily tinted black SUV stops in front of us and a man gets out quickly. I freeze, trembling a little at the mere sight of it. All three of them turn to look at me, and Justin comes over to my side. Madam gives me a small, sympathetic smile, and

Loren just watches me. I swallow and make myself walk again. Justin places his hand on the small of my back.

"You okay?"

"I just got a little light-headed. Hunger." I summon a light laugh to go with my lie.

I wasn't there the day my boyfriend Vinny got shot, but I made my brother recount the story so many times I can picture it as if I were. A black car slowed down and parked and shots rang out. It was like a scene out of a horror movie, Gio had said. Gio, who's heavily involved in illegal shit himself, had called it a horror movie. Then again, how else would you describe it when your best friend gets gunned down in front of you? It's something I think about often. I was home, in the house we'd moved into together six months earlier. We were getting ready to start a life together, ready to finally just be together, and then . . . he was gone.

Somehow, I make myself move and get in the backseat. The guy holding the door open for us isn't much older than me and doesn't look very kind at all, except when he looks at Madam Carmen, then he smiles. She pats his face gently, as if he were four.

No one brings up my shell-shocked reaction as we ride to the restaurant, and I'm thankful. Once we get there, we're introduced to the rest of Madam Carmen's family, including her husband Silvio, who spends the first few minutes smiling at her and asking me how it was to have her as my teacher.

"It was the most incredible experience of my life," I answer truthfully, smiling at the smile she gives me. "Where's your daughter?"

"Oh, she's in Chicago." Madam smiles wide. "She's a corps de ballet dancer there."

"Oh wow."

I remember her daughter being much younger than me. Young enough that she never rehearsed with me. I look around the table as everyone talks and picks at the sharable food in the middle of the table. They're all friendly, so friendly in fact, that I feel instantly at ease, which is more than I can say about my own family dinners. I spend the better part of an hour raving about how amazing she is and he spends it agreeing with me. Loren, who's sitting to my left, closest to his uncle, doesn't say a word to me the entire time but something about his stance tells me he's brooding. Whether or not it's about me or the call he was on when we left the ballet, I don't know and I tell myself it doesn't matter. So what if I lied about who I was? He's just a teacher. He shouldn't care about that. Hell, I shouldn't care about it, but I do.

"So, Catalina, what else do you do besides dance? Do you go to school? Do they pay you to dance? Will you become a teacher like Carmen?" the man across from me asks. A brother of Silvio's.

The way he's looking at me with those hooded eyes that don't do anything to hide where his interests really lie, makes me uncomfortable, but I smile because it's what I've been doing my entire life around creepy men like him. Beneath the table, I feel Loren's leg press against mine and I still, my heart ricocheting at the feel of it, large and strong against mine.

"At the moment, I only dance, and yes, they pay me," I respond.

I don't tell him that I didn't re-sign my contract with the company because I want to take a season off to see what happens. Not even Justin knows that yet. Not even Madam Carmen, who I usually call with important decisions like that. No one but Emma knows.

"That's good," he says. He turns to Justin. "And you dance with her?"

Justin puts his hand over mine on the table. "We've been dancing together for almost two years."

"You have wonderful chemistry," Madam Carmen says with a smile.

"Are you together?" the man asks.

"We're not," I say quickly.

"Not anymore," Justin adds with a wink. "But you never know what the future holds."

"Have you thought about what you'll do after dance?" The question jolts me because it's from Loren.

"Yeah, to no avail," I say in a small voice.

"Teach," Madam Carmen says with a bright smile. I return the smile and move my shoulders in a *maybe*.

"Where are you originally from?" Silvio asks.

"Chicago, but I grew up in European boarding schools, so I feel more like a European baby."

"Fancy," Loren says beside me. He makes the word sound like a curse.

"Interesting," Silvio says. "Why'd you go there?"

"Things were a little hectic at home, so my sister and I were sent to London for high school. My cousins in Colombia went to the same school, so it wasn't out of the ordinary for us," I respond, surprised by how at ease I feel speaking the truth in front of them. Maybe it's because Madam is here and she's always understood me and Silvio has kind, understanding, brown eyes. "We came back our senior year."

"Oh, so you've been here a while," Silvio supplied.

"Not really." I hesitate. "I moved back to London and was dancing with the Royal Ballet. I just moved to New York two years ago."

"I assume things are better back home now?"

"I . . . I'm honestly not sure." I pause, swallowing past the lump that always forms when I talk about my parents. "I have a rocky relationship with my parents."

I look at my lasagna again because the cloud of sadness is too much for me to bear in this setting and if I'm being completely honest with myself, I miss the hell out of my parents all the time. I just wish they felt the same about me.

"You miss them," Silvio says.

I nod silently, unable to form the yes over the knot in my throat. Beneath the table, Loren places his hand on mine, which is resting over my thigh. It's a simple gesture, one that is so contradictory of how he turned me away yesterday, and somehow it warms me all over. His calloused fingers brush against the back of my hand and it becomes too much for me. I turn my hand over and link my fingers through his just so that he stops. I can't handle the kindness right now. That seems to jolt something inside of him because he jerks his hand out of mine and moves his leg so he's no longer touching me at all. And just like that the room feels arctic.

"What does your father do?" the man across from me asks.

"This is not an interrogation or interview," Madam says before I get a chance to answer. "Please leave my girl alone. I don't want you scaring her away."

Loren makes a grunting sound beside me and I try not to overanalyze the fact that I think even *that* sounds hot coming from him. While Justin is distracted, talking to the man in front of him, I turn to Loren.

"Well, I guess I don't need to go to your office?"

"I expect you there by twelve." His gaze heats. I swear it does. My stomach flips.

"I have dress rehearsals. I don't think I'll make it."

"I'll wait until twelve-thirty. If you're not there by then, I'll assume you're not serious."

"I need the class."

His eyes search mine. "Do you or does Emmaline Álvarez need it?"

"Same difference."

He ignores me and looks at Justin's hand still on mine. "Does your ex-boyfriend always hold your hand at restaurants?"

"Only when he's trying to get laid."

"How often does that work out in his favor?"

"Not as often as he'd like."

"What are the odds looking like tonight?" The way he looks at me, like he's trying to climb into my head, is unnerving.

"I'm not sure yet. Is that what you're into? Odds?"

"Maybe," he says, a hint of amusement in his eyes. "So, what does it depend on?"

"How tipsy I am when I leave here." I bring the glass of red wine to my lips and take another sip. His eyes heat as he watches me lick my lips.

"Come home with me instead."

My pulse quickens. "I thought you didn't do things with students."

"You're not my student."

"*Yet.*"

At this, he merely smiles. His eyes are still on mine as he scoots his chair back and stands up, placing his napkin on the table.

"I'm looking forward to hearing your explanation for that on Thursday." He looks at his uncle for a long moment, some kind of unspoken conversation transpiring between them before he looks around the room. "Good night, everyone. I have work to do."

What? He literally just invited me to go home with him. How is he leaving? It dawns on me that he expected me to say no. How messed up is that? I should've said yes just to fuck with him. Just to fuck him, too.

He leaves with the wave of his hand and I find myself staring after him, wishing he were still sitting beside me because the rest of the dinner feels awkward, which makes no sense. I've known Madam forever and Justin a lot longer than Loren. And yet, that's how this man makes me feel—a little awkward in his presence and yet somehow worse in his absence.

SEVEN

CATALINA

ON THURSDAY, I'm scrambling to get to the university, pulling my freshly washed, wet hair into a high bun and letting it fall right back down when I realize I left my hair tie back at the studio. Oh well. I rush into the subway right before the doors close and let out a relieved breath as I catch the rail just as it starts to move. I'm fifteen minutes away from the school and I'm going to make it. My phone rings as I step out of the subway and rush down the platform, but I ignore it. I need to run up the stairs and get on the sidewalk. That's my end goal right now and I'm pretty sure it's just my sister calling to ask about the status of the class so it doesn't matter. When I get to the sidewalk and stand at the red light, I fish my phone out of my bag and look at it. Missed call from Gio. Wrong sibling, same pain in the neck. I dial him back because he's the kind of person who will blow up your phone until you answer it.

"Yo, I'm in town," he says by way of greeting. "Let's hang out tonight."

"I can't. I have a performance." I rush to the other side of the street with the mob of people crossing. "Why are you here anyway?"

"Uh, the bar I'm opening?"

"Oh shit. Right. Dammit, G." I cringe, remembering the bar. He bought a warehouse in Brooklyn and has been remodeling it for over a year. It's been so long since he got it and so many times that he's said the opening will happen soon, that I completely forgot it actually was finally happening this weekend. "I have a ballet thing on Saturday that I can't skip out on."

"What ballet thing? You promised you'd help out." I hate it when he uses his ten-year-old voice because it makes me genuinely feel bad that I can't comply with what he's asking for. My brother is a master manipulator.

"It's one of those fancy schmancy daytime events for our sponsors. It'll be done early."

"Did you ask some of your girls to come dance?"

"Must I remind you that you literally just called me to tell me that you're here and you need this by Saturday? So, no I haven't asked any of them. I'm sure I can get you some strippers, though."

"I can get myself strippers, Cat. I want regular dancers. I don't want people stripping or looking for tips."

"I'll try to put something together but you can't just expect people to drop everything for you."

"Of course I can," he says. "Tell them Giovanni Masseria is opening a new Devil's Lair and that they can keep their morals low and their asses high."

"You're disgusting, you know that?"

"I'm aware." He says something that's muffled by his hand over the speaker and I press my phone to my ear a little harder.

"Who are you with?"

"Frankie and don't get any ideas."

I grin. "Tell Frankie I say hi."

"No. I don't need the two of you starting trouble while we're here on business. Go get your girls rounded up and keep me posted," he says. "Oh, one more thing, it's a secret society, high-class gentleman's club, so I'll need to send them NDA's."

"Not much of a secret if you keep blabbing about it to all of New York."

"Good point. Talk to you later." He hangs up the phone before I can respond.

I look at my screen and gasp. Shit. I only have five minutes. I take off running toward the faculty building and ignore the way my calves burn like hell with each step I take. As I reach it, I start cursing, realizing that I'm at the back of the building. There's a door, but I doubt it's unlocked. I run up to it and try anyway. I pull the handle and open it easily, fully intending to propel off into a sprint again when I slam into someone with an *umph*. It might as well be a wall, as hard as it feels. The impact of it kicks me back and I lose my balance, but a hand reaches out and wraps around my waist, pulling me up before I land on my ass. My damp hair is covering my face when I hear the door shut us out of the building. It takes me a moment to stutter an apology and another to swipe my hair out of my face, only to meet with Loren's hazel eyes.

"I'm on my way to your office," I gasp out. He hasn't let me go and our faces are so close if one of us breathes too hard we'll be kissing. We might as well be with the way my heart won't stop stuttering.

"You're late," he bites out.

"You left early." I gape at him because for a beat I'm frozen in shock, the adrenaline that pushed me through rehearsals this morning and to come over here, quickly fading. I try to shimmy out of his arms but he holds tight. "You can let me go now."

"I don't think I will." He stares at me for so long I think he may just kiss me. And I might let him. Or maybe I'll slap him. I don't even know anymore. I just know my heart is beating out of control and suddenly I'm unsure whether this attraction is a burden or a refuge. He doesn't kiss me though. He eases his hold on me and sets me down so that my feet are on the ground and I'm able to find my balance. "I didn't leave early. I left at twelve-thirty, just like I said I would."

I look at my watch and back at him. "It's twelve-thirty right now."

"Like I said, you're late."

"No, I'm . . ." I take a deep breath and let it out with a growl. "I need this class."

He comes into my space so quickly I have no choice but to move back on instinct, but my back meets the rail behind me and I know there's nowhere to go. I've been around menacing men all my life and Lorenzo Costello will not be the one I cower from, so I hold my head up high and meet his challenging gaze.

His gaze narrows on mine. "I'm not letting you in the class."

"Why the hell not?"

"Because I don't fuck my students."

I blink, completely thrown by this. Out of all the things in the world he could have said, that was the last one I was expecting. I open my mouth and close it several times, willing my heart to chill out while I sort the thoughts running rampant through my brain. I settle on one.

"You're assuming I'm interested in you."

His lips form a slow, seductive smile. "I know you're interested."

"Maybe so, but I can resist going down that road. What I can't do is not get into this class."

"Right, because your sister, whom you're posing as, which is illegal, by the way, wants it on her transcript and being that it's her last semester here, this is her only shot."

I hesitate. "How do you know that?"

"I made it my business to find out a few things about you and in turn, her, since she's the one you're doing the favor for," he says as he looms over me. I'm feeling so many things at once that I don't know what to do with myself, so I grip the metal rail behind me and continue looking at him.

"Why?"

"I already told you, I want to fuck you. I wanted to gauge how difficult it would be to get from point A to point B."

"Do you investigate every woman you want to fuck? Why not just ask?" I shake my head. His past is the least of my worries. "What else did you find out?"

"Not nearly as much as I'd like to know."

"I don't sleep with strangers," I say, because it's true. Every guy I've ever had sex with has been a friend who became more, but I think I'd make an exception for Loren.

"We're not strangers. You met my family the other night."

That gives me pause. He has a point. *Still.* That doesn't mean I know him. Actually, I know absolutely nothing about him. He barely spoke during dinner.

"Come out with me tonight," he says before I can respond. "We'll get to know each other then."

"I'll go out with you tonight if you promise to think about letting me in that class, or at the very least, give me all of the material you're planning on teaching this semester."

"Give me your phone number."

"Are you agreeing to my terms?"

"What are you, a lawyer?"

I raise an eyebrow. "Is that a yes?"

"Give me your phone number and you'll find out."

"Fine." I put my hand out. "Give me your phone." He does. I speak as I type in my contact information. "I'll be available after six."

He takes the phone back, drops it in his pocket and leans in slightly, pressing his mouth on my forehead and inhaling. He groans as he does so, and as much as I want to think it's weird, I can't because the groan rumbles through my body and awakens butterflies I was sure were dormant until he barged into my life.

He straightens and pushes away from the rail, bending to lift his helmet off the ground before he walks away.

"I'll see you at eight," he calls out once he's a few feet away.

My eyes follow him until I can no longer see him. My heart is beating so wildly that I legit have to take a few deep breaths before I feel like I can move my legs again. I don't understand how or what just transpired, but I have a date and I'm officially freaking out.

EIGHT

CATALINA

NOW I KNOW that at the very least I can get her the notes for this class, I gather up the nerve to call my sister and tell her everything from start to finish. The last date I went on was with Justin and most of those were group dates because we'd get out of rehearsal and collectively go hang out at a bar or restaurant or someone's apartment. I hate to take away meaning from what Justin and I had, but to me it never felt real. Vinny was real, the stolen moments we got whenever I'd come home for the holidays, those felt real, but I was a teenager and any attention from a guy, especially an older, more experienced one like Vinny was bound to make me fall head over heels. And that was the issue I was having with Loren Costello. He wasn't that much older, but clearly more experienced, and had an edge about him that drew me to him like a magnet. I'm no longer a teenager. I'm surrounded by gorgeous half-dressed men for twelve hours a day and somehow none have made me feel the way Loren does when he looks at me.

"It's scary," I tell Emma. "But I mean, it's fine. He just wants to have sex. Keep things casual."

"Do you think you can keep things casual?"

"Yeah. I mean, why not?" I frown. "Anyway, I won't let this jeopardize your class. I'm going to get that class on your record and take your tests when I have to."

"I trust you." She laughs. "That's so interesting that he's Madam Costello's nephew. What a small world."

"I know, right?"

"Crazy small world," she says, "but I'm excited about your date with him. You need to get back out there and meet men you don't work with all day."

I smile. "How's work going?"

"Like shit. I'm trying to write an article about the black market and every time I think I'm getting somewhere, I hit a brick wall. Everyone here is protecting someone. You know how it is."

"Why not call Dean?"

She's silent for a beat. "I don't know."

"He'll help you," I say. "You know he would."

"I doubt it," she whispers.

"I'm sure you'll figure it out," I say, trying to sound cheerful. "Please be careful though."

"Careful is my middle name."

"No it's not. Christine is."

"Such a party-pooper," she responds. "I'll be careful. You be careful with mister FBI. Remember who your family is."

"Speaking of family, did Gio tell you about the club? The opening is on Saturday."

"Soft opening," she said, sounding distracted. "Only super secretive men are going that day. Why?"

"How do you know?"

"I'm staying at Dad's house, remember? I hear everything even when he thinks I don't."

"You should write about him in your little investigation."

Emma snorts. "Yeah, so I can be the next one in the river? No, thanks."

It's a joke, but it settles us into a weird, uncomfortable silence that begs the question: *he wouldn't kill his own daughter to shut her up, would he?* According to the documentary, he's done unthinkable things. I shiver at the mere thought.

"So, question of the day, is the professor as hot as they say he is?"

"Hotter."

"No way."

I laugh and talk to her about what I should wear. We hang up so that I can go get ready, which I do fairly quickly, considering how nervous I am. I gasp when the doorbell rings and stand up quickly. *Oh my God how is he here already?* I sent him the address and apartment number earlier, but I expected him to text and let me know he was on his way or something. *Isn't that what people usually do?* I place my hand on the door and lean in as I check to make sure it's him, my heart nearly pounding out of my chest when my eyes meet his through the peephole. He's wearing jeans and a black t-shirt that hugs his frame perfectly. I don't know what his body looks like beneath his clothes, but I'm sure it's nothing short of amazing. His gaze smolders, as if he knows I'm looking at him, but that's impossible. The way his lips form a slow, sinful smile catches me off guard. I back away from the door for a second, gathering my wits before unlocking and pulling it open.

He gives me a slow, purposeful once-over that makes my nerves haywire. "You're not wearing any shoes."

"You never said where we were going, so I was waiting for you to get here before I decided what shoes to wear."

"Normally women wear killer heels on a first date."

"Oh, is this a date? It sounded like blackmail."

"When two people who are sexually attracted to each other go get dinner together, it's usually called a date, even if there is blackmail involved."

My stomach dips. I can't even retaliate because if I deny my attraction to him I'd be a damn liar. I push the door closed behind him as he steps into my apartment. It's not much, but the location is great and it's the best my sister and I can afford right now without asking our father for help, which we refuse to do, though Gio has helped here and there.

"I guess I should apologize then." I start walking toward my room. "My thighs are sore, my calves are sore, my toes are sore, and I have a million blisters right now and the only way I'd subject myself to closed shoes or survive wearing anything but these flip flops is if I'm carried all around the city, so you're just going to have to deal with the shoe selection and my ugly feet."

I might as well stomp and say, "so there". I don't even wait to see what his expression is before walking into my room. I have no idea where we're going, but he's dressed down, so I think a black maxi dress and flip flops will work just fine. I'm pushing my feet into them when I feel his presence, and glance up to find him standing by the door. My pulse quickens. The way he stands, like he commands the air around him, the way a simple t-shirt fits on his muscular frame, the way he's looking at me like he wants to devour me on the spot, it all makes my throat go dry.

"I'm ready," I whisper.

He tears his gaze away from mine, looks at the sandals on my feet, and nods, his throat moving as he swallows right before he turns away. I stand and follow behind him, picking up my purse and keys on my way out, my chest drumming with each step I take. At the ballet, I'm surrounded by good looking guys, but Loren's level of good looking makes them all look like peasants merely playing the roles of gods on stage. The thought rocks me, because even those playing gods on stage turn into mortal men when the house lights come on.

NINE

CATALINA

I MARVEL at how tall he is. I've never been out with a man this tall before. I barely reach his shoulders, but it's not only that, it's how big he is, too. He's massive, like he belongs in the NFL or something. I wonder if he's big everywhere. A shiver accompanies the blush creeping on my face at the thought. Thankfully, he's not looking at me.

"You have a roommate?" he asks as we near the elevator.

"My sister."

"Right. Emmaline."

I smile. "The one and only."

"You're a good sister," he says as we step into the empty elevator. He pushes the B, which surprises me. I don't know anyone who drives here. Then, I'm filled with instant dread.

"You brought your bike?"

His gaze slides over to mine. "You'll be fine."

"Um . . ." I hesitate.

He already mentioned heels he was expecting me to have on, which I'm not wearing. How bad would it be if I told him that I'm terrified of motorcycles right now? I hate first dates. Hate them. File that under the reason I've only ever dated guys in the ballet and Vinny, who was a long-time family friend I grew up with. First dates make me queasy. The elevator doors open. We step out into the garage, which I've never actually been in because I don't have a car to park here and I always take the train or a taxi everywhere.

"You okay?" I can hear the amusement in his voice. When I look up at him, sure enough, he looks like he's trying really hard not to laugh at my expense.

"Yeah, of course." I shrug, hoping my uneasiness leaves with it.

It doesn't. My stomach is still in a knot as we walk toward his bike. What am I supposed to say? *I'll meet you wherever you want to take me?* Jesus. Even my palms are sweating. I haven't felt this nervous since I danced last night, but performance nerves are good nerves, they're adrenaline and power that propel me forward. These kind of nerves make me want to run away. He reaches into his pocket and the lights of a Mercedes truck we're nearing light up. My heart launches into my throat. I look at Loren, who's practically grinning, a chuckle rumbling through his chest. I'd find it sexy if the urge to punch him wasn't so overwhelming.

"You're a bastard," I breathe. "You knew I was freaking out, didn't you?"

"She doesn't wear heels, doesn't want a ride on my bike, and now she calls me a bastard," he says, his eyes glinting with amusement at each point he checks off.

I open my mouth to argue, but then he starts walking over to me with all that swagger and I can't even think of a word to say. His eyes are set on mine but I swear I feel the heat of his gaze everywhere. When he reaches me, he puts his thumb and forefinger on my chin and closes my mouth. His thumb lingers on my bottom lip and I remember that I forgot to wear lipstick. Talk about first date fail for real. His gaze heats as he looms over me and I swear I feel like he's going to lean down and kiss

47

me right now. I'll let him. There's no doubt in my mind that I'd let him do that and more, but he drops his hand and walks past me. I hear the faint sound of the car door opening behind me.

"You coming or what?"

I blink and move, turning to face him and climb into the truck quickly as he holds the door open for me. He shuts it as I'm clicking my seat belt in place. I take in the interior of the car, which smells brand new. He opens his door and settles into his seat, clicking his own seat belt on as he starts the engine.

"I've never been inside one of these before," I comment, looking around. "It's interesting."

He chuckles. "You don't sound impressed."

"I'm impressed that you didn't bring your motorcycle and try to kill me."

He shakes his head as he drives out of the parking garage.

"Honestly, I don't think I've been inside a regular car in like . . . five years or something," I say, frowning as I ponder that.

"You live in the city. You don't really need a car."

I glance over at him. Even the way he drives, with his right hand casually hanging over the wheel in a way that makes the muscles on his arms flex, is sexy as hell. I look away. I'm built of muscles. Justin is built of muscles. I'm surrounded by muscles every day. *What the hell is wrong with me?*

"You don't live in the city?" I watch him shake his head, but doesn't add more. I look forward. "So, where are we going?"

"Pizza parlor in Brooklyn."

"I like pizza."

"Thank God for that."

I smile, shaking my head. "You know, another woman would feel offended by all the things you've said about me only . . ." I look at my watch. "Fifteen minutes into our first date."

"Another man would probably also be offended by how unimpressed you seem."

"You have such a big head."

"You have no idea."

I blush fiercely and laugh. "I totally fell into that one."

"You did." He gives me a sly smile when he glances at me. "So, how old were you when you started dancing with my aunt?"

"Fifteen."

"Hmm."

"It was right after I got to London the first time," I continue. "She was all anyone could talk about in dance school and she was only there for a few months and taking just a handful of students, so I felt like I needed to land that audition."

"She's very protective of you."

I bite my lip and glance away in hopes of keeping my emotions in check. I'm not a big crier, but talking about Madam and how much she cares about me may just do the trick. It makes me miss my own mom. I push that thought out of my head. I don't have room for heavy emotions right now. The whole point of coming on this date was to get lost in something other than my thoughts, emotions, or past.

He parallel parks and comes around to open the door for me. We cross the street, and even though we're walking side-by-side and he's not touching me, I can feel him stiffen beside me when we get to the corner of the pizza place and near a group of men standing outside. He puts a large hand at the small of my back and it feels like a brand. I'm not sure how I feel about him being possessive, but right now I'm grateful for it because the four men standing there are giving me leering gazes that make me feel uncomfortable, and I'm never uncomfortable in my skin. The hostess smiles when she sees Loren and I walk in. She glances at me briefly and says hello, but her full attention is on him.

"Usual?" she asks.

I look up at him to see what his reaction to her is, but he doesn't really give one. He simply nods and glances over his shoulder once more and I wonder who the hell those guys are and why a college professor would have an issue with them, but it's clear there's something there. The hostess walks us to a table for four in the back and places the menus on it.

"Val is caught up right now, so give me a second to take your orders."

She leaves. I move to sit, but Loren grabs my arm and ushers me to sit on the other side of the table, the one facing the restaurant. He takes the seat next to mine. It's clear he's still brooding.

"Do you know them?" I ask, finally, because I can't stand the silence.

"Who?"

"The guys outside."

He glances at me, then outside, then at me again as he pushes his seat back and stands up. "I'll be right back. Go ahead and order for us. The white pizza is great if you're into that. I'll eat anything."

I watch as he stalks toward the front door. Even the hostess makes a face as he passes her without a second glance. She walks over with two bottled waters and a notepad.

"Do you know what you want, honey?"

"Not yet." I smile at her and glance outside again. I can't see much, but Loren is definitely telling the guys something they don't want to hear. It makes me uneasy. Who are they and why is he even talking to them? Maybe it's the former FBI thing. I settle on that.

"You want me to make any recommendations?" she asks.

I force my attention away from Loren and back to her. "He said the white pizza is good."

"He always gets the same thing." She shakes her head, a smile on her face as she shrugs. "It is good though. You want anything else?"

I skim the menu. "Maybe meatballs?"

"Meatballs and white pie it is. Anything to drink besides water?"

"Nope, I'm good." I smile as I hand her the menus.

"I'm Gianna, by the way. If you need anything, holler."

Once she leaves, my eyes are back on Loren. He bumps fists with the guys and walks back inside the restaurant. They all turn, flicking their cigarettes to the ground as they stroll away. Loren and I watch each other as he walks over to me, sitting beside me again. He puts his hand over mine on the table, sending a wave of electricity down my spine.

"You ordered?"

I nod, licking my lips. "Is everything okay?"

"Yeah."

"What was that about?" I ask, nodding toward the front door.

"Nothing you need to concern yourself with." He runs a flat hand down my back. I stiffen, arching a little more than usual, which is a lot. My posture is always stiff, my back muscles always tight. As if he knows it'll bring relief, his hand makes its way down my back in a massaging motion that all but makes me moan. "How many days a week do you dance?"

"Including practice?"

He gives a nod.

"Seven."

"How many performances?"

"Five. Twice a day Friday to Sunday. Tuesday and Thursday only at night, like the one you saw, assuming you were watching."

His gaze meets mine. "I couldn't take my eyes off you."

"You really know how to turn on the charm," I whisper, my heart throbbing in my ears.

He smiles, not with his mouth, but his eyes. He drops his hand from my back and I make a protesting sound that makes him smile for real, but he doesn't bring his hand back to the spot.

"What do you do when you're not dancing?"

"It feels like I'm always dancing." I lean back in my chair. Not acceptable posture but to hell with it. "Monday is my day off and I do nothing all morning. It's glorious. In the afternoons, I go to a women's shelter my friend runs and help out. To be honest, I've been so exhausted and haven't gone much lately."

"A women's shelter? What do you help out with?"

I shrug. "Whatever they need."

"And when you're not doing that?"

"I'm starting to feel like a bit of a loser," I admit sheepishly. "I don't have much of a social life, if that's what you're getting at."

"You obviously have time to do things though. You were dating that ballerina guy."

The way he says it makes me laugh. "You have a problem with male dancers?"

"Only if they're fucking the woman I'm interested in."

"What sparked this sudden interest?" I pivot my body toward him, hoping the butterflies in my stomach settle, but when I do, he does the same and his legs end up on either side of mine, effectively closing me in. The butterflies flap their rampant little wings again.

"My interest in you?" He brings a hand up to my face and tucks my hair behind my ear.

"Was it the way I took over your class?"

He chuckles, that sinful mouth moving into a ghost of a smile. "I think it was when you called me an asshole."

"Interesting."

Gianna brings over the pizza and meatballs and sets them in the center of the table. She asks Loren a hundred times if he needs anything else as she wipes her hands on the apron she has on. She really is pretty, with her cinnamon hair and big green eyes. I wonder if they've ever had a fling or if she's still trying. She smiles politely at me again and walks away.

"She's really fond of you," I comment, taking a sip of water.

"I'm a good tipper."

I roll my eyes. "I doubt it's that."

"You're right." He reaches for a slice of pizza and sets it on a plate, which he places in front of me, and does the same for himself, his eyes glittering when he meets mine. "I only go places where I know the women will gawk at me."

I bump him with my shoulder. "How'd you end up teaching? The FBI wasn't paying you enough?"

A low rumbled laughter rings out that seriously makes my heart bang so hard against my chest I have to take a minute before I bite into the slice of pizza in my hand. "It kind of fell in my lap, actually."

"How does a profession like that fall in your lap?"

"A friend of mine teaches the class, but he's out of town for the next few weeks. I covered for him." He shrugs.

"Wow. You're a good friend."

"You can say that." He pauses, tilting his head. He has a look on his face that I recognize as one of contemplation, like he's trying to figure out how much he wants to tell me. "It's kind of an exchange of favors. He's doing something for me and I'm taking over the class for a few weeks."

"Wait." I set my slice down and watch him chew. "So you're not the hot teacher everyone talks about?"

His eyes crinkle. "Disappointed?"

"I mean . . . no, but now I'm dying to see this friend of yours. You know, for the sake of comparison."

His mouth tilts into a ghost of a smile as he takes another bite of his pizza. My phone buzzes on the table, where I set it in case my sister called. What I see is a text from Justin in a group picture with the rest of the company. They probably just finished the evening show. A part of me wishes I'd been there to see it, but I know sitting out and letting Riley dance was the right move. It's part of my agreement with the board. I'd have to let other dancers step into my role for two shows of my choice and this was the one I picked. Everyone else thinks I took a sick day and I'm lying in bed coughing up a storm.

Justin: *We miss you!*

I feel myself smile as I type, "*Miss you too.*"

I blink away and look up at Loren, who's watching me intently. We stare at each other for a moment, the air around us charging, feral with that look he's giving me, like he wants to possess me. The fact that I'd let him is what scares me the most. I'd sworn off all men with the power to make me feel this way – all gooey and shaky inside, and here I am.

"Does your ex know you're on a date with me?"

"It's not really like that between us."

"What's it like?"

"I don't know." I shrug. "He's cute, attentive, we're together a lot—hazard of being a principal dancer. And we just click."

"Why'd you break things off?"

"I guess I just got bored. That sounds horrible, I know, but dating someone you're with twenty-four-seven gets exhausting."

"I can see that."

"So, what's up with the whole *you don't sleep with your students* thing if you're not even the real teacher?"

"My friend would never sleep with a student. I can't tarnish his rep." He shrugs. "Besides, I don't really find any of those girls interesting."

"You're a pretty good professor," I say. "Or maybe you'd just make a great con-artist. I totally bought the teaching thing."

"I'll jot that down on my list of business ventures."

"Con-artists aren't on the level of killers." I raise an eyebrow. "Though the people in that class would argue that."

Loren laughs. "Right, but you'd be okay with it."

"I'm not sure actually." I tilt my head to think about it. I'm really not sure.

"Why are you so interested in criminals? Have you dated one?"

I open my mouth and close it quickly. How do I answer something like that? Surely, he's joking and expecting me to joke along with him but I don't have it in me to turn something like that into a joke.

"I'm kidding," he says.

"Yeah, I know." I blink away from the meatball on my plate. I literally took one bite of it and had half a slice of pizza before I got full and now I definitely can't go back to eating. I shake my thoughts away and focus on him again. "What do you do aside from taking over people's classrooms?"

"This and that. I went to law school, moved back here, passed the bar and took on a few clients." He shrugs nonchalantly.

"A few clients can afford you a Mercedes truck? Aren't those things really expensive?"

He stares at me for a moment. "I'm a smart investor."

"Hmm." That makes sense. Maybe he's a trust fund man.

"The other night you left because you had to go to work," I comment.

"Right."

I stare at him for a beat. "What kind of law?"

"Criminal."

"Oh." I glance away and fiddle with the meatball. "Where'd you study?"

"Loyola."

"In Chicago? Really?" My eyes snap to his. "Criminal law, huh? Are you on the right side of the law or the wrong side?"

"What does the right side of the law look like?"

"I'm not sure."

"Yeah, me either." He eyes me peculiarly.

I feel myself getting small, as if there's a chance that he knows about my past, about me. I shake it off and stick to the subject at hand.

"You definitely sound more Jersey than Chi-town."

"I'm surprised you can pick up any accent, as absent as you've been."

"I've been back a couple of years."

"A couple of years," he says, as if marveled by it all. "And your sister's been here the entire time?"

"Yeah. Here and Chicago."

"You've been dancing for City Ballet all that time?"

I nod, still chewing.

"Had you seen my aunt before the other day?"

"No." I pause, frowning. "Why?"

"Just wondering." His eyes flick to mine again. He catches me staring at him. "What?"

"I don't think I know any sexy lawyers."

"Ah, so she does think I'm sexy."

"Shut up." I look away to tear my crust apart. At this point, I've made playing with my food a sport. "So, being that you're not really the person who's supposed to be teaching that course and my sister really needs to get in there, do you think you can just let me in or at least give me the notes that this date was contingent to?"

He chuckles. "You ever thought about going to law school?"

"No, but this is the second time you've mentioned it."

"You'd be good in that arena."

"I'm good in my arena."

"You're incredible, but that doesn't mean you need to stay there forever. Where would you be if you didn't have ballet?"

"Married with kids."

"Really?" He stares at me for a moment, those golden eyes serious as they flicker between mine. "How old are you? You're not even thirty are you?"

"Twenty-eight."

"And you think you'd already be married with kids?" he asks.

"I like to think so." I feel myself smile. It's probably a sad one, but it's a smile nonetheless.

"Why can't you have both?"

"Nah." I shake my head. "I want to be there. It's hard to be present and live the life I live right now. Maybe if I slowed down."

"Do you feel like you have a deadline for dance?"

"It used to be that women my age were considered too old for the ballet and now we're the norm, so that's pretty good. I can dance professionally for a while."

"But you don't want to." He says it as if he can read my mind. Maybe it's in my tone. Who knows.

I shrug. "It's all I've ever known, but I'm not sure anymore. I know that doesn't make sense when I say it aloud."

"Huh." He narrows his eyes as if he's trying to read into me, but for some reason decides to let it go. "What does your sister do when she's not skipping out on classes she's supposed to be taking?"

"She's a professional psycho," I say, smiling at his low chuckle. "She's an investigative journalist."

"That's a good job."

"Yeah, not when you go to Chicago to shake down the mob, it's not."

Loren's chewing slows way down as he processes that. His eyebrows pull in slightly. "Why would she do that? She got something against them?"

"Like I said, she's a psycho. Anyway, she was hired to write a piece on the black market and the organization. She won't say their names or whatever." I shake my head. "I honestly don't know what she's thinking."

"But you're worried."

"Of course I'm worried."

"What about you?" His gaze meets mine again. "Who's worrying about you?"

"What do you mean?"

"You're in this big city all alone, no sister, no brother, no father or mother," he says. "Working your body so hard you can't even wear heels or walk long distances. Who's worrying about you?"

I'm shocked to silence. I have a million arguments I can make at the tip of my tongue – *I don't need anyone. I can take care of myself. I'm strong and don't ask for help.* My words fall short though because the way he's looking at me makes me wish I did have someone to look after me.

TEN

CATALINA

WE WALK into the record store next door to the pizza parlor and walk around, pointing out our favorite covers.

"For someone who spends the day dancing classical music, you sure like a lot of rap," he says.

"We listen to all kinds of things during rehearsal. Including rap."

"Interesting. What are the odds Madam Costello listens to rap?"

"Slim." I laugh, picturing Madam Costello listening to J. Cole. "Definitely only classical music in her class."

"I figured."

We walk around a little more, not holding hands, but our fingers brushing every so often as we talk about music and artists and rappers who mumble that Loren happens to like and I can't stand. He turns the car on from across the street and opens the door for me again. I bite my lip as we drive back toward my apartment, wondering how this is going to go down. Will he invite himself in or should I say something? I think about the long day I have ahead of me tomorrow. Thankfully, we don't have any big performances, only the one for the donors and benefactors who donate a shit ton of money to the company, but I still have Gio's club opening to worry about. As if on cue, my cell phone vibrates with a call from my brother. I stiffen as I watch the call continue, knowing if I don't answer he'll just keep calling.

"You need to pick that up?"

"It's my brother." I glance at Loren. "I'll only be a second. Sorry."

He waves me off like it's no big deal. I answer it as Loren starts driving with one hand on the steering wheel and the other on my leg. That alone has me on edge.

"Hey, G," I say upon answering the phone.

"You haven't sent me a list of names."

I sigh. "I don't have a show today. I'll get you the girls though, but I already told you I can get you—"

"I swear to God if you say strippers one more time."

I shut my mouth. There's an edge to his voice that tells me it hasn't been a good day. I answer calmly, "I'll send you sizes for the costumes. They'll sign the NDA's when they get there."

"Fine. Make sure they bring their slippers. You'll perform four to five songs. Sexy but classy."

"Since when are you into classy?"

"Since I'll have twenty men I can't control," he says. "You'll be wearing masks, don't worry."

"Are people going to . . ." I take a deep breath to brace myself to ask the question. As if he senses my discomfort, Loren strokes my thigh. Butterflies swarm my belly. My gaze flickers to him briefly, catching the intensity in his. I lower my voice as much as I can to try to hide the question from Loren, but I know it's impossible. "Are people going to have guns?"

"Don't worry about that."

"My girls can't get hurt, G."

"They'll be fine."

"But like if a fight breaks out—"

"Catalina." His tone quiets me. "You think I'd ever let anything happen to you?"

"No."

"Okay then. Don't fucking worry about that." He pauses, covering the phone as he talks to someone, and then he's back on the line. "Are you home?"

"No." My heart pushes up against my throat.

Gio is notorious for showing up uninvited. If he decides to come over while Loren and I are there . . . well, it would not be good. I'm still not convinced that Loren isn't FBI, and knowing he was practicing law in Chicago is another thing to worry about. The chances of him never having heard of the last name Masseria are exactly zero.

"Where are you?"

"Out."

"Out where?"

"On a date. What does it matter to you?"

"A date with who? What's his name? He Italian?"

"Jesus, Gio. You're here for a week and you wanna act like dad?"

"I want to know what my little sister is up to, that's all."

"You don't seem to want to know anything about me unless you need something." The words come out with a lot more force than I intend, but once they're spoken I won't apologize. Gio stays quiet for a moment.

"I'll see you tomorrow. Have a good rest of your night."

He hangs up before I can say another word and I instantly feel guilty, as if I'm the one who did something wrong. I shove the phone into my purse and look out the window. He's not worth my anger or my tears. Somewhere between coming back from London and Vinny's death, my brother became a person I barely recognize. He's so like my father it's scary and worrisome.

"You have two shows tomorrow?" Loren asks. I startle.

"Sort of. During the day, we're doing a private matinee for the benefactors who donate the big money to the ballet. It's not really anything major. We dance for like twenty-minutes and then change and mingle with them."

"And at night?"

I swallow. "Another private show."

"One that requires NDA's."

Our eyes connect when he stops at the light on the corner near my apartment building. The unspoken question here is: *are you going to tell me about it? how much do you trust me?* Maybe if we were different people I would tell him, but I can't lead the cops to Gio. Regardless of how much I disagree with what he does, his underground gambling has helped pay for mine and Emma's rent more times than I care to admit. I glance away. My answer. He takes his hand off my lap as he illegally parks his car in front of my building and comes around to open the door for me.

"They'll tow you."

"I'll only be gone a minute."

"Oh."

I follow him inside, trying not to let the wave of disappointment take hold of me. He tells the doorman to keep an eye on his car, the silent promise that he'll be compensated is laced into his tone. We walk to the elevator and take it up to my floor and I can't help the emptiness I feel as we walk the empty hallway toward my apartment. Yesterday I was unsure about this, tonight I want nothing but this. When we reach the door, I unlock it, hold it wide open with my back, letting my intentions be known. Loren stands in front of me, not quite inside the apartment, not quite outside either. He brings a hand up to cup my face and lowers his head slightly.

"Tonight was nice."

"It could be nicer." I bring my hand up to cover his on my face. "Stay."

A myriad of emotions seems to flash in his eyes—lust, regret, doubt. "I can't tonight. I have some work to do."

"Oh." I frown. "Okay."

I'm stumped. He hadn't mentioned work before. *This and that* he says he does. What kind of *this and that* would require him to work at night? And why so suddenly? I shouldn't have picked up the call from Gio. It totally killed the mood. Maybe I messed this up before we had a real chance at anything. Concern starts to eat at me, but then Loren brings his other hand up to iron out my frown and cup the other side of my face, his eyes not straying from mine.

"You're beautiful, Catalina."

"Thank you," I whisper. *Not beautiful enough to pull you from work, though.*

"Any other day," he says, inching closer, "Any other situation, I'd stay. Nothing would keep me away from this."

"But not today."

He shakes his head, brushing his nose against mine lightly, his mouth is even closer to my own. My heart thunders as his lips touch mine. It's a soft kiss that deepens as he pushes himself against me, his hands traveling down my sides, to my ass, which he squeezes, groaning into my mouth as he lifts me so that I'm forced to wrap my legs around his waist. Every flick of his tongue against mine is accompanied by me grinding against him, unable to pull away, unable to stop myself from needing that friction. He groans against my mouth as he pulls away, setting his forehead against mine and exhaling.

"What are the odds you'd invite me in another day?"

"Very high."

He sets me down slowly, my body sliding against the length of his. He's hard everywhere. The fact that he's going to just walk away from this is insane to me. Even I know I'm going to have to run inside and get myself off. He turns and walks toward the elevator, one hand in his pocket, the other swinging lightly at his side.

"Loren," I call out. He stops and turns to shoot me an expectant look. "What are the odds of me getting in that class?"

"After that?" He chuckles, shaking his head. "I'd say they're very low, but I'll see what I can do about getting your sister's name on the roster."

I'm halfway inside my apartment when he calls out my name, so I step back out, holding the door open with my right hand. "Yeah?"

"For the record, I would've carried you."

"Huh?"

"You said your feet hurt too much to wear heels," he says. "I would've carried you."

And then he leaves. I bring my hand up to my chest, letting the door of my apartment bump into my side as I stare at the now empty hallway. That may just be the nicest thing anyone has ever said to me.

ELEVEN

LORENZO

"GIOVANNI IS OPENING up Devil's Lair Saturday," I say.

"Shit." Dominic looks over at me wide-eyed. "How'd you find out?"

I stay quiet. What am I supposed to say? I was tracking his little sister, then lost track of her, then re-gained it and now I'm trying to fuck her? Nah. I'd rather lose a pinky before I confess to that. Not that Dominic has the power to take one from me, but he also doesn't have the rank to be questioning me, so I don't answer either way.

"Old news," Dean says from the backseat.

Dominic and I turn around to look at him. He's on his phone typing away. Doesn't even bother looking up to acknowledge our stares.

"Why didn't you say anything?" I ask.

He shrugs a shoulder. "What difference does it make?"

"For starters, it means he'll be here more often," I say. "He's bound to find out about this and he'll want in no doubt."

Dean's phone rings. He glances up at us as he answers it. I turn around and look straight ahead. We've been waiting longer than usual for the damn cargo plane to get here. I check my phone again to make sure it's still on its way. Six minutes the tracker says. Dean barks out an order on the phone and tosses it in the backseat. I look at him through the rearview.

"They arrested Joe."

"What?" I turn around. "What the fuck for?"

Here's the thing, I don't give a fuck about Joe. In fact, my uncle's beef with Joe runs so deep, that I bet he'll be celebrating his arrest within the hour. I don't give a fuck whether or not he rots in a jail cell or in his mansion, but if they have something on him they may have something on us as well and if they don't have something on us and he talks we're all as good as dead.

"I don't know yet," Dean says. "But I'm going to find out. Where the fuck is the cargo?"

God damn where the fuck *is* the cargo? I look at my phone again. "Two minutes."

Dom zips up his jacket. "I'll drive it to the warehouse, boss."

I nod. He gets out of the car and runs over to the security guard, one of his cousins. Another pro to having him on my payroll. It also happens to be the upside of this run, everything is simplified. We have guys on the inside who we take care of for their cooperation. It works out for all of us, but mostly for me. Dean gets out of the back and moves to the front seat, sighing as he shuts the door.

"This Joe arrest is going to be a problem," he says.

"Don't I know it." I glance at my watch. "I hate having everything in one spot, but I'm going to have to pay Gio a little visit and move the rest of my shit to Jamaican Mike's vault."

Dean nods, looking straight ahead as the cargo plane drives in our direction. "How much money did they say this one is holding?"

"One mill in cash. Not sure how much the jewelry's worth yet."

"How's the gas business?" he asks. My attention whips in his direction. He smiles slightly. "What? You think I wouldn't find out about it?"

"Who told you?"

"Silvio. Should've been you."

Why the fuck would my uncle tell anyone about the gas station business? It's not even a sure bet. I haven't seen the numbers. I say this aloud. Dean chuckles.

"Yeah, well, you have the Midas touch. I'm not worried about whatever money I put in."

I think it over because, fuck, I hate splitting my pie with too many people, but if Dean already knows about it and he wants in, he's not going to stop until I give him the option. I look at him again.

"It would be a small percentage."

"How small?"

"I don't know. I'm not sure how much money is going to come in yet. It's not cut and dry," I say, knowing that no matter how hard I try to explain it he won't get it. Dean isn't a numbers guy. He doesn't cut pie; he just eats it.

"Just let me know how much money I'd need to put in and how much I'd make." He shrugs. "That's pretty cut and dry."

"We'll talk next week."

After what feels like an eternity, the gates open and the red semi-truck drives out. I put the car in reverse and head to the warehouse by the Hudson. I try to think about the million dollars in cash and the extra in jewelry in the truck behind me, but my mind is on Joe Masseria's arrest and what that'll mean for his family and the rest of us.

TWELVE

CATALINA

I CHANGE into the flowy dress I brought and re-apply my makeup in the mirror, more natural this time, not the stage makeup we use under the lighting beamed on us. Once I'm finished, I pop my head into the dressing room next door, where the rest of the girls are. Bella beams a pretty smile in my direction when she spots me. I take in the curve hugging little black dress she's wearing and raise an eyebrow. She laughs as she walks over to me, linking her arm with mine as we head out to where the cocktail party is taking place.

"I'm ready for this club opening thing," Bella says. "Better than the bore we have to endure right now."

She's one of the dancers I knew would go for it because she's young and completely reckless. Lilly and Darcy are the other two. I limited it to the four of us because I really don't want to get more people involved and because Lilly, Darcy, and Bella are the three I trust to keep this a secret, because NDA aside, dancers talk a lot. Gossip is how we survive twelve-hour-days without strangling each other. I don't normally mind it. I actually enjoy a little bit of tea time, even when it revolved around the state of mine and Justin's non-existing relationship.

It's as if every single person here, girls and guys alike, is dying for us to get married. All it tells me is that we have great chemistry on stage, which is good enough for me. What I don't enjoy is knowing that come Monday, tea time will be centered around Gio and his . . . questionable actions. It's something I've fought against the majority of my life, and here I am again.

"Yeah, well, keep that in mind when we're over there," I respond.

"How do you know Giovanni Masseria anyway?"

"Family friend."

"Wow," she breathes. "If he were my family friend, I would've married him already."

I laugh. "You say that because you don't know him."

"I follow enough gossip magazines to know some things about him." She glances at me and lowers her voice to a whisper as we near some of the patrons. "He's dated like three supermodels."

"Right, and we're mere ballerinas."

"Well, if you believe the rumors out of Chicago, he's dating a soloist over there."

I feel myself stiffen. Why would my brother date someone in my realm, knowing how hard I try to stay away from the family?

"You know how ballet gossip is," Bella says with a shrug.

On that note, we walk out and start going up to our sponsors. I never thought spending a couple of hours around people who make you feel like you're a doll in their expensive collection would be a welcome change, but with the information Bella just gave me, the attention from the benefactors is a welcome distraction.

"I FEEL LIKE A DOMINATRIX," Bella says later, when we're in the Devil's Lair trying on our costumes.

"More like Natalie Portman in Black Swan."

I snort-laugh at that because she's totally right. "We should've brought our black pointe shoes for this."

"I can get you black pointe shoes." The voice comes from my brother, who's suddenly standing at the threshold of the dressing room. The girls startle. I merely glance up at him.

"You can't buy us pointe shoes," I say. "Even if you could, we'd need to condition the shit out of them before wearing them."

He shrugs. I wonder if they can see the resemblance. While my sister and I look more like our mother—with our dark red hair and pale skin, Gio looks like Dad—tall, lean, with dark hair, dark eyes and even darker thoughts. He's always been like that, even as a kid. I've never seen him in a good mood that lasted longer than five minutes. He's broody. Intelligent and business-savvy, even witty sometimes, but moody as fuck. I think of Loren and feel myself smile. I wonder if they'd get along. Gio lifts the brown bag in his hand and shakes it as he walks to the center of the room. He sets it down on the table and looks at me, only me. He hasn't even really acknowledged the other girls.

"The masks."

None of the girls have said a word. It's as if Gio has the ability to make even the loudest women quiet. I'm not sure whether to call it impressive or depressing. Surely someone out there ought to stand up and challenge him every once in a while.

"Thanks," I say, and because no one else will, I add, "What's the status on the payments?"

He glances at his watch. "Currently being wired."

"Hmm. Where's Frankie?"

"Taking care of some things. You'll see him after. Did you speak to the DJ?"

I nod. "And the girl in charge of lighting and the caterers—they brought food over a little while ago."

Gio finally looks away from me and glances at the other girls. "Thank you for being here, ladies. I trust you'll find two-thousand-dollars per song is sufficient."

My jaw drops. The girls gasp and scream and jump, all saying thank you twenty-billion times. I smile at him because he's so extra-over-the-top, but I know these girls need that money. It's not like the city is affordable and even though I make decent money, most of the dancers are not on a lucrative salary. Any extra cash helps. A hint of a smile touches Gio's face as he looks at me before he walks out of the room. The minute he does, everyone, including me, lets out a relieved breath.

"He's so hot," Bella whispers.

"OhmyGod, yes," Darcy agrees. "Can you believe how much he's paying us?"

"I'd do him for free, but holy shit," adds Lily.

"Let's look at these masks." I reach into the bag and take them all out.

They're all black with feathers, with the exception of one, which is gold. I assume it's for me. I wonder why he wants to differentiate me. I try so hard not to think it's for any cynical reason, and I know my brother would never in a million years hurt me, but why then? Why?

"Are we going to perform '*Weak and Sober Up*'?" Darcy asks. I nod. She smiles. "We did those in rehearsal the other day and it was so good."

"So much fun," Lily says, smiling.

"Are we going to work the pole a little? I've always wanted to," Bella says.

"We can." I shrug.

Why the hell not? It's not like I've never worked a pole or

anything. Not that I've done it for money, but back home when I came back after high school, Gio had just opened his first club and I used to perform in the VIP section. No stripping, just dancing, and only as a way to eavesdrop.

Thirty-five minutes later, we're standing on a stage with four poles on it that are clearly for the strippers he claimed he did not want at his club. I'll have to ask him about that later. There's a sheer black curtain in front of us that I told them to drop as a cue when the song hits.

"Can you adjust mine? I want to make sure it doesn't fall off," Bella says, turning to me.

I reach up and fix her mask. They hit us right above our mouths and the material was well-thought-out in the sense that it seems like they won't slip off with sweat.

"There are a lot of men here," Lily whispers. "Thank God they can't see us."

"They're wearing masks too. It's not like we can see them," Darcy whispers back. It's true, their faces are all covered by masks as well. With the kind of company my brother keeps, I'm surprised they agreed to it.

"Some of their bodies look promising," Bella adds.

"And others look like my dad," Lily says.

We all laugh at that. We stand in our places and positions— feet in fifth position, arms altering between fourth and first. Butterflies swarm my belly the way they always do right before the music starts, and then the AJR song drops and we move. To break up monotony during rehearsals, we switch up the music and dance to all kinds of music, pop, house, country, rap—you name it, we dance it. It's the most fun we have together and this is no different. The sheer black curtain drops to the floor past the stage and the four of us find the poles, using them as an accessory to our dance. In our series of *releves* and *sautes* we add in regular dance moves as if we were at a club. I don't have to look out to the audience to know the men are enjoying themselves. Between the hoots and hollers and the whistles, they're obviously liking the show. "Sober Up" starts and the girls and I share a laugh because it's late and I'm pretty sure no one in this room is sober. Our amusement is cut by the sound of the violin in the song. We start our contemporary dance, moving in synch, the way we do so often. The music switches once more, to a hip-hop/house type of song, that we move to before closing the show with a twerk that we've only done in class as a joke, but the men get a big rise out of it. The last piece we perform is a classic from the Nutcracker, in which we all act like dolls.

Finally, we take our bows and make our exit, one by one, showing them that graceful ballerinas can do it all. There's a roar of applause and hoots and hollers that make us all laugh as we catch our breath. We walk back to the dressing room and change into our street clothes. Lilly leaves first, she always calls her parents in Japan at this time. Bella and Darcy stay behind for a little while, but leave after drinks and a few snacks are brought back to the dressing room. Once I'm left alone in the room, I lay flat on the floor and close my eyes.

"That tired, huh?"

I don't open my eyes to look at my brother, but I smile and nod. "That was nice what you did."

I hear his footsteps inch closer and then take in the scent of his cologne as he sits on the floor beside me. It's a comforting smell, reminds me of birthdays and Christmas and the time he punched that kid in London who spread rumors about me being a prude because I wouldn't jerk him off in the custodian closet.

"Me? Nice?"

I open my eyes just so I can roll them at him. "You're a cheap ass and you paid them a lot because you knew they needed it. So yeah, nice."

"Huh."

"What?"

He brings a hand down and runs it over the top of my hair. "Nothing. Never thought you'd think something I did was nice."

"Yeah, well, maybe you should do nice things more often."

"I'll keep that in mind." He smiles. "Did you hear about dad?"

I sit up. "What?"

"Police took him in last night."

My chest constricts. "Why?"

"Conspiracy to murder."

"What?" I breathe. "Jesus." I bury my face in my hands.

"I didn't think you'd care," Gio says.

I can't even look up at him right now. I can't. How can I not care? Sure, I don't speak to my father. I don't even answer the phone when he calls. After mom left, I just . . . I can't bear it. I can't. I was never close to Mom, I was always a daddy's girl, but that doesn't mean I didn't hope to one day win her love. When she left, she took that opportunity away. When she made it clear that she would not be staying in touch, it broke my heart. All of our hearts. Dad changed, became a different person. I stopped speaking to him, stopping calling home and definitely stopped going home. Still, he's my father. He's the person who taught me how to ride a bike and took me to ballet every day when I was a kid. Other girls in the class had their mothers in the waiting area, I had dad. I lower my hands, wiping my wet face as I do.

"Is it true?" I whisper.

Gio's expression gives nothing away, but he shrugs. He doesn't say yes or no, and that kills me.

"Who?" I whisper. "Who are they saying he killed?"

"I can't tell you that, Cat." His voice is soft, his eyes sympathetic. "It's better you don't know."

Right. Because then I'd be one more person they could come after with questions.

"I need you to do me a favor if you're up for it," he says, standing up. "It's for Dad."

"Yo. You over here?" Frankie calls out, stomping toward us.

We both look in the direction of the door and watch as he walks in. He's the shortest one of the group, and even then he's taller than me by a lot. We were raised like cousins, but he's like a brother to me.

"Hey Frankie," I say, smiling.

"Hey, Kitty Cat."

"Don't call me that." I groan. I've always hated that nickname. It was given to me by my ex-fiancé. Or dead fiancé. I've never really been sure what to refer to him as.

He laughs and wraps an arm around me. "I loved the show you put on. Maybe you can give me a private one later."

"Fuck off," Gio scolds, tearing Frankie's arm off me as we laugh.

"The Little Italy and Hell's Kitchen locations were broken into," Frankie says suddenly.

"Did they take anything?" Gio asks, his voice incredibly low.

"A shit load of stuff and set some other locations on fire."

"On fire?" Gio shouts. "Who the fuck—"

I pull away from them, knowing I shouldn't be listening to this conversation. If the girls needed masks to protect their identity, I'd need my entire head chopped off. I busy myself with packing up instead. They step into the hallway and continue their hushed conversation. When I'm done picking up, I idle about, walking around the room that I'm sure will be used by strippers or future performers.

"Some. Took all of Costello's shit."

"Fuck!" Gio slams a fist into the door. I flinch at the fist and the name Costello. My ears perk up. My brother shakes his head, breathing hard. "As if I need one more problem with that bastard."

"He's here."

Gio's quiet for a beat. "I'm surprised he showed."

"You know he gives no fucks."

"Still." Gio punches the wall again. "Fuck. Find out exactly what they took."

Silence hangs again. Gio walks back into the room and gives me a sheepish look. "Sorry. You up for that favor I mentioned?"

Frankie steps in to the room. "G, I don't think—"

My brother puts a hand up to shut him up. "I'm speaking to my sister."

"Whatever. I'll be in the club figuring shit out," Frankie mutters, turning around.

"What's the favor?" I ask.

"I need you to dance in the VIP room and eavesdrop on some people."

"I thought you had cameras everywhere."

"No audio in the VIP rooms."

"Am I supposed to strip?" I ask.

"No stripping. Just dance. The dancers just started on the main floor. Everyone's playing poker, so they're just there for show. You'll be in there for show too. They won't talk to you. It'll be like having a TV on while you're cooking dinner. Background noise."

Declining the offer and asking him to find one of the other girls and have them do it is on the tip of my tongue. I'm tired. My body is aching. I have a performance tomorrow night. Normally, saying no would be a no-brainer, but it's my brother and he just told me Dad got arrested and obviously one of their business locations was broken into. I can't really say no, so I say yes.

I look around. "What do I change into?"

THIRTEEN

CATALINA

I'M NOT NAKED, but I might as well be. At least I still have the mask on. To add to that, I have heels on. Fucking heels. Wearing heels right after taking off pointe shoes for the third time today is like sticking my foot in a blender. It doesn't help that I haven't conditioned or stretched my feet today. I try not to wobble on them as I make my way over to the main VIP room, which is on the far end of the club, past the stage I was on earlier. Gio's right about the men playing poker and not paying attention to anything else. They're laughing and conversing about God knows what. They're no longer wearing masks and I get the feeling that they'd prefer not to have any women here at all.

I pull the VIP door open and step inside, pausing as I close it behind me. There are four men in here, all wearing dark suits, no masks. The light is dim and red, so I can't see their faces, but I can feel their eyes on me, like they're waiting for me to hurry up and get on the stage. I keep my head down as I head to the center of the room. It's a small, low stage, one meant to welcome advances. It creeps me out, but I find the steps none-theless. I take the heels off. It's one thing to agree to this and an entirely different one to jeopardize my career over it. If I twist my ankle doing one of these movements I'm fucked. Hell, as it is I'm already worried about my wrists.

The men are engaged in hushed conversation again, one I can barely hear over the hum of the bass coming from the other room and the tempo of the music in this one, as I head onto the stage, directly to the pole. Luckily, I've taken pole dancing lessons for years. It's one of the ways I condition when I'm not in a show. Pole dancing, hot yoga, Pilates, you name it.

"I found him in Florida," one of the men says. I twirl around the pole and close my eyes to listen more closely.

"Does Dean know?"

My eyes pop open at the sound of that voice. I stop moving. They stop talking. I make myself move again, heart thundering, but they don't pick up their conversation again. Instead, I hear him say, "Get out."

I make myself look up at them. The three men to his right are all frozen on the couch, waiting.

He repeats, "Get out."

I straighten and start moving off the stage, but the men also get up and walk out of the room in a single file line. I'm walking toward the little stairs on the side of the stage when his voice stops me.

"I didn't mean you."

My pulse quickens. I move back toward the pole. Does he know it's me? There's no way he does. I have a mask on my face. My hair is up and even if it weren't he couldn't make out the color due to the muted lighting. There's no way he knows. He must think I'm one of the dancers who works here.

"Dance," he says, his voice commanding. "Isn't that what you're here for?"

I go back to the pole and do what he's asked, twirling my legs around the pole. I'm upside down, my legs clenched around the pole, when he walks over to me. I smell him rather than see him, my eyes are hazy as I slide down, gripping on to it with one hand. I bite the inside of my cheek to keep a straight face, but inside I'm freaking out. Does he know? Does he know? And what the hell is he doing here in the first place?

"No heels again, huh? Not even in here?" he asks, his voice low.

I stumble over my naked feet, my ass nearly hitting the floor. He somehow manages to grab my hand and stop that from happening as I gape. He can't possibly know who I am. Can't. There's absolutely no way. I'm wearing a mask!

"How—"

"I want a lap dance," he says before I can ask the question. He steps away from the stage and takes a seat.

Oh my God. *I can't give him a lap dance here.* My brother is probably watching the cameras right now. No. Scratch that. He's not watching, but he will and when he does I'm going to get yelled at and Loren is going to get shot. The whole point of me being in here is to eavesdrop and I only heard one thing. Gio will be in here soon for sure. He'll stop this charade.

In the meantime, I step forward, slowly descending the stairs to stand between his legs. He's watching me closely, those eyes burning embers into me, igniting a needy feeling in the pit of my belly. He grips my thigh with one hand, it's a possessive hold that warms me throughout.

"Move."

His words rumble through me, but somehow I manage to rest one knee on the couch beside him and bring a hand up, running my fingers through his soft hair. He makes a little growling sound in the back of his throat, closing his eyes briefly. When they open, his gaze catches mine again, this time hot, feral. My pulse spikes. I rock my hips against him. He sinks his teeth into his bottom lip and groans as if he's savoring the moment. My grip tightens on his hair, his tightens on my thigh, my ass, my hips. I move my other leg so I'm straddling him completely. He moves his hands so they're on my waist, his thumbs caressing my rib cage. I'm glad I'm wearing my leotard, even though his touch feels like it's burning holes through it.

"How many people are watching us right now?" he asks.

"I don't know." My voice is a breath, barely audible over the swishing in my ears and the music playing, but I manage to keep my eyes on his as I rock my hips against him.

"I want to feel how wet you are for me," he says. "Would you let me? Would you let me play with your clit? Would you rock into me like you're doing now?"

My eyes glaze over. I moan, but keep moving, faster, my hips gyrating in a way that's not even up to tempo with the music, but I can't seem to stop. Even in the darkness, I can see his gaze darken, his jaw clench. He licks his lower lip slowly, rocking into me, letting me feel how hard he is in his slacks. Now it's my turn to bite my lip. He doesn't say a word and I don't either even though there are millions of thoughts running through my head. Millions of questions I want to ask. Loren makes it impossible not to get lost in the moment though.

He makes it impossible not to play this game of dry-humping. He leaves me wanting more, needing a release and he's barely even touching me. But the way he looks at me like he wants to flip me over and fuck me? The way his hands hold my hips like he'd damn well take ownership of my body? All of it sets me ablaze. The door opens behind me. I instantly stop moving.

"Time's up." It's Frankie's voice.

I push off Loren's shoulders and stand, wishing like hell I could lock that door and bash the cameras and just finish what we started. Instead, I walk over to the door without turning back. Frankie walks me to Gio's office. I relay to him the conversation I heard, which isn't much. He looks at Frankie beside me.

"Who's in Florida?"

"I don't know," Frankie says.

"Find out." Gio looks over at me. "Thanks, sis. Frankie will take you home now."

"You're welcome." I give him a quick hug and start to walk away.

"While Dad's in jail, we need to keep our eyes peeled," Gio says.

"No one knows I'm here," I say. "I use mom's last name for a reason."

"I know, but I want you to be extra careful. Stay close to your dance partners."

I nod. "What about Emma?"

"She's fine. She's walking around with a federal marshal."

I smile. I like that.

"Lock your windows and doors."

I frown. "I live on the eighth floor."

Gio shrugs. "You never know."

I shake my head as I walk out. Who sleeps with their windows and doors unlocked anyway? I follow Frankie to the street and get into the car he unlocks. He rented a red sports car that looks more expensive than my entire apartment building.

"You know, this is exactly why you guys get a bad reputation," I say as he swerves through Manhattan.

"Because we drive recklessly?"

"Because you get these flashy cars *and* drive recklessly."

"Vincent always had the flashiest cars," he says, glancing over at me. "You didn't mind those."

I swallow, glancing away. I don't mind talking to Emma about Vincent, but talking to someone who was like a brother to him makes me uneasy. How do you talk about someone who was there every second of the day and in the blink of an eye was taken? It's a difficult subject to broach. Vincent and I might've been dating for two years, but most of it was long distance.

Even me coming back every holiday and him going to London to visit every once in a while wasn't really enough. When he died . . . when he was killed . . . murdered . . . I was able to cope with it by not going home anymore. When the burn of the grief shot through me, I could pretend he was away on business, unable to answer my calls. I did that for the first year—ignored the reality. He was gone and never coming back.

"I know you don't like to talk about him," Frankie says, "but I live with the pain every day, and I think in a way his death set you free." My gaze snaps to his. I can't respond because of the ball in my throat, so I let him continue, "You always wanted to be free. How was that going to happen if you'd stayed with him? You knew what he was, Cat."

"I loved him," I whisper. "I didn't want to be free of him."

"He was in this life, always at death's doorstep." He pulls into my building's parking garage and turns into a spot right beside the door. When he switches off the engine, he looks over at me. My arms are still crossed, trying to hold in the tears burning in my throat. "You weren't meant for this life, Catalina. I'm glad you've stayed away as long as you have."

He opens the door. I open my own, grabbing my duffel bag as I get out of his car. I glance around the parking garage quickly. The few times I've come in here, I hop straight into a car or straight out of one and into the building, but today I feel hyperaware of my surroundings and it feels like I'm being watched. I look around once more.

"Everything okay?" Frankie asks.

I rush over to the door he's holding open for me. "Yeah. Fine. You don't have to walk me all the way in. You can just go."

"Okay. I'll be around." He wraps an arm around me in a familiar side hug. I do the same.

"Like around here?"

He nods. I nod because I still have a knot in my throat, but knowing he'll be around makes me feel a little more at ease.

Still, I close the door and practically sprint to my apartment. Once there, I lock the door behind me and check them once more to make sure I'm safe. Maybe it's what Gio said that has me paranoid, but I'm sick with the feeling that someone may have followed us here.

FOURTEEN

CATALINA

I TAKE a quick plunge in an ice bath and clean before continuing my foot care routine. I called my sister when I got home, but she didn't answer. She sent a text that included a picture of what looked like a nightclub and said she'd call me in the morning. I reach for my phone again, this time, I text message Loren. Five simple words: *what were you doing there?* I wait, and wait, but his response never comes. I tell myself he was just at the strip club. A regular guy at a strip club. No harm, no foul.

He's not involved in any of the stuff my brother is into. At least I know that much. Men like my brother don't take women to hole-in-the-wall pizza parlors. They wine and dine them and show off their expensive cars and watches. Loren's too humble to be in that life. I'm applying my muscle pain cream to my calves when there's a knock on the door. I freeze. Fucking Frankie. I hate it when he stakes out and watches us. It always leads to a knock on the door and us having to invite him to sleep on the couch. I stand up with a sigh, pulling my silk robe around me and tightening the belt as I walk over.

I stand on the tips of my toes and look through the peephole, only to gasp at the sight of Loren on the other side. I stand flat on my feet, then on my tip toes once more to look again. He's still standing there, wearing a black suit, white button down, no tie. His dark hair unruly, his piercing eyes on mine. He looks imposing and menacing and sexy as fuck. That sinful mouth of his pulls up slightly. *Shit*. He must know I'm right here. I debate not opening. Everything tells me not to. Every bone in my body begs me to send him away, to pretend I'm sleeping. I should be sleeping. Everything except that ache in between my legs, and that's why, against my better judgement, I open the door.

"Hey."

I half-expect him to apologize for coming unannounced, but something tells me Loren isn't the type to apologize for his actions. His eyes rake down my body slowly. In the few seconds it takes his gaze to travel down my body, to my bare feet, exposed legs, and back up to meet my eyes, I feel like I've lived and died ten times. He stands there for what feels like an eternity, which is probably closer to a couple of agonizing seconds, without saying a word and normally I'd call someone out for that because it's awkward, but I can't seem to find my words around this guy.

"What are the odds you'd invite me in?"

I swallow. "High."

I move out of the way, letting him step inside before I close the door and lock it again. As I face it, I take a second, then two, to breathe, but all I can smell is that cologne that's as sexy as the man wearing it. And, *holy crap*, I just invited him into my apartment where I'm alone and wearing nothing but underwear beneath my robe. Not even sexy underwear at that. *Shit*. I take one last breath before turning around to face him. He walks toward me, his fancy shoes tapping against the hardwood as he closes the distance between us. My heart hammers, but I manage to tilt my head and meet his gaze. There's a wicked promise in his eyes that makes my knees quiver. A look that says, *I'm going to devour you and you're going to enjoy every second of it.* He's still watching me like that, through hooded eyes, as he brings his hand up to my neck and closes it there, his thumb brushing directly over the center of my clavicle. My pulse throbs. I swallow, unable to help myself.

"You're nervous," he says, his voice a deep husk that nearly makes me come undone.

Am I nervous? Yes. Yes, I am because I know that if I let myself go with him, the fall will be hard. With a man like Loren the aftermath won't be pretty. But still, I lean into his touch and fall into his kiss when his mouth finally hits mine. The moment his tongue sweeps into my mouth, the nerves melt away. All I can do is feel, with his fingers expertly undoing the knot of my robe and sliding over my stomach, my waist, until they reach my breasts. He stops then, and pulls back to look at me, his eyes cloudy with a lust so powerful I swear I feel it between my legs. It's half a second, yet it feels like an eternity.

I'm not sure if he's asking if this is okay or if he's waiting to see if I'll tell him to stop, but my entire body is alight with want and there's no way I'm going to stop this. I reach up, wrapping a hand around the back of his neck and pull his lips to mine once more. He groans into my mouth. This time, the kiss isn't slow, but frenzied. He brings his hands down and lifts me up with ease. I tug at his shirt. We stop kissing long enough for me to pull the shirt over his head and toss it. With his hands still squeezing my ass, I bring mine to the button of his jeans. He pulls back, his eyes burning with lust.

"Fuck I can't believe how much I want you." It's a whispered growl that vibrates through me.

He buries his face in my neck and breathes me in as he carries me away from the front door, through my apartment, straight into my bedroom. How he knows it's mine is something I dwell on for all of five seconds because he sets me down on my mattress ever so slowly, and pulls away. I'm laid out on full display before him as he looms over me. It's only then that I really realize how fucking sexy he is. His skin is tan, a light caramel color that I can only achieve with tanning lotion. Without his solid chest pressed up against mine, I'm able to see every cut on his abdomen, every slope of his muscular arms. Geez. Dancers have muscles most people have never heard of, but Loren? Loren looks like a god. When I catch his gaze again, he runs his tongue along his bottom lip and shakes his head as if he's imagining this whole thing.

He reaches for me then, uncovering whatever is actually being hidden by my flimsy robe. With the way he's looking at me, I thought I was naked. That's how Loren makes me feel. Bare and open to him. It scares and thrills me. He runs the back of his right hand down the center of my chest, between my breasts, which aren't very large but I've always been fond of them because their size doesn't leave much room for them to sag at all. His hand continues down my stomach, to my underwear, which are the cheeky silk kind I bought on sale recently without having a clue that I'd feel every. single. touch over them. I arch off the bed slightly, my breath quickening as his fingers dip between my legs.

"So fucking sexy," he says, his eyes on mine again.

I quiver. "Maybe you should finish undressing."

"I will."

Instead of complying, he brings both hands to my ankles and pulls me in a quick sweep so that I'm closer to him. His hands make their way slowly from my feet to my underwear, which he, in turn, drags down my legs in a way that makes me want to beg him to hurry the fuck up because coming without foreplay would be embarrassing. He gets on his knees and parts my legs, his lips caress my inner thighs, making their way up my body. Every kiss beckons a new wave of shivers from me. He stops when he reaches my breasts. Wordlessly, I sit up, letting the robe slide down my arms. We're nose-to-nose as Loren puts one hand beside me on the bed and brings the other to cup my face. We're mingled breath and wanton eyes. I try to make sense of the myriad of emotions I'm feeling but they continue to elude me, leaving me to only feel his touch. He presses his lips against mine and it quiets the darkness lingering behind my eyelids, it silences my brain. He pulls away and drags his mouth over me again, stopping at each breast. I arch with each motion, each lick, each suck. He drags his lips down my body. I hold my breath when he spreads my legs and dips his head between them.

"Fuck." He groans deeply.

I bite my lip to keep the mewl I feel in the back of my throat from forming, but then his tongue flicks my clit once, twice, and by the third time I can't help it. My hips begin to sway, to move against his mouth, searching for release on his tongue. He glances up, catching my gaze, and whatever he finds there makes him growl against me, the sound sends waves of pleasure through me as he clasps his mouth closed over my clit and sucks. I press my head against the mattress, squeezing my eyes shut, my back bowing from the bed in ecstasy as I find my release.

I'm still seeing stars as he stands up, but manage to open my eyes. Through my haze, I watch him take off his jeans, his boxer briefs. My legs fall open on their own accord as he looks at me, using one hand to stroke himself. Like a magnet, my eyes find what he's touching, and I gasp audibly. There's absolutely no way. I back up on the bed. I'm trying to be in the moment, but how the hell am I going to stand up tomorrow, let alone dance? Clearly sensing my hesitation, Loren drops his hand as he climbs between my legs. He kisses me then in a way that sucks all the air out of my lungs and brings a hand between my legs, his fingers playing with my clit and dipping in. I gasp into his mouth, rocking against him.

"You're going to kill me," I whisper against his lips. He

merely chuckles and bites down on my bottom lip, pulling another orgasm out of me with his skilled fingers.

My entire body is shaking with my orgasm, but I watch through hazy eyes as he slides on a condom. The tip of his dick hits my clit once, twice. I bite down on my lip, unsure if I can take any more of this, but then he thrusts into me achingly slow, as if to let my body adjust to his girth, and I feel like I'm going to die if he pulls out. He does pull out then, despite my complaints, and pushes in again, deeply, groaning with each thrust like he really feels it. It does something to me, that groan. If I wasn't suddenly feeling so shy, I would tell him that I'm ready. I'm ready for him to lose himself inside of me. Loren doesn't give me the chance. His hands make their way back up my torso and find my breasts.

He pinches my nipples as he looks down at me, his expression masked with a hunger that our hands and mouths can't seem to sate. He lets go of my breasts and drags his hands down my body to my legs as he continues his slow rhythm. He grabs my thighs and spreads them further, pushing in deeper, causing a wave of pleasure to rock through me. I can't contain the sounds coming from my mouth. I should be embarrassed, but there's no stopping the screams or moans or pleas. Then he starts fucking me, really fucking me, pounding into me so hard and so deep that I can't even think straight. He leaves my legs spread open like that, gripping one of my thighs as he brings the other hand in to rub my clit. I start shrieking. Not even the bed creaking or banging against the wall can hide my sounds now, but Loren leans down, and still fucking me, brings his mouth to mine, sweeping his tongue in a frenzied kiss.

"You feel so fucking good," he says. "Like heaven, Little Red. Fucking heaven."

My chest starts heaving and I realize, as he's pounding into me relentlessly, that I'm crying. The combination of his hands everywhere I need them, his penis working some sort of magic

I've never experienced, and his tongue in my mouth is making me feel too much, it's too strong. His fingers find my clit again and I'm sure I can't take anymore.

"Loren," I say, gasping, "Oh my God. Loren!"

He kisses me deeply then, his tongue exploring my mouth as he growls into me. I scream so loudly into the kiss, I'm sure I won't have a voice tomorrow. Someone bangs on the wall, and I don't even have it in me to be embarrassed, but Loren chuckles. His amusement is short lived because his own orgasm rocks through his body and it's the most marvelous thing I've ever seen—this statue of a man, who's perfect in every way, suddenly shivering. He throws his head back and mutters a string of curse words as he empties inside of me. He's wearing a condom, but I swear I can practically feel every single drop of his semen through the latex, and even that manages to turn me on.

The second he pulls out of me, my entire body quivers in aftershocks. *Holy shit.* I don't think that's happened to me with a human in like . . . *ever.* It's a jarring realization, one that I can't afford to dwell on. I've been avoiding complicated relationships my entire adult life, and what just happened between us is way beyond complicated. He gives me one more of those long, earth-shattering kisses before rolling off the bed. He lands on his feet with the grace of a cat, not making a sound, and I idly wonder if this guy's a ninja.

"You can stay," I whisper.

My throat is hoarse from the screaming and I instantly kick myself for inviting him to stay. That further complicates things. *What am I even doing right now?* Loren doesn't respond. He simply walks over to the bathroom like he's been here a million times. I take a deep breath, wipe my face, and let it out. I am officially bone tired. Before I find out whether or not he's going to take me up on the offer, I fall into a dead sleep.

FIFTEEN

CATALINA

MY PERFORMANCE IS shaky at best. The reason I don't have sex the night before I dance is because I need all of my muscles to cooperate fully and this was a shit-show. Thank God the audience doesn't seem to notice, but Justin does. And thank God Justin is partnering me right now because he's able to catch me and make every misstep I take look like it's part of the choreography. Fuck my life. He's going to ream into me about this afterwards. I know it.

The piece ends, the applause starts, the flowers come, and I instantly know they're from my brother. He's the only person who would give me sunflowers, my favorite as a little girl. After the final curtain call, as we're walking backstage, Justin pulls me aside.

"What the fuck was that?"

I close my eyes. "I know. I'm so sorry."

Justin sighs heavily, shaking his head as we walk toward the dressing rooms, where everyone is jumping to and fro from one to the other, naked or half naked, depending on how far they've gotten in changing into their clothes after the set. Sundays are always a celebration around here since for a lot of us, Mondays are our days off. One of the other principal dancers comes up to us and starts talking to Justin about his plans and I dip out before he starts going off on me again. Most nights, I wait to shower when I get home, but tonight I need to wash away the disappointment that follows a performance like that. Once I'm finished showering, I've managed to move past it. Mistakes happen. We're allowed off nights. The end.

I step back outside, wearing skinny jeans, a frilly white blouse, and leopard loafers. Justin, who's changed into joggers and a t-shirt, comes right up to me. I groan an obvious *fuck, do we need to do this right now?* The look he gives me says *yes, we do.* I cross my arms over my chest and hear him out, trying not to tune out because I know he means well and is only trying to help. I nod along, *yes, I'll keep my head in the game on Tuesday. Yes, I know we're due to perform for the president on Wednesday. Yes, I know it's a big deal.*

"Who's the lucky guy?" he asks once he's done.

I blink. "What?"

"I know you. You're only this distracted when you're sleeping with someone and normally I'd be flattered because it's me, but clearly that's not the case. Is it someone in the company?"

I look away from him, my eyes catching movement over his shoulder. Everyone in the hallway is parting for the person who's coming and staring as if Moses himself were moving past them. The hair on the back of my neck stands up in anticipation, and then I see Loren, and my pulse spikes through my veins. Justin's attention follows mine and he mutters, *I knew it,* under his breath. My gaze snaps to his momentarily.

"I hope you know what you're getting into," he warns as he shakes his head and walks away from me.

I don't have the time nor the inclination to question him because the only thing I can do is look at Loren again. He's dressed in a navy suit, brown shoes that look like they cost more than my rent, and a white button down that he has casually unbuttoned up top. My mouth waters at the sight of him as he walks toward me, one hand in his pocket, the other swinging at his side. His eyes are hot and locked on mine. I swallow the nerves crawling up my throat as he reaches me. He doesn't say a word as he stands in front of me, towering over me, and wraps a hand behind my neck. My eyes fall closed, anticipating the kiss, but it never comes. Instead, he leans his forehead against mine, his calloused thumb running over the side of my neck, and waits until I re-open my eyes to speak.

"You were beautiful out there," he says, his voice a husky whisper.

I open my mouth to refute that because I wasn't, but I leave it alone. "I didn't know you would be here."

"I'm addicted to watching you dance."

"Yeah?" I smile shakily, my breath caught in my throat.

I lick my lips, still waiting for his mouth to come down on mine. I feel eyes on us—a lot of them—as if I never left the stage at all, but I don't acknowledge them. I can't bring myself to break this spell. His eyes are a darker shade of that brown-green mix today, and the look in them makes every muscle in my body pull with want.

"Or maybe it's just you I'm addicted to." He pulls away slightly, his hand still on my neck, his thumb still moving in a motion that makes my nipples harden. "Who gave you the flowers?"

"My brother. I'm supposed to have dinner with him tonight."

"Hmm. I guess I'll just have to make do with this moment."

"You can come over later," I say, before realizing I won't be home later. I'm about to retract my statement, before he shakes his head, his nose brushing mine.

"I have to work."

"So late?"

"Hmm." And then his mouth is on mine, his lips moving slowly yet possessively, his tongue diving into my mouth and colliding with mine, he releases a deep groan that rocks through me. He pulls away too quickly, looking down at me one last time. "Tomorrow night."

"Tomorrow night," I agree. He starts walking away from me, when I stop him by calling out his name. I walk over to where he is a few steps away. "What were you doing there yesterday?"

For a moment, he just looks at me, and I think he's not going to answer. "I was hanging out with some friends. Getting some work done," he says.

"Working," I repeat. "At a strip club."

"What were you doing there?" He raises an eyebrow.

"Working."

"At a strip club." He narrows his eyes slightly. I bite my lip and look away, feeling like I'm wedged between a rock and a hard place. He brings his hand to my face and caresses my cheek. I look at him anew. "Tomorrow night," he says again. I nod, letting my questions go.

He walks away for real this time. I hear a few claps and hoots from my fellow dancers, and then another large, imposing body nears me and I instantly stiffen, knowing it's my brother. When he confirmed that he was coming, I reminded him that I didn't want him making a huge fuss over me, mostly because I didn't want people knowing that Giovanni Masseria and I are related. It's messed up. I know, but I can't help it. My entire life my last name has loomed over me like a rain cloud and I don't want it to follow me into this arena. After a beat I decide to hell with it. My happiness for his presence here is greater than my shame over my last name. I glance up at him and take in the curious look in his eyes.

"Was that—" he frowns, looking in the direction where Loren just walked.

My heart launches into my throat as I wait. I should ask

him. I should tell him Loren's name and have him tell me what he knows, if he knows anything at all. I think about what he said, that he was working, hanging out with some friends. I have to assume that was the little meeting I walked into that he quickly canceled when he saw me. My brother shakes his head, his frown disappearing as he looks back at me, the confusion cleared. I decide I don't want to ask. I'd rather find out for myself. Besides, whatever it is we're doing isn't anyone's business.

"You ready to go?"

"Ready." I smile. "Thanks for the flowers, by the way."

"You're welcome." He smiles down at me. I put my hand on his bicep as we start walking. "I haven't seen you dance in so long. I forgot how good you are."

His words send a warm feeling through me. I squeeze his arm, then sigh. "I was off my game. I'm kinda bummed about that."

"Well, no one in the audience knew that. Promise. Every single person around me was in awe of the way you move."

I smile at that as we walk outside. As usual, there are a handful of people, mostly kids, waiting for autographs and pictures. I let go of my brother's arm and walk over to them. The hair on the back of my neck pricks in awareness as I'm signing a four-year-old girl's ballerina book. I glance up mid-signature and look around but don't spot anything out of the ordinary. I move on to the next kid and the next, signing ballet slippers and photo books before waving goodbye. I'm no Misty Copeland, whom everyone wants a picture with, but to these kids anyone who walks out of those doors is important. I scan the sidewalk for my brother, who's standing in the corner with his hands in the pockets of his dress pants, grinning as he watches me walk over. He puts an arm around my shoulder.

"Damn. My little sister is famous."

I laugh. "Shut up. If you didn't look so grumpy and imposing they'd think you were a dancer too."

"Yeah, well, don't get cocky. I can *plie* and *demi plie* like a pro."

I pull back, raising an eyebrow at him. "You know this is a very small world and according to the gossip I'm hearing, you're dating one of the dancers in Chicago."

"I don't know about *dating*, but I'm seeing someone yeah." He shrugs, his lips moving into a smile as he fishes out the keys to his car and unlocks it.

"Interesting." I climb in the SUV as he goes around to his side and does the same.

"What about you? Are you seeing anyone these days?"

"I don't want to talk about it." I bite my lip and look out the window. "I don't want to jinx it."

"Fine."

We FaceTime Emma on our way to wherever it is we're going for dinner to rub it in her face a little, but also because we miss her. We haven't hung out just the three of us in years. It's a thought that makes my heart ache because I know some of that is my fault. My fault for holding this massive grudge against my father. My fault for not swallowing my pride the way Emma did, and returning home with an apology. She's a bigger person than I am.

Gio pulls up to the sidewalk on Second Avenue and I instantly feel sick.

"We're going here?" I ask, watching as the valet guy walks over to us.

"I have to make my presence known," Gio says. Now that dad's away, I can't have people thinking we're not handling business."

"Right." I take the hand the valet offers me when he opens my door and walk out to the sidewalk.

It's chilly tonight. I should've really worn something

warmer. I follow my brother inside the restaurant, which is our family name, the one I refuse to use. Gio thinks it's because Emma and I got scared when we saw the documentary and decided to live our lives in hiding. As if my sister would ever know what living a low-key life actually looks like. She's literally on social media all day, every day. Emma uses our mother's maiden name because she doesn't want her reputation dragged through the mud. I use it because I'm embarrassed. I know that my father and brother aren't bad people, but breaking the law, laundering money, strong-arming people, and putting out hits don't exactly make them great citizens of society either.

The hostess greets us warmly. She looks shocked to see me, and the fact that she even knows who I am makes me want to hide a little more. Instead, I hold my head high as I follow them to the back of the restaurant, and then down some stairs that lead to the wine room. I haven't been here since I was a teenager. My family lived in Chicago, but we came to New York quite often for business and pleasure. I scarcely remembered a wine room at all, but now that I see the long table sitting in the middle of the room, the memories pop back into my brain and I remember all of those late nights we spent here as a family. A real family. Talking about normal family things and laughing as our parents kissed and hugged and made us want to look away from their over-the-top display of affection. Tonight, it's only my brother and me. My heart feels heavier as I think of Dad and what he must be going through in a holding cell. Once we're seated and order wine and water, I ask my brother about him.

"Have you gone to visit? How's he doing?"

"He's holding up." Gio sighs heavily and shrugs. "Has mom contacted you at all?"

I shake my head and look down at the unnecessary menu. I can recite the entire thing by heart. A part of me thought mom would call after the news I got the other day. The fact that she hasn't, hurts. I'm not going to lie.

"Maybe she doesn't know," I say, finally. "She's probably in Barranquilla with Grandma."

"Probably."

"Has she ever called you?" I whisper, looking at him. I brace myself for the answer, for the blow I'll feel if the answer is yes.

"Once."

The blow comes anyway. I feel it take my breath away. "What'd she say?"

"She apologized for leaving."

"Hmm." I bite my lip and look at the menu again. I hate that she called him and not me.

"She's hiding out you know," he says. "That's why she hasn't called you guys. There are some really bad people out there who want to make dad's life miserable and the only way they know they can get to him is through her."

I meet his gaze. "Is she safe?"

"As long as she stays out of sight, yes, but if she starts making phone calls she'll get caught."

"Who's after her?" I whisper.

"People who are upset that she married dad in the first place."

"Her brothers?"

He nods.

"Why did she go back to Barranquilla then?"

Gio smiles, a small smile that speaks of all the secrets he keeps. "I never said she was over there."

I want to ask so many things, but I know better than that. Not only because I know he won't tell me, but because I want my mom to stay safe. I don't want to be the reason anyone catches her and does anything to hurt her.

"Maybe now that Dad's in jail . . ." I start, but leave it at that because I don't even know what would happen. She'd come back? Probably not.

"We'll see," he says. "She just needs to stay put."

I nod. We order our food. His phone rings as we're eating our salads, talking about the upcoming presidential election. He looks at it, sighs, and lifts it to his ear.

"What?" he says. I watch his eyes grow big as he listens to whoever's on the line. "What the fuck do you mean?" Another pause. "I want you to find him. I don't care." Another pause. "Frankie, I swear to God if we don't get to the bottom of this we're as good as dead." My heart lurches into my throat. I set my fork down, suddenly losing my appetite. My brother exhales. "We're meeting tomorrow. Right. Well, fuck him. I'll make sure he knows we're coming for him." He hangs up the phone and slams it on the table. I flinch.

"Everything okay?"

"Fine."

"Okay, then," I say. "When are you going back to Chicago?"

"Soon. A lot is going on and getting out of hand." He shakes his head looking tired. "I need to make sure things with the restaurants here are in order."

"And Devil's Lair," I add.

"Right." He closes his eyes briefly. "If I'd known dad was going to get arrested, I would've held off the opening. Just as well. I'm taking down all the stripper poles and firing the dancers. It'll be a true gentlemen's club from now on."

"Sounds boring."

He shrugs. "Men don't want to talk business in front of women."

"So sexist."

"Not sexist. It's not because they're women and they can't handle it, but because we don't know who they're fucking or where they're loyalties lie."

"You act like you know where any of those men's loyalties

lie." I raise the wineglass to my lips. "And you don't know who the men are fucking either."

He looks at me, eyes narrowed as if he's trying to read me, but shakes it away when his phone rings again. He's on the call the rest of the time we're at dinner and half of the way home.

"The annual charity party is tomorrow night," Gio says as we pull up to my apartment building.

"That can't possibly still be on this year," I say. "Dad's in police custody."

"His lawyers are posting bail. Besides, his indictment is all the more reason to hold it." He pauses, shooting me a glance. "The money goes to the orphanages. It's not like it's going into dad's pockets."

"G." I shake my head. "I haven't even attended the event in years. Emma's the one who always goes."

"I know, but she can't come this year," he says. "And we need to walk into that room and let people know that we're a united front."

"But we're not." My eyes flash. "We're a crumpled up, tattered store with a fake welcome sign."

"Emma can't make it," he says. "She always comes. I don't expect you to go and mingle with everyone, but I'd appreciate it if you were there for me. Please."

"Fine," I agree.

I think back to what Frankie told me the other night about how I'm better off without Vinny here and I decide he's right, as much as it pains me to think that, because I wasn't built for this life. I wasn't built for the worry and the sorrow and the deception.

SIXTEEN

CATALINA

IT'S MONDAY, so I spend the morning sleeping in. That is, until my stomach starts growling so loudly and so often that even I can't stand it. I eat some left over Chinese, shower and change right back into my pajamas because on days off I don't do regular clothes. Slipping my feet into the unicorn slippers my sister got me for Christmas, I toss the clothes I took off into the hamper and wheel it to the laundry room in the basement.

I set the washer, the timer on my phone and go back to my apartment. The moment the elevator doors open up on my floor, I feel uneasy. It's the same weird energy I felt the other night when Frankie brought me home. It's the same feeling that often grips me when something really bad is about to happen. I've been on edge since Gio dropped me off last night. Fear does that to you – it pulls you under and holds you until you feel like you're suffocating. This is why I should've stayed in London. I never felt this way when I was over there. Maybe I just talked myself into believing I was safe in another country, who knows. I walk to my apartment in slow motion, the hamper-on-wheels I'm pulling rattling behind me. There's no one in the halls, so I know I'm alone. That doesn't make me less afraid. I unlock my door and secure the lock quickly behind me, letting out a breath, my heart pounding hard in my chest. My cell phone rings and I nearly jump out of my skin. I reach for it shakily and relax slightly when I see Loren's name on the screen.

"H- hey."

"Hey," he responds, "You busy?"

"Not unless you count lounging in pajamas and doing laundry busy."

"Hmm." The way he groans makes my pulse quicken. "What would you say if I told you I'm walking through your lobby right now?"

My heart launches into my throat. I open my mouth, close it, and open it again. "I'd say I look a mess and you probably shouldn't come up here."

"Too late." He chuckles. "You said Mondays you were off."

"Yes, which is why I'm wearing pajamas at two o'clock in the afternoon."

I hear the distinct sound of the elevator chime. Oh God. He's really here? He's really here. I hang up the phone and set it down, my eyes darting to the mirror beside the door. I undo the bun on my head and re-do it. He knocks on the door, a thump, thump, thump that I swear matches the way my heart is beating. I pull the door open without even looking through the peephole and sure enough, there stands Loren in all his glory, totally relaxed in black joggers and a black shirt that looks like it was made specifically to showcase his muscular body. I bite my lip thinking about him naked. His eyes flare as he steps forward. I suck in air, but with it comes his scent, and only intoxicates me further. He brings his hand around the nape of my neck, stepping into me and I'm suddenly fully aware that I'm not wearing a bra because my nipples tighten painfully underneath my light cotton shirt.

"I couldn't stay away." His voice is deep, raspy, the timbre of it hits me between the legs.

The statement rocks me. I hadn't asked him to. I hadn't expected or wanted him to, but the fact that this Adonis of a man says he couldn't stay away from me, sets my skin aflame. His mouth lingers over mine, his eyes still captivating mine in a way that makes me not want to look anywhere else. I'm about to plead with him, beg him to kiss me, to ease this intense lust I feel for him, when his mouth comes down on mine. My hands instinctively move into his hair, threading into his incredibly soft mane.

It may just be the only soft thing about him. He groans as he deepens the kiss, his tongue hot and heavy against mine, his body pressing me into the counter behind me. My knees shake from that alone, and suddenly I'm spreading my legs and he's hoisting me up. I wrap my legs around his waist and grind against him, needing the pulse between my legs to stop. He pulls away slightly and pushes me against the counter to hold me steady as he takes his shirt off and drops it beside us. Mine goes next. While I'm working on pulling down his joggers, his mouth moves to my nipple, taut and begging for him as I press into his palm, his wet kiss. He looks up at me suddenly, his face inches from mine.

"I wasn't supposed to come here today," he says, his voice a deep husk. "But I can't seem to stop myself when you're concerned."

"Please." I grind against his jeans. *Please what? Please don't stop yourself. Please do something. Please, please, please make me come.* When have I ever said those words aloud? Never, but I must have said them now because he growls as he takes my mouth in his once more. He rears back slightly so that my legs touch the floor. I'm in a haze, about to question what happened, when he pulls my pajama bottoms and underwear down in one swift movement and turns me around, grabbing my messy bun in a fist as he flattens my chest on the kitchen counter.

"Tell me if you don't want this," he says," his jeans brushing up against my naked backside. He leans down, still gripping my hair. There's an edge to his tone that makes a shiver rock through me. I've been around dangerous men before I even knew what the word meant, and that's the vibe this tone of his gives me. It makes me rock against him, like a magnet to whatever it is he's offering. He grips harder, his mouth coming down to my ear. "Tell me and I'll go."

I shake my head. "I don't want you to go."

"You should."

I push back again in response.

He hisses through his teeth. "Fuck. All I can do is picture you when I close my eyes." He moves behind me, but he's still holding my hair so I can't move. "These beautiful legs spread wide open for me." I bite my lip, spreading my legs into a split. He brings his free hand between my legs, teasing me there. "This tight fucking pussy." He pushes his thumb inside me and rubs my clit with his other fingers. I moan, moving against his hand. He brings his mouth to my ear again and tugs my earlobe with his teeth. "I keep thinking of all the ways I want to fuck you out of my system." His hands flick, and flick until I feel heat spread through me. I twist my hips in a fast motion against his moving hand, in perfect synchronization, trying so hard to find release.

"Please, Loren," I groan. "Please."

And then, his hand is off of me. I inhale sharply, shocked, and move to stand, but he flattens me to the counter again. "Not done with you, Little Red."

"Please. Please. Please." I squeeze my eyes shut, moving my hips side to side.

Both hands grip either side of my ass. I feel him drop to his knees behind me before he pulls the lower region of my body off the counter, his mouth between my legs and his grip on my ass the only thing anchoring me in place. He licks from my clit to my ass slowly once, twice, three times, and then he stops and sucks in my clit. The orgasm rocks through me hard and fast. Through my haze, I hear the rip of a condom, but don't have enough time to open my eyes, let alone move to question him before he's slamming into me.

"Oh my God!" I scream.

He's so big that I swear I feel his dick touching my lungs. He pounds into me like that—hard and fast, gripping my ass, holding me off the floor. My chest is heaving with uncontained sobs. Another orgasm crashes through me, and then another, until he's growling my name and filling the condom, making me feel like he's filling more than just that, and that scares me. When it comes to men like Loren, mysterious and dangerous, I'd have to accept that love and fear come in one shiny, fucked up package.

He sets me down gently, a different man than the animal who just fucked me, though I'm not gonna lie, I loved every second of it. I stumble a bit, but Loren doesn't let go of me, his arms sustain me as he turns me around to face him, his hands cup my face again. He's looking at me with a broken expression on his face, like a man asking for forgiveness. I lift my own hands to his face and rub his cheek softly with my thumb.

"Did I hurt you?"

I shake my head in a daze, unable to take my eyes off his. "No."

"Good." His mouth twists into a smile. "I ordered food, by the way. I don't want you to think I came over here just to fuck you."

"Oh." I blink.

Would I care if that's all he came here for? I decide I would because I like being in his presence. I also decide that's a very bad thing. If this is going to escalate, I need to be honest with him about who my father is and who my brother is. I owe him that. The way he's looking at me makes my nerves go haywire. I decide to tell him later. I can't ruin this yet, and that's what'll happen. It'll ruin everything. There's a knock on the door and I step back quickly, grabbing my clothes off the floor and heading to the bathroom as he walks over to handle the food.

When I return, Loren is fully dressed. He glances up from where he's setting the pasta on the table. I don't know what he ordered but it smells like heaven.

"Is that what you sleep in?"

I sit down across from him and look down at myself, as if I need another look at what I'm wearing. I just put it back on. It's a black long sleeve shirt that says Revenge that I got from the Drake concert Bella and Lily dragged me to last summer and black cotton bottoms.

"Not really." I shrug and start serving the lasagna. "I sleep in a t-shirt and boy shorts most of the time. What do you sleep in?"

"Nothing."

My gaze snaps to his. "You sleep naked?"

"Uh-huh." His eyes dance. My mouth goes dry at the thought. I lick my lips. "Keep looking at me like that and I'll have to tear your clothes off again."

The pulse between my legs tells me I may just be fair game. "Maybe I'll let you."

"Hmm." It's a growl that comes from the back of his throat. Sexiest thing I've ever heard.

We stare at each other across the small table for a while. His gaze heats up like he's seriously thinking about tearing my clothes off. I can't even breathe normally around this guy. Maybe that should be a red flag because if I can't even breathe how will I ever do regular things like hold a conversation in public?

"So." I clear my throat. "There's this thing tonight that I have to go to."

He raises an eyebrow. "What kind of thing?"

"A gala. It's to raise money for the Covenant House," I explain. "My mom is . . . was . . . an orphan. It's a cause that's dear to our hearts."

"I didn't realize she'd passed," he says with a sympathetic look in his eyes that makes me want to kiss him.

She hasn't passed, I hope. I don't say that because it's better for everyone's sake to pretend she's no longer here. I mean, she's not. Not for me anyway. Besides, how do you explain that she left because she was embarrassed and then stayed away because trouble has a way of finding the people you love most? You don't, that's how.

I take a deep breath. "Do you want to go with me?"

His eyes widen. "To the gala?"

"I know it's super last minute." I glance at the time on the microwave on the other side of the counter. "And I wasn't really planning on taking anyone, but you're here and I like you and I thought—" I shrug. "I don't know."

He's silent for a while, watching me with an unreadable expression on his face. "This is a problem."

"What is?"

"You. Me. *Us.*"

"Oh," I whisper.

I glance down at the barely touched lasagna on my plate. It hadn't occurred to me that this was just sex to him and he'd only humored me by taking me on that date and letting me get to know him better. It hadn't really dawned on me that it was all for show, to get in my pants. It makes sense, obviously, now that I'm thinking about it. It's logical. Yet it doesn't stop the crushing feeling in my heart.

"Cat," he says.

"Yeah, no, it's totally fine," I say, licking my lips and trying to find my voice again. I manage a smile and meet his gaze. "Forget I asked. This is just sex. I know."

He scowls and goes back to his food. He doesn't say another word as he finishes the lasagna on his plate. Obviously my poor, crushed, little feelings have no bearing on his appetite. Loren's phone has been vibrating incessantly for the last fifteen minutes. He keeps glancing at it and ignoring it. A dreadful feeling grows in the pit of my stomach because, *oh my God*, does he have a girlfriend? A wife? My attention shoots his way.

"You're not . . . I should've asked this before but I just assumed because it's a normal thing to assume but I guess maybe one should never assume anything at all," I say, rushed, letting the silverware in my hands clunk into the sink and turning off the water so that I can turn around and face this possibility. Loren's watching me expectantly. "You're not like, in a relationship, right? With someone else?"

"I don't do relationships," he says. "With anyone."

"Oh."

He drops his phone into the pocket of his joggers and walks over to me, pulling me into his chest. I breathe him in, relishing the scent of him for the last time. When he pulls away, he looks directly into my eyes.

"I'm not fucking anyone but you and I won't, if that's what you're worried about," he says. I nod. I'm not even sure I'm okay with just fucking him, but I nod anyway. He smiles. "Is seven okay?"

"Huh?"

"To pick you up for the gala. Is seven okay?"

"Oh. *Yeah*." I nod, wide-eyed. "Seven is perfect."

Without another word, he leaves my apartment.

SEVENTEEN

CATALINA

I WEAR a gold dress that matches the Gatsby theme. It's always a Gatsby theme. I wore this same dress the last time I attended the party eight years ago. Thankfully, ballet keeps my weight and measurements steady. I never have issues with clothing sizes because of it. The knock on my door comes at seven o'clock on the dot. He's nothing if not punctual. I walk over and open it without even looking through the peephole, freezing on the spot when I see him on the other side of the door. He's wearing a tuxedo that fits him like it's custom made and, *damn*. If I thought Loren naked was out of this world, Loren in a tux is my second favorite. I lick my lips, probably taking off the little lipstick I'd applied in the first place.

"You look . . ." I start.

"You look incredible," he says, in a voice that makes me feel incredible. He steps into my space, lowering his mouth to mine in a slow kiss that makes me let out a strangled sound when he finally pulls away. His eyes are liquid heat as he looks at me. "And you're wearing heels."

"Had to." I smile, picking up my clutch and keys and

ushering him out the door. I lock it behind us. "You may have to carry me at some point later tonight."

"I don't mind." He sets his hand on my lower back and I feel tingles everywhere.

I can't imagine a man like him not doing relationships. He's too flirty, too attentive to just be a one-night-stand kind of guy. It's a shame, really. Instead of pushing down the button to the garage, he pushes the lobby.

"I have a car waiting for us," he says. "Didn't want to deal with parking tonight."

"That also means less walking for me, so it's a win-win." I smile.

He shoots me an amused look as we walk out of the elevator and through the lobby. When we get outside, that uneasy wave hits me like a nasty, unexpected gust of wind. Loren speaks to the driver, a tall, built-like-an-ox man with an angular face and sharp blue eyes that scare me. He's holding the door to the black SUV open for us and I'm about to step in, but something makes me look around. When I do, I see a man standing by the door of my apartment building. He's wearing jeans and a hoodie that covers most of his face, but somehow I know he's watching me. The wave of uneasiness rocks through me again. I stall, one foot inside the vehicle, the other out. I look right at him and I swear that even though I can't see his eyes I feel him staring right back at me. Loren's hand on the small of my back startles me. I blink away from the guy and up at him.

"You all right? Did you forget something?"

I shake my head, glance back toward the door, but the man is now gone. *What the fuck?* I climb into the car, shell-shocked. Loren gets in behind me.

"Is it black SUVs?" he asks once the driver closes the door.

"What?" I blink and look out the window again. *I couldn't just have imagined it right?*

"Is it black SUVs that freak you out?"

"Oh." I shake my head, remembering that time I went to dinner with Madam and him. "No. Well, not typically." He just stares at me as if he's waiting for an explanation, so I give him one, "My ex. He was shot in broad daylight by some guy in a dark SUV. Whenever I see one it brings back memories."

"Were you there when it happened?"

"No." A shiver rocks through me at the thought. I look down at my dress, pick at the little tassels. "It's stupid. I heard about it and it kind of stuck. I feel like I was there."

He brings his hand over mine and leaves it there as we drive. I bring my free hand and caress his knuckles with my fingertips. They feel rough, like he beat someone up with them. I wonder what he uses his hands for so much. Definitely not law. *This and that.* Whatever that is. I bring my attention to the side of his perfect face and wonder how many secrets this man hides. I really don't know much about him at all.

"Where are your parents?" I ask, because I need to stop thinking about relationships with him.

His gaze flickers to mine. "Italy."

"Ah, I've always wanted to go." I feel myself smile. "Where are they going?"

"They live there." He smiles at the shocked look on my face.

"So you're like actually Italian," I say.

"Not pretend Italian like you." His eyes twinkle when he says that. "Where does Álvarez come from? I know you said your mom, but what's her origin?"

"She's Colombian." I smile proudly. "From Barranquilla."

"Have you been?"

"Of course." My eyes widen. "Before boarding school, we went every summer and stayed with my grandmother. Sometimes Dad surprised us and took us during the winter months."

"When was the last time you went?"

I stiffen, biting my lip. "Not in a while."

"Hmm. I moved here when I was in ninth grade. We'd come

for the summer and I fell in love with New York." He chuckles. "Ask me if I like it now."

"Do you like it now?"

"Fuck no, but I'm stuck. I made a life here, a career." He shrugs a shoulder and glances up toward the driver. "Dom, you think I should go back to Italy?"

Dom looks at us in the rearview. I wasn't even expecting them to know each other. I figured the driver was a hire-by-the-hour kind of guy. He smiles, and it's one of those genuine ones I'm not used to seeing often.

"I think your folks would ship you back if you tried," he says. Loren chuckles and it makes me smile.

"How long have you two known each other?"

"Too long," Dom says.

"Long enough," Loren answers.

He hits a button on the side of his door that makes a partition start going up between us and Dom. He casts one last amused look in the mirror and shakes his head as if to say *here we go*.

"How often do you do this?"

"What?"

"Have a driver take you and a date somewhere, raise the partition." I raise an eyebrow toward it now. Loren's eyes bounce between mine.

"You jealous, Red?"

I *am* jealous. So fucking jealous. I keep my eyes forward and grind my teeth together because I refuse to answer him.

"I told you I'm not fucking anyone else," he says, as if that's supposed to make me forget about whoever he fucked before me. *WHY DO I CARE?*

"I don't care," I say, finally. *Liar. Liar.*

"Good."

That's all he says. *Good.* As if good is good enough. It's not because now I'm thinking about when this will all be over and some other woman comes to take my place. Maybe it's for the best. I focus on breathing and by the time we pull up to the hotel where the event is, I feel completely fine. I push all thoughts of other women away and focus on walking. Loren offers me his arm and I take it until we walk inside and at least five women look over and check him out, giving him obvious looks. Then, I let go of his arm because I can't stand it. We make our way to the ballroom, look at the tables and find ours. We're seated with Gio and Frankie. I was expecting it, obviously, but the thought of introducing Loren to them makes the hairs on the back of my neck stand up. I don't want to do it. I also don't want to hide it. Besides, he made it clear that all I am to him is a fuck, so who cares what he thinks of my family?

"Do you know many people here?" Loren asks.

"Not really," I say, but I can't deny that every single person we've walked by thus far has stared openly at us.

Loren puts his hand on the small of my back again. A part of me wants to tell him to drop it, that if these people think we're together like that, they'll crucify him. I spot my brother before he spots me, but only by a second. When he does, he lowers the glass in his hand and gapes at me, or maybe it's at Loren beside me. Either way, he looks pissed, so when he walks over to us, Frankie at his tail, I step in front of Loren.

"I came," I say before he can say anything stupid.

My brother is still gaping. He narrows his eyes at Loren behind me. It's not like I'm tall enough to block him completely, the top of my head, with heels, reaches his nose.

"What the fuck," Gio roars, "are you doing with her?"

The question is obviously not for me. I frown.

"He's my date. Obviously."

"Lorenzo Costello is your date." Gio practically spits out. "Are you fucking crazy, Catalina?"

I feel myself stumble back a bit at the power in his words

and the fact that he knows his full name. I hit Loren's hard chest. His hands come down on my shoulders to steady me.

"You know each other?"

"Do we know each other?" Gio raises an eyebrow. He's still pissed. I can tell. "Costello, do we know each other?"

"We're acquaintances," Loren says behind me.

"What the fuck are you doing with my sister?" Gio asks again.

"Maybe we should talk about this in private," Loren suggests. "I also have something that may interest you in the car."

"What interests me is the answer to my question."

"I don't understand," I say, and I know my voice sounds like a small rumble between their thunder, but I just don't understand what's happening.

Gio and Frankie take a step to the side. Loren lowers his hands from my shoulders and presses his lips to the back of my ear. "I'll be right back, beautiful."

The three of them walk out of the room. Every single pair of eyes follows, including mine. My heart is still pounding in my ears when I finally get the urge to move my feet and walk to the table I'm assigned to and away from the center of attention. When I reach it, I find a woman sitting there. She's wearing a black dress that look similar to mine, but then again, so do most of the dresses in this room. Gatsby themes are prone to copycat wardrobe. We smile at each other as I sit one seat down from her. I look over my shoulder, my leg bouncing as I wait for them to come back. What's happening? Are they fighting? How do they even know each other? Fuck I hope Loren didn't have a case against one of Gio's friends. Or worse—my father.

"You're Catalina," the woman at the table says. I turn my attention to her. "I'm um . . . I'm here with Giovanni."

"Oh." I take a moment to really look at her, she has dark

long hair and big brown eyes, a similar build to mine. It dawns on me that she's probably the girl in Chicago. "Are you the dancer?"

She smiles. "Violeta. We've met. I mean, we were both younger so you probably—"

"Oh my God. Madam Costello's daughter? He said he was dating a dancer but he didn't specify who."

She blushes. "He said we're dating?"

"Yeah." I'm not entirely sure what he said actually. I look over my shoulder again.

"We're not really dating," she says quietly. I meet her gaze. "He's a little old for me. Don't you think?"

I smile. I remember her being much, much younger than me when Madam brought her to class. "How old are you?"

"Twenty."

"Wow, you are young." I let out a breath. "In that case, he is too old for you. You should date guys your own age."

"Yeah." She purses her lips like she's not really interested in doing that, but doesn't say anything else about it. "I saw you come in with my cousin."

"Yeah. I didn't know he knew my brother."

"Small world," Violeta says, shrugging, but it's the way she looks around when she says it that strikes me as odd because yeah, the ballet world is small, but the rest of the world isn't so small that they'd be likely to know each other.

"What do you mean?" I ask.

"I mean with the business they do, the clubs and stuff."

"Loren's a lawyer." I watch her closely as I say the words.

"He is." She nods in agreement.

"I feel like I'm missing something. How does a lawyer end up having anything to do with Gio?"

She watches me for a long moment as if deciding something, finally, she says, "He helps my dad out a lot—Loren does. Dad owns restaurants and stuff."

"Oh." I feel my brows pull in. "I wasn't aware."

"He still practices law though," she adds.

I nod, smiling even though this conversation doesn't bode well with me. I've been around liars my entire life and I'm not calling her one because she may not know the half of what her father or Loren do, but it is unsettling. Maybe it was the way Gio looked at him, that flash in his eyes like he really wanted to rip me away from him. My brother's not overprotective like that. He's always trying to set me up with his friends, so why not Loren? What am I missing?

Loren, Gio, and Frankie walk back to the table. I feel myself let out a relieved breath. Loren sits beside me, Gio beside Violeta, and Frankie beside him. Two other men join our group and introduce themselves, both Wall Street guys. I would've guessed it before they said it. They all carry themselves a certain way, like they're on another level. Yet sitting at this table, they seem shy, boyish even.

The keynote speaker, a woman who grew up in one of the orphanages my parents funded, begins to speak. It's a moving tale about loss and unsteady feet, and the appreciation she had for the orphanage. Loren puts his hand on the back of my chair and runs his fingertips down my back. I watch him as we listen to the woman speak. His expression is closed off, completely void of emotion. He'd make a hell of a poker player. I'm almost in tears and I'm barely even paying attention to her.

The night goes like that, with us not saying much. Violeta talks a lot though. Enough for the entire room, and I like that. She's young, but she's not shy. My brother watches her with keen interest as she talks about school. When she finishes saying her bit about why she decided on nursing school, Gio opens his mouth to get a word in.

"Cat didn't go to college and she's doing well." he says. "Maybe you can just stick to dance."

Violeta shakes her head. "I love school. Besides, in less than two years I'll have my nursing degree. At that point I'll figure out if I want to keep dancing or not."

"Not a true ballerina," Gio says. "What does your mother say about that?"

Violeta blushes, biting her lip. "She says I need to do what makes me happy."

"For the record," I say, deciding to throw her a bone. "I wish I'd gone to school when I was your age."

She smiles brightly at me and turns to Gio. "See?"

My brother shrugs.

"I never wanted to be one of those girls who got married and pregnant young," she says.

Gio says nothing but I can tell it bothers the hell out of him.

"Maybe try dating a guy your own age," Loren adds beside me. I sip some water to swallow my panic because my brother has been known to lose his cool over things like this.

"And maybe you shouldn't date your dead cousin's ex, but here we are," Gio says.

It takes a moment for his words to sink in. A moment, in which my senses are slowed way down. I play them back in my head. *And maybe you shouldn't date your dead cousin's ex, but here we are.* I feel stupid, so stupid that it takes me longer than a second to realize he's talking about me. About Loren. About Vinny. My eyes shoot to Loren. He's watching me carefully, the way you watch a feral creature, unsure of what they'll do next.

"Is it true?" I ask, my voice a mere whisper.

"I can explain," he says.

My hands shake as I lift the napkin from my lap and set it on the table. I push my chair back. Loren does the same. I cut him a look.

"Don't."

"Cat, I can—"

"Give me space, Lorenzo."

He flinches like I hit him, but lets me stand up without making it into a scene. I walk to the bathroom as if I'm stuck in a dream, or a nightmare, depending on how you look at it. I feel eyes on me, watching every move I make and a part of me wonders if it's because they know Loren was Vinny's cousin. I wonder too if they know he played me. I don't need a mirror to tell me that my skin is completely flushed from embarrassment, from the absolute horror and deception that he's been lying to me about who he is this entire time. Oh my God. I'm so stupid. I've been sort-of-dating, and totally hooking up with my ex's cousin, and I didn't even know they were related. By the time I reach the bathroom door, I'm on the verge of having a full-blown panic attack, something that hasn't happened to me in more years than I can count on one hand.

When I feel somewhat settled, I step out of the bathroom and hear men shouting. I'm pretty positive one of them is my brother. Instead of going back toward the tables, I head to the exit. I can't deal with this right now. I don't even know where I'm going, I just know I need to get out of here. My heart quickens with each step I take but when I finally push the back-door open and step out into the alley, I feel myself calm down. I'm opening my clutch to get my phone and walking toward the sidewalk when someone grabs my arm. I turn around with a gasp, my heart in my throat.

"What the hell, Frankie? I could've killed you."

He stares at me. "With what? The spike of your heel?"

"Well, yeah." My frown deepens. "What are you doing out here?"

"Gio and Loren are arguing so I figured I'd come check on you," he says. "Why are you out here?"

"I want to go home." I sound defeated. I *am* defeated. I just want to go home and go to bed so that a new day can start already.

"I'll take you."

I let him lead the way to the front and wait beside him while the valet gets the car. I've managed to block out everything I just learned from Loren—for now. I'll dwell on it when I get home and don't have a chance to break down in front of anyone.

"You should stay at Gio's tonight," Frankie says as we drive away from the hotel.

"Why?"

"I just figure it's a good place for you to stay. You know, so you won't have to deal with Loren when he comes looking for you." He glances at his watch. "I'd bet money he's probably on his way to your place right now."

I cross my arms and look out the window. "He's not going to come looking for me."

"Yeah he will." Frankie snorts.

My heart thumps in my ears. "Is he really Vinny's cousin?"

"Yeah."

"Why would he . . . why wouldn't he just tell me?"

"Men are weird creatures, Cat." Frankie shrugs. "You know this."

"Still," I whisper, looking out the window. "I feel so stupid. So, so stupid."

"Don't feel stupid." His tone makes me look at him again. "It's not your fault, and it sucks that you feel that way, but Lorenzo's made a career of omitting shit. He's a lawyer for fuck's sake." He pauses and smiles. "He's not a bad guy. I know that's not what you want to hear right now but it's true and I'm sure there's a reason he did this. Hopefully your brother doesn't kill him before he can explain himself."

"You think Gio would do that?" My heart throbs in my throat.

Frankie shrugs like he thinks it's a possibility. I shouldn't dwell on it. I'm so angry with Loren and more so, with myself, that I shouldn't ever want to see him again, but the thought of not seeing him ever again doesn't sit well with me.

By the time we get close to Gio's place, I'm crying angry tears. Frankie just stays quiet the entire time. He doesn't tell me it'll be okay and doesn't tell me it won't be. I'm grateful for his silence, but it doesn't help me understand or process it, probably because there's nothing to understand. Loren played me. He saw how stupid and vulnerable I was, and he played me. He obviously knows Gio and knows Frankie and runs in these crowds and he just wanted to use me. For what though? I wipe my face as Frankie parks his car in the visitor space and we get out. The only reason I agreed to stay here is because I don't want to be alone. It isn't until I'm settled down in the guest bedroom that I realize that I'm alone nonetheless.

EIGHTEEN

CATALINA

MY LAST NAME IS A CURSE. It's always been one. I stare at the revolver in my hand. The one I got from Gio's room moments after Frankie left, locked the door, and told me he'd tell the security to watch anyone coming up here like a hawk while he went off to do whatever it is he does. I took the revolver into the bathroom with me while I was showering. I took it to the kitchen when I went back for water and now I'm holding it as I sit in the dark living room. It's the only kind of gun I know how to shoot because it doesn't require cocking. Point and shoot. Point and shoot. Would I do it? I'm not sure. I turn it around and around in my hand and finally set it down on the table in front of me.

I'm not sure how long I sit before the front door opens loudly, like someone has kicked it in. I grab the gun and stand, holding it with both hands and aimed toward the hallway. It's probably just Gio drunk or something, but if it's not, I want to be prepared. The sound of dress shoes rings out through the apartment. I should've turned on the lights. Only the kitchen light and moonlight illuminate the apartment and it's not enough to see. When Loren steps into view, I feel the breath sucked out of me. My hands start to shake hard, the gun rattling against the bracelet I'm wearing.

"I'll shoot."

"I don't doubt it," he says, his voice low.

"Where's my brother?"

"He's probably still with Vi." He glances at his watch. "I'm sure he'll be here soon."

"Why are you here?"

"Are you going to lower that?" He raises an eyebrow.

"I'm not afraid of you."

"Only cowards with weapons in their hands say that." He puts his hands in his pockets and steps closer casually, as if I'm not aiming right at the center of his chest.

"I'm . . . I'm not kidding. I'm not afraid to use it."

"No one's afraid to use guns in theory," he says, tilting his head. "That is, before we shoot and take a life. The life of some-one's brother, son, or father, and we have to live with that guilt forever. And it does haunt you forever, Catalina." He steps even closer, closing the distance between us, until he's directly in front of me. I grip the gun tighter and tilt my head and meet his eyes. I press the barrel into the center of his chest.

"I hate you," I whisper.

"I know."

"I really, really hate you," I say again, despising the way my eyes are brimming with tears. "You lied to me. You tricked me. You *played* me."

Loren's jaw clenches. "I did."

"Why?" I whisper, unable to stop the tears from flowing.

"It's a long story and if I'm going to explain myself, I don't want to do it with a gun pointing at my chest."

"What difference does it make?"

"You're going to be angry."

"I'm already angry!"

"Trust me."

I scoff. "It's too late for that."

"Put the gun down and I'll tell you."

I narrow my eyes as I look up at him. Tears cascade down my face. His expression seems to crack.

"Oh, Cat."

"Stop it," I whisper harshly, bringing a shoulder to my cheek to wipe it.

If I set the gun down, I'm giving him the advantage no doubt. He'll have me in a headlock or something before I can think. He seems like the type. Gio will be here soon, which means Loren won't get far if he kills me, and if I'm being honest I don't even care anymore. If the point of me being here is playing this game with these men, I'd rather check out. Stupid, I know, but I never claimed to be smart. I take a step back, then another, and another, until I reach the coffee table.

I set the gun down and put my hands up in surrender but stay right beside it. "Talk."

"Vinny and I were close cousins, more like brothers. If I had a business idea, he'd be the first to know," he says. "Blood over everything, right? That was, until he decided to go after my wife."

"You have a wife?" I feel those words like a knife to the chest, digging in and turning.

"Had." He pauses. "I was out of town when I found out she was cheating on me with him." He pauses. "Tabby and I lived here. Vinny was traveling back and forth from Chicago at the time because you were there."

I clutch my stomach, shaking my head. "You're lying."

"I'm not." He shoots me a sympathetic look. "When I got home, she admitted to it. Called me every name in the book, told me all I cared about was law school and money." He chuckles darkly, shaking his head. "I confronted Vinny. We got into a fight. My wife moved out, moved into his place. Asked for a divorce shortly after."

"You're lying!" My bottom lip quivers. "I lived with him."

"You lived in the suburbs in Chicago. In that house with the white picket fence," he says. "She lived in his condo in Brooklyn."

"You're lying. Lying!"

"Why would I lie?" Loren shrugs. "Ask around."

"That doesn't explain why you did what you did. It doesn't explain why you didn't tell me who you were." I wipe my face. "Is this some sort of sick revenge? A way to get back at your cousin's ghost?"

"No."

"So then?" I step back even more, allowing the entire living room between us for distance.

"It's complicated, Cat." He looks pained as he swallows. "I saw you at his funeral."

"Oh God." I clutch my stomach, hoping to ease the knots forming there.

"You looked devastated. I'd heard of you, but I'd never seen you in person." He licks his lips, pausing again. "I followed you for a while, but then you skipped town and never came back."

"You followed me?"

"I was curious."

"Why?" I whisper. "Why would you follow me? Why would you . . . why?"

He runs a hand over his face and exhales, looking away. He looks tired, with his bowtie undone and his tuxedo untucked and disheveled. When he looks at me again, he doesn't look as sure of himself as he normally does. He looks like a man who has lost and is resigned.

"Come home with me," he says. "Let me explain everything."

"You lied to me. You made me . . ." I shake my head, the sob launching into my throat making it impossible for me to finish my sentence. "I'm not going anywhere with you."

"Fair enough." He nods his head and exhales again, his eyes searching mine once more before he turns and walks away.

When I hear the door close behind him, I crumble down on the couch and start to cry.

NINETEEN

LORENZO

I SHOULDER past Gio as I step out of the elevator into the lobby. He looks shell-shocked to see me there.

"What the—"

"Go check on your sister."

"If you hurt her—"

"Fuck you." I turn around and meet his gaze.

He looks taken aback by whatever expression he finds on my face. I hated every second of that torture I spent upstairs telling her about Vinny. More than anything, I hate leaving her there. I hate not touching her. Not kissing her. Not holding her as she cried. Not getting to explain to her why I did what I did. I walk away from Gio. Frankie follows me. I'd know his footsteps anywhere. He wears expensive dress shoes he buys from Mike's store that make him sound like a damn tap dancer.

"What do you want?" I ask as we step outside.

"You care about her."

My eyes cut to his. "What the fuck makes you say that?"

"I've known you since we were kids, Lor. Give me a fucking break."

"Yeah, well, I shouldn't care about her."

"Because she's Vinny's ex or because she's Joe's daughter?"

"I don't know." I sigh, running a hand down my face. "I need feelings for Catalina like I need a hole in my head."

"I feel you." He pops a cigarette into his mouth and lights it. "You ever think about getting out?"

I stiffen. Do I think about it? Fuck. That's all I think about. I'd never admit it to anyone though, not even someone I've known since I was a kid. *Especially not* to someone I've known that long. Getting out or wanting to get out, is a sign of weakness and weak I am not.

"I think about it," Frankie says, answering his own question.

"Yeah, well, don't say shit like that out loud." I start walking away, heading to my bike. "See you."

"Yo, Loren."

I turn around.

"He'd be okay with it, you know," he says, blowing out a cloud of smoke. "Gio, I mean. He'd be okay with you and Cat."

I scoff, turn back around and keep walking. Gio would be okay with digging my grave and burying me in it alive, too. After what my cousin did to Catalina, I know for a fact neither Joe or Gio would be okay with me stepping in.

TWENTY

CATALINA

I FEEL groggy and I have a killer headache. Two things I can't afford, but that's what happens when you cry yourself to sleep. I make myself get out of bed and walk to the en-suite bathroom. I shower again, hoping to rid myself of this groggy feeling. I can't believe Loren lied to me. I can't believe . . . *God, I'm so stupid*. Beneath the shower head, I start to cry, shivers racking my body as I try to hold myself together. I haven't cried like this in years. I was probably due for it. I haven't felt this foolish . . . ever. I think about Loren, the way he looks at me. The thought alone sets my skin aflame. I push it aside. How could I have been so fucking stupid?

My phone vibrates on the dresser and I half hope it's him. Stupid me. It's Emma.

"Hey," she says. "Just calling to check up on you. You okay?"

"No." I sigh sadly.

"I'm sorry," she says. It was what she said last night over and over. I called her after Loren left and poured my sorrow into the phone call.

"It's okay. I'll get over it."

"Well, I'm kinda calling to tell you something but I don't want you to freak out."

"Oh God. What now?" My heart stops. Of course I freak out.

"I want to preface this by saying that Loren is no longer teaching the class you're taking for me," she says. *Oh God.*

"You need me to go back there?" I squeak.

"There's a quiz today. Remember?"

"Are you serious? Not today, Em. Any day but today."

"I'm sorry," she whispers. "But he's not there. I'm serious. I checked."

"How do you know?"

"I messaged one of the girls taking the class," she says. "Have you even logged onto the online portal?"

"No." I set the phone down to slip my underwear on. "I don't even have the log in. Wait, so you have all the notes?"

"Well, I have the notes Loren gave you to give me. The online portal is where I turn in the homework assignments." She exhales into the phone. "Anyway, it doesn't matter. Someone mentioned how the real hot professor is back and the other hot guy was just a sub."

"Oh."

Emma spends another ten minutes explaining the quiz to me and begging me to go on her behalf.

"I'll go." I sigh. "But only because you're the first person in our family to get a college degree. Otherwise, I'd tell you to fuck off."

"You're the best sister in the world," she says.

"I know." I set the phone down again and pull on a t-shirt. "So, you think the Daily is going to offer you a full-time position?"

"We'll see." She doesn't sound as excited about that prospect as I thought she'd be.

"Do they know who your dad is?" I ask.

"God no."

"Gio says Dad went home on bail yesterday," I say. "Five hundred thousand."

"It's a hell of a lot of money," she says. "You think he did it?"

"I don't know. Clearly I'm an awful judge of character."

"Yeah. Well, he says he didn't do it, but I guess he would say that to me no matter what." She sighs. "Gotta go, babe. Call me when you're done with the quiz."

I hang up and finish getting dressed. Frankie and Gio are in the kitchen and they both look at me without saying a word. Last night, we didn't talk much. Gio came upstairs and gave me a long hug but didn't say anything about Loren. He told me about Dad being out of jail and that I could stay here as long as I wanted. I'm sure I'm going to get one of his long-winded speeches today though. I can see it in the way he's frowning at me as I pour my coffee.

"How could you not have known?" Gio asks. "You went out to dinner with his uncles and you didn't know?"

I glance up at him. "I went out to dinner with Madam Costello's family and he happened to be part of it. I assumed he was forthcoming like the rest of them."

"*Assumed.* That's cute." Gio chuckles, turning to Frankie. "When was the last time you had the privilege of assuming?"

Frankie shrugs. "Probably never."

"Right." Gio nods. "Don't assume things, Cat. Especially not when it comes to a man like Lorenzo."

He's obviously right. I assumed a lot of things about him without question. I opened my door to him, as well as my legs. And worse, when hope fluttered inside my chest, I didn't knock it down and cut its wings. I should have. I should've known he was too much like my brother, like my father, like every man outside of the ballet world who's ever paraded into my life trying to control me. He seemed different though. He showed me he could be kind. He could be caring. I saw it. And yet . . . I sigh heavily, hating the fact that tears are swimming in my eyes again.

"I pointed a gun at his chest," I whisper.

"Should've pulled the trigger," Gio responds.

I glare up at him. "So I could be just like you? Just like Dad?"

"Blood is blood."

"Yeah, well, I wish I could drain it out of me."

"You're so fucking mellow-dramatic."

"I'm not mellow-dramatic," I say. "I just don't think shooting people for lying is the answer."

"Yeah well, we'll have to agree to disagree." He shakes his head as he walks away. "For the record, stay away from Loren and after rehearsal, you come back here."

"I have things to do after rehearsal," I shout.

"So do I and here we are—stuck babysitting you."

"I don't need your help," I shout louder.

He slams the door to his bedroom, making items around the apartment shake and clatter.

I set the mug down hard beside the sink. "I need to go."

"I'll drive you."

"I can take the train or a cab."

"I don't really want to find myself buried six feet under, if you know what I'm saying." Freddie stands up, walking around the counter to set the mug in the sink. "We don't have to talk."

I cross my arms over my chest and follow him out, shooting one last glare at Gio's door. With the commotion of last night, I didn't even remember to grab my black duffel bag from my apartment. I just grabbed stupid shit like deodorant and underwear. Well, not stupid shit, but not any of the things I need for dance and now I don't even have time to pass by there. The whole situation makes me want to scream at the top of my lungs. It makes me feel like a child without any power. That's their favorite thing to do to women—render them powerless.

It's the only positive I've been able to think of, God forgive me, to come from Vinny's death. If he were still alive, who knows what would have become of me. I'd definitely have kids running around, probably no dancing career, probably no career at all. Vinny wasn't the kind of man who wanted a working woman. I'd been willing to give up all of that for him back then. Now, not so much. Once you taste a bit of freedom, you become addicted.

TWENTY-ONE

CATALINA

FRANKIE DROPS me off at the studio. He glances over at me as he sets the car in park. "I'll be around."

"Meaning?"

"I'm tracking your phone."

"Oh." I frown. "So you're not gonna like follow me?"

"No. Your brother made it clear that I should let you have your freedom." He pauses momentarily. "Stop talking to Lorenzo."

"Oh my God. I get it." I roll my eyes. "You guys say that as if I'd *want* to talk to him."

I get out of the car and head into the studio, walking to the back and looking for my name on the sheet on the wall. I find it quickly and head down to the dressing rooms, where I find the costume designer. Marta glances up at me from the tutu she's sewing.

"Uh-oh. Why aren't you dressed?"

"Long story."

"Well, we don't have time for one of those. Are you okay?"

"Yeah. Thanks."

Marta sighs loudly, beckoning my attention once more.

"Someone dropped this off for you." She lifts a black duffel bag from the floor. "I assume some of your things are in there. Or maybe just your pointe shoes? Either way, let me know what you need and I'll be happy to provide it."

I thank her, lifting the bag from her hand and unzipping it. My pointe shoes are inside—both the pink ones and the black ones. My heart warms, my eyes filling with tears again. I've never been so happy to see my shoes. I really don't have time to break a pair in before rehearsal. Hell, I don't have time to break in a new pair for the show tonight, but even though I have mine, I can't wear them tonight. They're tattered. I pick up the new ones she gives me, and the ribbon and the little tool set. I'll work on them on the subway on my way to Columbia for the quiz. The thought rattles me once more. Emma said Loren was no longer there.

"Who dropped off my bag?" I ask when I reach the door.

"A really handsome man." Marta smiles wide. "*Really* handsome."

"Did he have a name?"

"Lorenzo, he said." She shrugs. "He could've said his name was Jesus and I would've followed him through the red sea."

"I'm pretty sure that was Moses." My voice sounds steady but my trembling hands betray me.

Loren dropped it off?

If I didn't hate him so much I would have the urge to kiss him for thinking of me. Of course, that also means that he somehow broke into my apartment and took it. The same way he broke into Gio's yesterday. The fact that he can do those things is unnerving. I turn around and head to the dressing room two doors down, stripping as I walk. These halls have seen more naked people—men and women—than your local strip club. No one will be offended and no one will find it strange either. I change as quickly as I can and walk as fast as I can without doing too much damage to my calves. Mister Paul is not very happy with my late arrival. His icy glare says it all. He doesn't interrupt the class though and I don't expect him to. I take my place at the barre and pick up where they are. I'm only ten minutes late. It's not a huge deal.

We go over the choreography for *Glass Pieces*, which is the repertoire I'm headlining tonight. Justin doesn't say a word to me as we dance, but he makes sure to pinch me every time he feels how stiff I am—a warning—*don't fuck this up for us tonight.* When we're finished, I'm the first one out of the studio.

"Miss. Álvarez, may I see you in the office?" Mr. Paul asks.

I nod, sighing, knowing I'm about to get my ass handed to me. I follow him into the office at the end of the hall, my heels bouncing. Normally, I'd take a quick shower and leave to the university for the quiz, but today I won't be able to. I'll need to switch out my shoes, hopefully slip on some pants to cover my ass, and attend class in my stinky, sweaty state. Fuck it. I fold my hands on my bouncing knee and look at Mr. Paul.

"You haven't signed up for next season."

"I spoke to Mrs.—"

He puts his hand up to interrupt me. "You know that if you take an entire season off and want to come back, you will have to condition doubly?"

"I'm aware. Yes, but the company agreed to give me a sabbatical."

"You know that dancers your age cannot afford to take time off." He raises an eyebrow.

Dancers my age. There are dancers double my age still performing nowadays. He's in his forties and still performs every so often. But I know what he means. My knees and aching back remind me every day that it's a short-lived career.

"There is a new company. Very small, *very* small," he emphasizes and waves a hand. "An investor bought a sinking ship and wants to restore it, you know the type."

I don't bother to interrupt because when Mr. Paul gets on

one of these tangents, he doesn't like anyone to stop him, but I have no idea what he's talking about. To make matters worse, the convoluted way he speaks rivals Master Yoda on a good day.

"They need a principal. I told them I'd let them borrow one of mine." He shrugs nonchalantly. "Money is good."

"Are you offering this to me?" I ask, confused.

"Stop frowning. You'll get wrinkles."

I stop frowning and sit up straighter, feeling like he took a ruler to my back the way they used to at school. "How many shows?"

"Only two per week. You'd be able to rehearse here and at Steps."

"Who's the choreographer?"

He smiles. "You."

"Me?" I frown, taken aback.

"Mr. Jerome recommended you."

I gasp, bringing a hand to my mouth. Jerome is my favorite choreographer. I've helped him here and there, sure, but . . .

"I've never choreographed a piece entirely by myself."

Mr. Paul continues to smile. "Mr. Jerome will be working with you."

"How much is the pay?" I whisper.

"Same as here."

I gape. "For two shows a week?"

"Well, you will be dancing as well as creating the choreography." Mr. Paul raises an eyebrow. "Are you interested?"

"Very interested." Who needs time off anyway? I was done fooling myself into thinking I was going to do anything besides dancing—but choreography? I'd be lying if I said I hadn't considered it a million times but I never thought I would actually be able to do it.

"You have a very important performance tomorrow night," he says. "The president will be in attendance."

"All of my performances are important, even if no one is watching."

"Good girl. Run along." He waves me away. "I'll email you the contract for Lotus."

I undo my ribbons and take my pointe shoes off as I stand up, stretching my feet, then I move as fast as I can. In the dressing room, I pull on a pair of black Adidas sweatpants and matching slides, grab my backpack and take off. I feel disgusting, but I have no time to dwell on any of that right now. I need to move. On the subway, I pull out my phone and go over the notes my sister emailed me, my stomach is still unsettled as I contemplate whether or not Loren will be there. While I study the notes, I work on my shoes—scoring the satin tips and beating the boxes, then I rip the shank in half, and finally begin to sew on the ribbons.

I do all of this on auto-pilot—bam, bam, bam. When I reach my stop, I shove everything into the black duffel bag and get to the auditorium as fast as I can.

TWENTY-TWO

CATALINA

I PULL the door open and all of the nerves I thought I'd gotten rid of shoot back ten-fold at the sight of Loren sitting behind the desk. Emma wasn't entirely wrong. There is another man here today. A tall dude with a nice tan and pretty blue eyes. His eyes fly to mine as soon as I step in the door. He assesses me for a second before going back to watching the classroom like a hawk. Loren is lounging in the seat that would otherwise be the professor's, one foot on the desk as he casually reads a book.

Everyone in the room has their head down as they take the quiz quietly. When the door shuts behind me, Loren's head snaps up from the book. His gaze moves over me slowly. I swallow, wishing my heart wasn't such a treacherous bitch, because if I'm being completely honest, I love the way he looks at me—as if I'm the only woman worthy of those eyes. Fuck I hate him.

"Take a test from the desk and find a seat," the real professor says.

I walk up to the desk, my head held high as I reach for the packet on the edge. There's only one left. He sets his hand down on it, over my hand, flattening it on the paper. My heart pounds harder. I swallow as I meet his eyes.

"We need to talk."

My jaw sets. "There's nothing to talk about."

He lifts his hand on mine, the tips of his fingers brushing over it softly. I grab the packet and pull my hand away, turning around quickly. I can't. I can't. I can't do this right now. I feel like I'm about to break down and I don't want to break down in front of all of these idiot kids and this idiot man and the real professor. My eyes scan the room for an empty seat. Behind me, I hear shuffling.

"You may sit here, Miss Álvarez," Loren says, his voice breaking into the silence that fills the room.

My heart is still beating stupid wild as I turn around to face him. He pulled out a folding chair and set it beside his desk, creating a make-shift desk for me. *Hell no.* I glance around the room once more. One of these fucking kids is bound to finish their test and vacate a seat.

"You have thirty-minutes to finish the quiz," he announces, and lowers his voice. "You were thirty-minutes late to class, Miss Álvarez."

Fuck him. I turn around, look at the real professor who merely shrugs, and then stomp to the chair he's unfolded, huffing and puffing as I sit down. I reach over his desk, grab a pen without even asking and scribble my sister's name on the top of the page. I'm going to kill her for this. I wasn't planning on it, but now I am. I focus on the questions, scoffing aloud at some of them.

"Something funny?"

My eyes snap to his. "It's funny that a criminal would be pretend teaching a course on how to catch criminals."

His eyes twinkle. "Life is full of twists and turns."

"You disgust me." I mean it. I look at the paper again.

Prohibition led to:

1. *A nation full of alcoholics*

2. *A return to the Victorian Age*
3. *Organized Crime*

THE ENTIRE TEST is multiple choice. Not all of the questions are easy. As it turns out, I don't know shit about organized crime. *Fuck you. Stop judging me.* I glare at every question. I turn the pages with displeasure. People are getting up, dropping their papers, and walking out by the dozen. I look back and realize there are only four students left. From my experience, those are the ones who are probably going to fail this. I turn back to my test, boiling furiously. I cannot be the last person left in this room. I also can't get an F on my sister's exam. I know this, but fuck. Another person leaves, then another. Three left including myself. Then two. I look at the guy behind me. He glances up at me, his blue eyes jumping right back down to his paper. He looks like a football player. He either doesn't know the material or he got here late, just before I did.

I turn and realize I'm on the last page. It's an essay, not multiple choice. My heart sings. I smile. Then, I read the text: *I'm sorry.*

I look up to find Loren looking right at me. I can't do this. *I can't.* My emotions have always had a way to getting the best of me. I feel the tears building before I can stop them. I blink rapidly and bring my hand up to clear my eyes as I swallow down the lump in my throat. I slap the pen down on top of the test packet and get out of my chair. I notice the real professor has stepped out and I'm only left with Mr. Football player, who saunters over and places his own packet down. He idles. I feel him staring at me, so I crane my neck to look at him.

"What?" I sound rude, but I don't care. I want to get out of here.

"You a dancer?" he asks.

"Yes," I sigh, and decide it's not his fault I'm in a pissy mood, so I add, "At City Ballet."

"I've never seen you in here." Mr. Football player smiles. "I'm Shawn, by the way."

I'm still frowning. *What is happening?* "Are you hitting on me?"

Shawn chuckles. "Trying and failing miserably apparently."

Despite myself, I laugh, *because what the hell?* There's no denying that Shawn is handsome and under any other circumstances I'd feel flattered, but right now, I feel too messed up to even consider it. But I try, dammit. I try to flirt back because Loren's watching and he messed up and then lied to me, and fucked me, and eventually told me he didn't want anything more than that—so fuck him. Fuck him. Fuck him. I smile up at Shawn.

"Who says you're failing?"

"Oh, in that case, how 'bout you slide me your number?"

"How 'bout you slide the fuck out of here?" Loren says, his voice menacing.

I hear the chair squeak as he gets up, feel his presence looming over my right side. He must have a scary look on his face because Shawn's reaction sends my heart galloping. I manage to tear my gaze from him and look at Loren. Sure enough, his expression is thunderous, his caramel eyes on fire. It makes me want to punch him. *Mister I don't do relationships. Mister I'm interested in you. Mister LIAR LIAR PANTS ON FIRE, who failed to mention he was my dead fiancé's cousin.*

"Mind your business, *professor*." I type in my number on Shawn's phone and hand it back.

"I swear to God, Catalina," Loren growls.

I smile wide as I hand over Shawn's phone and meet Loren's thunderous eyes. "You swear to God what?"

His eyes narrow as he searches my face.

"I'll call you later," Shawn says, walking away.

"Sure." I smile up at him.

"Delete her number," Loren says. Shawn's steps falter. He shoots me a confused look, and looks back up at Loren. "If you know what's good for you, you'll delete that number right now."

"If he knows what's good for him? Really?" I gape at him.

"I don't know what's going on," Shawn says, signaling between me and Loren, "but it's none of my business."

"If you call her you're making it my business," Loren responds. There's a threat in there. He doesn't say it, but his tone is undeniable.

Shawn walks out. I watch the door slam shut behind him and will my heart to go back to a normal pace because right now it feels like it's going to snap in half. When I realize it's not going to calm down, that *I'm* not going to calm down, that the rage inside of me is making me shake from how much I want to scream, I turn to Loren, my vision blurring with hot, angry tears.

"Are you fucking kidding me right now?" I seethe. "First you lie to me, and now you're trying to take over my goddamn life? What's next? You're going to barge into my apartment when I'm fucking someone?"

"Stop."

"Stop what?" I raise my voice again.

"Stop putting those thoughts in my head."

"What do you care?" I yell. "What the fuck do you care if I go out with Shawn or Justin or someone else? That's all I was to you wasn't it? A fuck. A revenge fuck, at that."

"Goddamn it, Cat." He slams a fist on the desk, making me jolt.

Thank God he's on the other side of the desk. I reach for the strap of my bag and put it over my shoulder, watching him warily.

"You have no right," I say, my voice lower now, emotion clogging up my throat. "You hurt me."

"I know," he says, his voice hard. "I'm sorry."

"So you say, but are you really? What are you sorry for? Are you sorry that you lied to me? That you took me on a date and fucked me under false pretenses?"

"I didn't fuck you under false pretenses." His voice is a low growl, as if he's trying to restrain himself. "I took you on a date because I wanted to get to know you. I fucked you because I wanted you. I still want you."

"You'll never have me again." I bite the inside of my cheek to keep my tears in check.

He shuts his eyes. "Let me take you home."

"Why?"

He opens his eyes. "Because I miss you."

"No." The word flies out of my mouth. My pulse quickens though. "You just saw me yesterday so spare me the bullshit."

"I just saw you yesterday and yet, I miss you."

"You said this was just a fuck. You don't do relationships." I blink away from him briefly because the look in his eyes is just too much. *Too much*.

"I know what I said."

My eyes flick to his again and I stare at this infuriating, gorgeous man. This liar, thief of a man, because that's what he's done. He's stolen my senses entirely. He must have if I'm actually considering going with him.

"Fine, but only because I need a ride and don't want to walk to the subway. And we're going to my place." I grip the strap of my bag. "Also, for the record, I still hate you and I think you're a massive liar."

"I'm okay with that." His lips twitch as if he's just won some case he's been working on.

Maybe he has. Who the fuck knows. Maybe I'm some kind of job to him. One that requires sneaking into my life under false pretenses and fucking the common sense out of me. Thankfully, he has his truck. We ride in silence. I turn my attention to the window and watch the city as we drive by. I can't look at him. As it is, my heart is still sputtering out of control from just seeing him and hearing the reckless words he said.

TWENTY-THREE

CATALINA

HE PARKS in an empty space and gets out of the truck. I wait. He doesn't come around to open the door for me. So I guess even his chivalry was bullshit. I open the door and step out, eyeing him curiously as he reaches into the trunk, grabs a gun, lifts up his shirt, and places it in the waistband of his jeans. He lowers his shirt again as he walks toward me, his mouth twitching slightly.

"I'm not going to shoot you, if that's what you're worried about."

"Yeah, because I'm really going to believe a liar when he pulls out a gun and tells me he's not going to shoot me." I shake my head and start heading up to my apartment. Loren follows.

"I would never shoot you."

"Whatever." I glare at him. "What else have you lied to me about? Did you know my sister would be in that class? Did your friend alert you to that too?"

He looks at me like he's debating something, finally he nods his head and sighs, "Yes."

I gape at him, but somehow make my feet move toward the door. "You are so fucked up."

"I know."

I'm reeling over his admission as I walk through the lobby. Normally, I wave to the guy behind the desk but I don't have it in me to do that right now, so I don't even see him when he starts gesturing frantically.

"The guy's calling you," Loren says.

I blink up and walk over to him.

"Miss. Álvarez," he says. "This was left for you last night."

I look at it for a beat before ripping the top. It's a plain white envelope but there's a bulge as if it contains something hard in it. I look inside. There's no letter, no paper at all, but I turn it over on my palm and shake it. The moment it lands in my hand the air gets sucked out of me. My eyes fly to Loren's.

"You did this?" I whisper, accusing.

"Did I leave you a letter? No. What is it?" He steps closer, closing the distance between us and looks down at the ring in my hand.

I pick it up and examine it because it can't be. It *can't* be, but there it is. C + V engraved on the inside of the silver band. I drop it.

"Oh my God."

"What's wrong?" Loren reaches down and picks it up. "What is this?"

My heart launches into my throat and sits there, blocking my airway, that's how little I can breathe. Loren puts his hands on my shoulders and squeezes, tells me to focus on breathing, to focus on him.

"Look into my eyes. Look at me," he says. I do. I look into his concerned golden eyes. "Breathe. Deep breath in, deep breath out, come on."

I try, goddamn it, I try, but I can't. "Th-th- that's my ring. That's my ring," I say, in a breathless chant.

His brows pull in and I can see the confusion clear as day. He has no idea what has me this freaked out, but one more

146

second of looking into my eyes and he sees it. Understanding dawns on him and he looks horrified.

"Vincent?" he asks.

I nod, my bottom lip wobbling. "Wh-wh- who would do this?"

Loren pulls me, crushing me to his hard chest and grips me like a vice. "When was this left here?" he asks.

"Last night," the security guard says. "Around seven o'clock."

I gasp. *No. No. No.* Loren's arm eases up a bit, but not much. His thumb rubs my shoulder gently as he speaks to the security.

"I need to see your security footage," he says, his voice rumbling in his chest and in turn, through me. The security guard must know he means business because he agrees. Loren walks me, still pressed up against him, behind the counter. I peak at the screen as the security guard rewinds the footage.

He points at the screen. "Here."

On the screen, I watch as a man walks in wearing jeans and a black hoodie. Fear ricochets in my chest.

Loren holds me tighter. "It's okay, baby."

"It's V-V-Vinny," I manage, placing one hand over my mouth. "I'm going to be sick."

"I got you," he says. "I got you."

What does that even mean? What the hell could it mean when I'm clearly staring at footage of the man I buried ten years ago.

"I buried him," I shout. "I saw his body. I SAW IT!"

That's the last thing I say before I keel over and puke on the floor.

TWENTY-FOUR

CATALINA

"I DON'T UNDERSTAND," I chant over and over in my apartment as I pace the living room. Loren's looking around everywhere for a sign of an intruder. I turn to him and point. "You snuck into my apartment last night. You took my bag."

"That was at nine o'clock, Catalina. He came by before then."

"I'm going to be sick again." I clutch my stomach. "How is this possible? I buried him, Loren. I buried him. I saw his body!"

He gives me a sympathetic look. "Go take a shower and pack a bag. You're coming home with me. I swear I'll explain everything in the car."

I open my mouth to argue but decide against it because I really need a shower. I give him a once-over, trying to figure out if I threw up on him at all. He waves me away as he lifts his phone to his ear.

"Meeting tonight," he says. "Urgent."

I walk away and do as I'm told. First, I open the blinds and brace myself. Loren already scoped everything out but I'm still scared. I can't shake this feeling. I check under my sink, too.

Not that Vinny fits there but who knows. I shower quickly and pack fast. Loren's in my room now, still on the phone, but watching every move I make. I haven't looked at him, but I know he is because I can feel his eyes on me and how sick is it that I'm yearning for him even in a time like this? Burning to have his hands on mine, his mouth on me. Wishing like hell he'd make me forget this nightmare for a second. He must see this in my eyes when I look up because his expression darkens.

"Not now," he says simply. "Hurry up."

I do. I finish packing fast and follow him out the door. He doesn't walk behind me or in front. He walks beside me, holding my hand in a vice grip as if he's scared of someone taking me at any given moment. I hold myself together, but when I get back in his car, I start to feel out of control again as I replay everything back.

"I saw him. When we got into the car yesterday, he was there, watching me. Watching us." I shiver. "Why? Why? What the fuck?" I rock in the seat and lean forward, putting my face between my thighs to try to breathe. Instead, I start to cry and hyperventilate. "Oh my God. Oh my God. Oh my God. Why?"

Loren makes a sharp turn and drives fast until he comes to a complete stop. I straighten. We're in an alley. He unbuckles my seat belt.

"Come here," he says.

My heart is sputtering out of control. Somehow, I make myself move to his lap because even though I hate him, even though I don't know what is happening right now, I need him. I need *something* and I decide his touch will do. He moves his seat back and positions me so that I'm straddling him. Then, holding my chin, he makes me look in his eyes. My chest is still heaving, but now my panic is muddled with emotions I can't decipher under these circumstances.

"I know you don't trust me right now. I know I fucked up, but you have to believe me when I tell you that I won't let anything bad happen to you," he says. "And I will tell you every-thing you want to know."

I nod slightly, eyes wide, because for some stupid, unknown reason I do trust him when he says this. "Okay."

"You feel better?" he asks. I shake my head, but my breath is evening out a bit, the pain in my chest lessening. Loren moves his other hand between my legs and dips it into my sweat pants. I'm rocking against him, still gasping, before his fingers even touch me. Slowly, he drags his fingers between my folds and dips them inside of me. I gasp, arching into him, rocking my hips against him. He's hard in his jeans and groans when I rock against him again.

"Fuck," he breathes. His hooded gaze is on mine as he licks his bottom lip slowly. "You're so fucking hot, Catalina."

I moan, his thumb on my clit sending a shock through me. I bring my hands to his hair and bury my fingers into it, rocking faster. "Please," I moan. "Please."

"Please what, baby?" His eyes open and shut as if they're being weighed down by something. "Tell me."

"I need you to . . . oh my God, please."

With his thumb on my clit, his fingers inside of me, he moves another to press onto my other entrance. It's all too much. This is too much. I feel vulnerable looking into his eyes like this. Vulnerable rocking against him like this, with aban-don. It feels too good to stop though.

"You're so fucking good at this." I rock against him once more.

He groans, his face moving an inch forward. He bites my bottom lip and pulls it into his mouth, sucking. That, and the way his fingers are playing my body, is what makes me come undone. I shiver and quake against him, and this time it has nothing to do with what had me shaking in the first place. All of the worries are completely forgotten. He pulls his hand away from me slowly. I whimper. He takes the same hand and wraps it around the back of my neck. I feel the slickness of my juices there. He pulls me toward him and kisses me then, his lips soft, like a cloud, his tongue lashing like a sword in battle.

He breaks the kiss slowly, with softer kisses and nips on my lips, and then stares at me with an expression I've never seen on him before. Without preamble, I start to cry. Loren holds me to his chest and runs his fingers through my wet hair for a long, silent moment.

"I have a performance tonight," I whisper.

"I know," he says. "I'll take you."

I nod against his chest and make myself move from his lap and back into my seat. I feel calm now, as if the orgasm took away my confusion and with it, brought clarity. Loren backs out of the alley and starts driving again.

"He's been alive all this time," I whisper, biting my lip as I look down at my hands. "All this time."

"He . . ." Loren clears his throat. "I killed him."

My gaze snaps to his.

"It's why your brother hates me." He chuckles. "Well, part of the reason. I think he just hates me—period."

"He thinks you killed him?"

"Everyone does." He shrugs nonchalantly. "It was the only way the plan was going to work. Vinny wanted out." He glances at me again. "People don't get fired. They get fired at. It's very rare that you see someone who joins this brotherhood step out and survive."

"Why?" I frown, shaking my head. "Why did he want out? Why didn't he take me?" My eyes widen. "What happened to your ex?"

Loren's mouth forms a smile. Not a kind one. "Tabatha was part of the reason he decided to come up with this plan in which I'd kill him so he could leave."

God, that hurts. I don't know why. It's been ten years, but the realization that Vinny had been cheating, and that he'd pick her over me . . . it feels like a stab in the chest. I make myself look at Loren.

"And you just . . ." I'm at a loss for words. Like, who willingly pretends to kill their cousin, one who stabbed them in the back, and never says anything about it?

"Blood is blood. If he hadn't gotten out, your dad would've killed him anyway. For hurting you."

"That's why you helped him?"

Loren exhales heavily. "I helped him because she begged me to. Tabatha did. She was pregnant with his baby."

I wrap my arms around my knees to shield myself from the pain, but it's impossible to protect yourself from blows that come from the inside. I bite my lip to keep from crying. I need to hear him out. I need to know why he came back and why he left me the damn engagement ring we buried him with. I think about that day, about the days that followed, and I realize that I hate him. I hate Vincent Moretti for fucking with me and fucking up my life.

"You don't have the same last name," I point out.

"His mom is my dad's sister. His father's a Moretti."

I nod as if that information was at all important in this equation. It's not. Vinny could be the fucking Pope and I'd still want to strangle him right now.

"Why come back?" I manage to ask. "Why even let me know he's back? Why . . . God, this is so fucked up."

"His mom died recently," he says, then retracts the statement. "His mom was murdered recently."

I gasp, covering my mouth. I met her a few times. She was a sweet, unassuming woman who'd feed you and give you the shirt off her back if needed.

"Who would do that?" I ask, dropping my hand.

Loren scratches his neck, looking like he doesn't want to answer, but finally says, "Your father."

TWENTY-FIVE

CATALINA

"PLEASE TELL ME YOU'RE KIDDING," I say. "Or that you're unsure. Or anything."

Loren shakes his head, his mouth set in a thin line. He turns onto a block. I haven't been paying attention at all, but now I look out and see that we're in a suburb with pretty houses. He pushes a button on the roof of his car and pulls into the driveway of a blue house with white trim.

"This is yours?"

"Yeah." He shoots me a small smile.

It's one I've never seen before and decide I fucking love. I try to smile back, but can't. I'm too wrapped up in everything he's just told me. He drives into the garage and waits until the door closes behind us. We get out of the car. Pulling my bag with me, I follow him inside the house. He punches in the code to the alarm system and the lights turn on automatically.

Loren steps out of my way and invites me into his space. It's . . . nice. It *feels* nice. Homey, like a place you can actually relax in. The walls are cool colors—whites, light grays. The furniture is also very inviting. There's really nothing that screams mobster except for maybe a large red and black painting of a revolver that sits atop one of the couches in the living room. It's not a big house. If I had to make an assumption based on what I see, I'd guess it's probably a three bedroom. It's beautiful, though. Meticulously kept, too. The dark wood floors are perfection—a grayish oak.

"Should I take my shoes off?" I ask, my voice comes out in a croak. I clear my throat.

Loren shrugs. "If you want. Doesn't matter to me though."

I take my shoes off and walk back to the garage entrance, dropping them there. He does the same with his, placing them perfectly next to mine. I tear my eyes away from the shoes and keep walking through the house. The kitchen is open, with a large island that faces a living room that has a cozy fireplace and television. It's a dream house, I decide.

"This is where you live," I say, unnecessarily.

Obviously it's where he lives. He shoves his hands in his pockets, watching me closely.

"You don't look very comfortable with me being here," I say.

"I'm fine with it, I just want to make sure you're fine with it."

"I . . ." My brows pull in as I consider that.

I don't know how I feel about any of this, but I know how I feel about him, more specifically about the way he makes me feel, so I walk over to him slowly, needing to feel his warmth against me. I wrap my arms around his middle and I know it's completely unexpected because his entire body stiffens under my touch, but only for a second. He wraps his arms around me and breathes out, holding me so tight I can barely breathe.

"I'm glad you're here," he says. "I'll keep you safe. I swear it."

I nod against him because, fuck if I don't believe him.

I CALL my sister and tell her everything and start to cry. She cries too.

"Oh God, Cat," she whispers. "I wish I was there. I can't believe this."

"I know."

"How can . . . I just can't believe it," she says again.

My sentiments exactly. I don't understand how this could happen. I don't understand how someone can purposely make you believe they're dead and vanish from your life. It hurts. It really hurts. After hanging up with Emma, I call Gio, but it goes to voicemail. I leave a message, then text him, and set the phone down. I have to warm up for my performance anyway. I change into my outfit and get into that, knowing I'll probably be running a little late and may not have enough time to warm up with my company. Loren's been in his office for over an hour now. He walked in there when I was talking to Emma and closed the door behind him. I haven't bothered to disturb him. Besides, I need to put distance between us to make sure that I'm not just clinging to him because I think the fear of what's out there is worse than what's in here.

"You hungry?" he asks behind me.

I straighten and look up from the floor. "Jesus. You're like a ninja."

His eyebrows shoot up. "Are you hungry? Can you eat at this time?"

"Not before a show. Especially not tonight. My nerves are already shot," I say, looking away from him and continuing with my warm-up stretches.

"What about a protein shake? A sandwich?" he asks. "A granola bar?"

"I'll take a granola bar." I stand and follow him to the kitchen. I eat the granola bar while he heats up some leftover lasagna for himself. My stomach growls when I smell the food but I know better than to eat right now, so I continue on with the boring granola bar and I down two large glasses of water.

"When did you start following me again?" I ask.

"You already know the answer to that."

"Okay, *why* did you start following me again?"

He watches me closely. "I changed my mind. Law enforcement would be a good fit for you."

"Then I'd have to chase you down and put you in jail."

"Are you gonna cuff me?"

"Probably."

"I think I'd be okay with that."

I feel my face heat up. I glance away. "Why now?" I ask again. *I can't get over it.* "Why would my dad do that now?" I don't even bother trying to ask why he would do it—period.

"Chances are, he didn't know Vinny was alive."

"How would he find out?"

"People are stupid." Loren shrugs.

"Yeah, but *that* stupid? He got out with a wife and a kid and then he got caught alone?"

He shrugs again. "It's not that difficult to believe. All it takes is one call to the wrong person and for that person to say something in public and boom, you're caught."

"It can't be that simple."

He tears his gaze away for a moment before he looks at me again. "I'm going to tell you something. Something I never even bothered to tell my ex because it's just not how I roll. I don't want people I care about knowing what it is I do for money because if someday I get picked up for something, the people around me will be the first they question." He stares at me for a while, his brow lifting.

"Tell me."

"I don't think you understand what I'm saying, Cat. If I tell you—"

"I get it, okay? Just tell me. I don't care how ugly it is, I don't care how it'll make you look, I don't—"

"But I do," he says, cutting into my sentence. "I care about how you see me."

I can't help it. I laugh. "How do I look at you now?"

"Like you want me to fuck you to oblivion." His lips twitch slightly.

I bite my lip, goose bumps spreading over my arms. I meet his gaze again. "Well, unfortunately I don't think whatever you tell me will change that."

"Good." His gaze darkens. "I used to find people. That was my first job when I started working for my uncle."

"Oh." I shrug. "That doesn't sound so bad."

"I used to deliver them to really bad men. Ruthless men. Fucked-up-in-the-head kind of guys, who did things I wouldn't wish on my worst enemy."

"They killed them," I whispered.

He nods once.

"Did you?"

"Kill people?" he asks. I nod. "I'm not proud of it."

"I always said I couldn't love a killer." Not that he cares. Not that I love him. I don't. I can't.

He stands up and walks around the counter, putting his empty dish in the sink, then walks over to me.

"I'll let you in on a little secret." He lowers his mouth to my ear and I swear I feel my nerves tangle up. "Anyone can be a killer. Even you, if you're pushed and have no other choice."

I stiffen. Maybe he's right. I wouldn't know. I've never had to choose. I look at him over my shoulder. He holds my gaze.

"Why did he come back? For revenge?"

"Yes, and I knew you'd be the first person he'd look for."

A shiver rocks through me. "You think he'd hurt me?"

"There's no telling."

"What about . . . what about the kid?" I ask, my voice barely a whisper.

"I assume he's with Tabatha. Vinny's not stupid enough to leave them without making sure they're okay," he says, his brows pulling in as he speaks. "Then again, I didn't think he'd be stupid enough to get caught either."

I glance away and focus on the granola wrapper in front of me. I can't believe I cried for him, mourned him, and the entire time he was living his life with his pregnant girlfriend and now child. That's the part that hurts most, if I'm being honest. That's the part that feels like a scalpel to my veins. She got her happily ever after. He got his. And I'm still here, just floating along.

"Are you okay to dance tonight?" Loren asks behind me.

I nod. "I'll push through."

I always do.

TWENTY-SIX

CATALINA

I POUR all of those emotions—fear, shock, and grief into my performance. By the end, I'm visibly crying, my shoulders shaking as I bow. Justin's hand grips mine, stronger than ever, and I appreciate it more than ever. It's good to have a real friend in a time like this when I don't know who I can trust. After our final bow, he pulls me into a hug, and with people still cheering, he brings his hands to my face and gazes at me.

"I got you," he says.

I start crying again because the words remind me of Loren and the fact that I'm barely hanging on by a thread. I don't expect it when Justin's lips come down on mine, but I don't feel entirely put off by it either. It's a chaste kiss, one a lot of us often share on and off the stage, an actor's kiss. The crowd goes wild as if he's just proposed. He does it again, deepening it this time. As we walk off stage, he has his arm draped over my shoulder. Other friends of ours come up to me and hug me goodbye.

"I'm not going to be gone long," I tell them, but I'm still crying. "It's only one season and I'll be practicing here."

"Still, I'll miss dancing with you next season," Bella says, giving me another hug. "Call me if you need anything."

"I'm having a house warming party next month once things are settled," Lily says, giving me a hug right afterwards. "I expect you to be there. Bring your boy-toy."

I smile through my tears and nod even though there won't be a boy-toy to bring by then. My relationship with Loren is shaky at best, especially now. Justin walks me to the dressing rooms, still holding my shoulder.

"You sure you're okay?" he asks.

"Yeah." I take a deep breath. "It's been a long couple of weeks. I'll miss dancing with you."

"I'll miss it too," he says, "but I'm hoping we'll be dancing together again soon."

I give him a hug, squeezing him tight before going into the dressing room. The shower is cold by the time I get to it, but I don't care. I wrap a towel around myself and walk back to the dressing room again, freezing at the sight of Loren standing there. He seems to take up the entire room. He also looks pissed-the-fuck-off. My heart hammers.

"Did anything new happen?"

"No."

"Oh." I clutch the towel tighter because his look is burning holes into me. "I need to change."

He crosses his arms and signals for me to change.

I blink. "Turn around."

"Are you serious?"

"Yes."

"I've seen you naked."

"Yeah but not when you're looking at me like that."

He closes the distance between us, bringing his hand to my neck. "Like what?"

"Like you want to hurt me," I whisper.

"You finally scared of me, Little Red?"

"No," I whisper.

"No?" He presses his thumb into my throat. I swallow again, my lips parting.

"No."

"Are you fucking him? Is that what's happening? You're fucking your dancer boy again?"

"No." My eyes widen. "He just did that. I'm not . . . I haven't."

"Hmm." It's a sound that comes from the back of his throat and vibrates through him. "I can have my way with you right now. Tear this towel off you, bend you over right here and fuck you raw," he says, his voice gravelly. "You'd scream louder than you normally do when I fuck you. You'd claw at me and I'd keep going. I'd fuck you until you screamed my name." He grabs a fistful of my hair hard, until tears spring to my eyes. "Maybe that's what it would take for that fuck-face Justin to get a fucking clue and stop coming after you."

My chest expands as I struggle to take even breaths, my nipples harden to the point of pain against the cotton towel around me. I rub my legs together, wishing like hell this wasn't arousing me as much as it is.

"You still not scared?"

I shake my head, trying to keep my expression clear of the emotion I'm feeling. It doesn't work.

"No," he says, bringing his thumb up to my lips. "I think you're turned on. I think you're wet for me already. Aren't you?"

I nod.

"Good." He drops his hand and takes a step back. A complaint rips from my throat before I can stop it. He raises an eyebrow. "You want to put on some clothes before I lose all control and make good on those promises."

I want him to lose control, God help me. I'm sick. Sick with lust. I hold Loren's dark eyes as I let the towel drop and reach for my thong, slipping that on slowly before pulling the cotton slip-on dress over my head. His eyes are molten, his jaw twitching with every movement I make. Butterflies swarm my stomach. They have no business being there.

"Fuck," he says, his voice low, barely audible. "The things you make me want to do to you."

Goose bumps spread across my skin. I should hate this man. There's no reason he shouldn't be number one on my shit list right now, yet here I am, trembling with this need for him that defies all rational thought. I'm completely fucked up. I reach into my bag and feel around for my phone, for his gun, not because I'm going to pull it out but to make sure it's there. I took it from the counter when we left his house earlier. My eyes widen when I realize it's no longer there. I look at him. He smiles, looking at me as if to say *surely you weren't expecting me to let you keep it were you?* That's the problem with men like him. Men like my brother, like my father. Some men pretend they want control. They play with handcuffs and floggers and remind you continuously that you're theirs. Men like Loren don't need to play a game. They don't need to remind you that you're at their mercy.

TWENTY-SEVEN

LORENZO

MAYBE MY AUNT was right when she told me to see a therapist after Tabatha left me for Vinny. It's obvious from the way I keep lashing out at Catalina that I need to rein in some of that anger and channel it elsewhere. It's not her fucking fault my ex-wife cheated. I also never reacted like this to Tabatha cheating. Sure, I flipped out because I was young and my ego was hurt, but I don't remember caring this much. I don't remember my blood boiling at the thought of my cousin touching her. Every time I think about someone else touching Catalina, I want to kill them.

"Where are we going?" she asks.

"I have a meeting to attend."

I feel her gaze on me. "What kind of meeting?"

"One that women aren't invited to, but seeing as your brother will be in attendance, I think you'll be okay."

"Oh God." She sounds like she's going to be sick. I lower her window.

"I don't mind you throwing up all over me, but I don't want that shit in my car."

"I'm not going to throw up," she whispers.

The girl doesn't eat enough. That's why she's always throwing up, and when she does she has nothing to get rid of except water. It's ridiculous. I pull out my phone and call Dominic, who answers on the second ring.

"What's up, boss?"

"Get me three pies from Roberta's. All cheese."

"Got it." He hangs up.

"Did you just order pizza like that?" Cat asks, looking at me. She pushes the button to put the window back up.

"Yeah."

"You didn't even say please or thank you."

I shoot her a look. "You sound like my mother."

She shrugs, glancing away. "I bet she wishes her politeness would've rubbed off on her son."

I can't help my smile. I park across the street from the warehouse and kill the engine and the lights. Cat makes to move, but I stop her with my hand. I like to scope out the scene before I get out of my car, especially here. I pull up the camera system on my phone. It's one that covers the entire block and sees every car, every person, every dog that's stepped foot on this street. Only four of us have access to it and we use the hell out of it. It's saved our asses from more than a few stakeouts by the FBI and DEA. They think they're slick but we're slicker. Once I know we're in the clear, I usher her out of the car and walk her across the street, opening the door and letting her in quickly. My heart is hammering loudly, I don't know what their reaction will be to having her here but I know it won't be good. It doesn't matter. I gave Dean a heads-up and his opinion is the only one that matters to me. Instead of leading the way and having her follow, I grab her hand in mine and take her to the other room.

"This is nice," she says, looking around in awe.

It is nice. We've made it a welcoming environment because some of the guys get kicked out of their house on the regular and this is their fallback place. We have bedrooms, a full kitchen—nothing fancy, a meeting room and a game room. It's an old firehouse that we bought thinking we'd turn it into a club. Instead, we turned it into a place that doesn't even allow women, let alone prostitutes. Those are definitely not allowed in here. I push the door open and feel Catalina press up against me as if she's taking cover. Four heads turn in my direction. I grin. Dean, at the head of the table shakes his head at that.

"What the fuck?" Gio roars. "Is that my sister?"

"Relax, I gave Dean a heads-up." I walk into the room and let go of Cat's hand as the door closes behind us. I put an arm around her instead and hold her to my side, my eyes on Gio who looks like he's going to fucking kill me. I'd love to see him try.

"You can sit here," I say to her, pulling a chair for her at the table, the one beside mine.

The one my cousin ensured he'd never get. The men gape at me. Dean just stares in amusement. Cat ducks out from under me and takes the seat. I don't exactly like that she's playing nice and doing as she's told, but given the circumstances, it's best that she does. She probably knows her brother's about to start a fight and I definitely don't want her in the way of that.

Gio stomps over to me and pushes me. It's all he needs to do. I punch him first. Bam. Right in the jaw. He holds his face for a second before coming at me. He punches me. I punch back. It's as far as we get before the door flies open and Dom comes barging in, setting down the pizzas before grabbing me. Frankie grabs Gio on the other side and they pull us apart. To be honest, I was done. I wipe my face, keeping my eyes on Gio's. He still looks furious.

"How could you bring her here?" he screams.

"Are you done with the foreplay?" Dean asks from the table.

He didn't even bother getting up. No, Dean Russo keeps his wits about him in every situation. It's one of the reasons I can't stand him. It's also one of the reasons I respect him. I straighten myself out and sit back down next to Catalina. Her hand covers mine on my lap instantly and I feel a sense of calm run through me. Gio sits across from me, hands folded, glaring.

"I brought pizza." I wave at the pizza in the center of the table. "Help yourselves."

Dom sits down on my other side, shooting me a confused look filled with a million questions I don't have time to answer. I turn to him. "By the way, Dom, thank you. For the pizza and for everything you do for me."

His brows pull in. "Um . . . you're welcome?"

Cat squeezes my hand. I chuckle and glance at her, smiling at the pink in her cheeks. She's fucking adorable this woman. I look back at the rest of the room. Everyone except Gio is eating pizza. I bring a box over to us, take out a slice and set it on a plastic plate in front of Cat.

"Please eat," I say. "It would make my night."

She blushes as she picks it up to take a bite, holding my gaze. "Thank you."

"What the fuck is happening?" Gio asks. "Why are you with him after what I told you? Do you need further proof that he's not the kind of man you want to be with? Do you need me to tell you that he killed your ex? Is that what it will take? Because he did. He fucking killed him. Murdered him in front of us."

I sigh heavily. I'm not even going to bother with it. Let her handle this shit. I want to hear her account of it anyway. She sets the pizza down the way she does everything, with grace and a serene disposition that drives me wild for some reason. Her gaze flicks to mine briefly, as if to say, can I talk? Is this okay? I nod. She nods back.

"I know you guys don't let women in here," she says, licking her lips. "But something happened yesterday and I guess Loren decided I should come." She shoots me a look like she wants me to save her from this, so I jump in.

"Vincent is alive."

Gio's jaw drops. Frankie's jaw drops. Dom's jaw drops. Dean just stares.

"What?" Frankie speaks first.

"Define alive," Dom says, eyes narrowed.

"You fucking lied to us, you piece of shit?" Gio asks.

"Let him talk," Dean says quietly.

"He wanted out. Tabatha was pregnant so I helped him get out." I shrug. "Joe would've killed him if he'd stayed and he would've found out he was fucking around on his daughter and got another woman pregnant. Tabby had suffered enough—"

"Yeah because you fucking cheated on her left and right," Gio roars. "Did you tell my sister that part?"

I sigh and rub the back of my neck. I glare at him. *I haven't told her that part yet, asshole.* So I fucked up. Sue me. I was young, stupid, and making more money than I knew what to do with. Women fucking threw themselves at me any chance they got. Was I proud of it? No, but what the fuck? Fuck you. You try dodging all that free pussy when you're in your early twenties. Catalina cares though. She pulls her hand back from mine and doesn't set it back. I look at her. She's not looking at me at all. She's so focused on that goddamn pizza I swear she's trying to figure out every single ingredient in it. I look up at Gio again.

"So you helped him get out," Frankie says, taking another bite of the slice in his hand.

"Right. He's been living in Florida with Tabatha and their kid for the last ten years," I say. "Their cover must have been blown at some point because the other day his mother went to visit and someone killed her. Strangulation," I say, raising an eyebrow. "And then they set the house on fire. Sound familiar?"

That's Joe's M.O. And Gio's. And Frankie's. And sometimes Dean's when he needs a job to look legit.

"He didn't stay quiet," Dean says. "He must have been in touch with someone here."

"Or maybe she was," I suggest. "Either way, Joe found out about it and got his revenge."

"But why his mom?" Cat asks. I'm surprised to hear her talk.

"Tabatha and the kid weren't home?" I ask rather than say because I don't know. I look at Gio. "You should know better than anyone. Why wait this long? Even if he was alive, why hold that grudge?"

For once, he doesn't look upset. His gaze flickers from mine to Cat's. "You didn't tell him?"

"Gio," she whispers, a warning.

Hell no. I told her everything. I risked everything by bringing her here. "Tell me what?"

Her bottom lip wobbles. I push her red hair behind her ear and cup her face so she'll look at me. When she does her eyes are filled with unshed tears and a sorrow I've never seen on her face, not even when she saw that ring from Vinny. I run my thumb over her cheek. With my other hand I pull the chair closer to me and turn my body in her direction so she's somewhat between my legs.

"Tell me what, baby?"

She blinks rapidly. I catch her tears and wipe them before they trickle down her face. "I was pregnant."

"What?" I don't know what I was expecting, but it wasn't that.

"When Vinny died. When he left," she corrects taking a breath. "I was pregnant. Dad made me . . ." she pauses, swallowing. She looks at Gio briefly, then back at me. I'm so shellshocked that I drop my hand from her face and gape at her.

"What happened?" I make myself ask her because I have to know, because that little charade of not telling her who I was from the get-go stings right now. Because I helped my asshole cousin run off with my ex because of a child but didn't even consider that he might be leaving one behind. What the fuck?

"My dad made me give it up."

My throat feels tight. "For adoption?"

"No." She shakes her head. "He made me get an abortion. He said I couldn't have a bastard kid, especially one with a dead father."

"He said you'd ruin the kid's life and your own," Gio finishes, his voice quiet, distant.

"I hate that I went through with it," she whispers. "Not because I think I'd be a great mom or anything but because it was mine and I gave it up, you know?"

I pull her to my chest and kiss the top of her head. She'd be a great mother. I want to say that but don't. I want to say a lot of things but don't. This isn't the time or the place to show emotion. Cat's the exception. I let go when I know she's okay and turn back to the rest of the room. I look at Gio specifically.

"Did he do it?" I don't have to specify what I mean. Did Joe kill Vinny's mom? My aunt, for fuck's sake.

He shrugs, but he might as well have said yes.

"Vinny left Cat's engagement ring at her building," I say.

"When?"

"Yesterday," she whispers. "We got it earlier today."

"Why the fuck didn't you call me?"

"I did call you." She pounds her small fist on the table. "I left you a voice message and a text."

"Dammit," he mutters. "Fuck." His eyes flick to mine. "You were with her?"

I nod.

"Would he come after her though?" Frankie asks. "If he wants retaliation, why not go after Emma? Or Joe himself?"

"If he goes after Joe, he kills him and then it's done. He

wants it to hurt," Dom says, shrugging. "It's what I would do. Wouldn't you?"

"Family is supposed to be untouchable," I say. "Joe fucked up."

"Vinny fucked up first," Frankie counters.

"Lorenzo fucked up first." Gio raises an eyebrow. "What does that make him?"

"We've all fucked up at one point or another," Dean says. "I killed my step-father. A made man. What does that make me?"

Un-fucking-touchable, I want to say, but don't. I bet we all think it though. He killed him over a decade ago and he's still standing, which means we don't need to vocalize that at all. It probably helps that he doesn't get out much. He's a hell of a recluse and he throws a hell of a party. When I was young, I used to take advantage of those parties and the twelve bedrooms in his mansion. Even when I wasn't so young I did. I glance over at Catalina and think those days must be behind me because the thought of going back to one of those parties isn't as gratifying as it once was. *What the hell is wrong with me?* Jesus.

"We need to find him," I say, finally. "Before he finds her."

"I'll take her to my place," Gio offers. "He won't look there."

"Fuck you. Let her decide where she's going. She's not a fucking pawn," I say, though I'm praying like hell she decides to come with me.

Gio considers that. "Every single one of us is a pawn."

Dean raises an eyebrow in agreement. Frankie and Dom shrug like he's right. The fucker has a point, but I'm not going to retract my statement now.

"I'll go with Loren," Catalina says after a moment. "Vinny might come for you next, G. And if his plan is revenge, I'm pretty sure he'll take it out on you. I don't think he'd hurt me. He was never . . ." she pauses as if it hurts her to speak the words. "He was always sweet to me."

"I think he was behind the robberies and the fire in Hell's

Kitchen," I add, trying not to think about her words or how much they bother me.

"Fuck," Frankie breathes. "It makes sense."

Dom's eyes widen on mine, probably realizing that all of the questioning he did on those poor guys was for nothing. At least we didn't kill anyone over it. Not yet.

TWENTY-EIGHT

CATALINA

WHEN WE GET to Loren's house again, he goes through the motions—checks the camera feed from the car, lets the garage door shut behind us, switches off the alarm, and locks the door. We head upstairs quietly, only the sound of our shoes—his dress shoes and my converse—on the wood stairs echoing throughout the house. I hadn't come up here earlier and I'm not sure what to expect, but he looks over his shoulder, takes me by the hand and leads me to a door down the hall. He pushes it open and switches the lights on, illuminating a large bedroom with a king-size bed in the middle and a couch off to the side. Everything is gray, white and blue. It feels cozy.

He shuts the door behind us and locks that too. I watch as he heads to his closet and switches the light on in there. He hasn't said a word to me since my confession during the meeting and I'm almost afraid of what he must think of me. I didn't really know if I was afraid of someone else's judgment for terminating the pregnancy until that moment. I judge myself daily for what I did. I live with the guilt of my actions. I have my good days and bad days. Most are good, and on those days, I remind myself what an amazing life I have and that I'm not sure

I could've offered a child anything on my own. On bad days, when I see kids that age running around, I feel hollow. Today is one of those days. I walk toward him because I want to take my mind off it. He's sitting on a small bench in his closet. I walk in, eyeing the suits on one side, dress down clothes on the other, trainers, and dress shoes. The back wall has a tall black gun safe that's directly across from where he's sitting. I lean against it and wait for him to finish putting the tongues in his dress shoes and look at me. When he does, his expression is guarded.

"You're judging me," I say.

"What?" He frowns, shaking his head. "No. I would never judge you for anything. I may not be a saint, but I'm not a hypocrite."

He stands up, I crane my neck as he does to keep looking into his eyes. His expression doesn't give away much as he turns around and places the shoes down and moves on to take off his watch, his dress shirt, his pants. He does everything quickly until he's naked except for his black boxer briefs.

"How are you in such good shape?" I ask.

"Home gym." He walks away, pulling a t-shirt from a drawer and underwear from another. I follow him out of the closet and into the bathroom. I freeze by the door. It has dark gray cabinets and nice white marble tile. There's a deep porcelain tub that looks like it was made in the eighteenth century and a large shower with one of those raindrop showerheads that comes out from the ceiling.

"This is nice."

"Thank you." He walks over to the shower and switches it on, pulling off his boxers and tossing them into a hamper beside the cabinets.

"Did you customize all of this?" I walk toward the shower and put my hand on the glass as he steps in and closes the door, feeling like I'm being left out of playtime.

"I did," he says.

I hate that he's being short with me and even though he told me he's not judging me, I can't help that the feeling festers. Why else would he be acting this way? I decide I've had enough. I take off my clothes quickly and join him in the shower. He doesn't even look surprised at this. He also doesn't look happy. His dick does though. At least a part of him cares. The only part, I remind myself. I'm just a fuck, I remind myself. But no. No, I'm not. He cares. I'm not imagining that.

I step forward, grab the loofa from his hand and set it aside. He looks down at me, the water flowing down his head, making his hair cover most of his eyes. I reach up and brush it back, letting my fingertips caress down his face, to his lips. I hold his gaze, which is broody and sexy as hell.

"What are the odds that you actually care about me?" I ask, the roar of the water and my heart in my ears making it nearly impossible to know if I whispered the words or said them aloud.

His lips form a sad smile. He doesn't give me a response beyond that. I don't like it. I don't know why, but I don't.

"Why is that a problem?" I ask. "Why don't—"

He silences me with a kiss. It's not a soft kiss that's asking for anything, but a hard, demanding kiss. One that speaks of a loyalty I haven't asked for, blood that hasn't yet spilled. He deepens it, lifting me and hoisting me against the glass behind me. He doesn't give preamble before he spreads my legs farther apart and thrusts into me slowly, gently, his mouth still on mine. I feel him so deep that my legs start to shake from it. He breaks the kiss and pulls back to look at me, his eyes searching mine as he continues to thrust into me, and I swear my heart splits in two right there.

"The odds are high, Cat," he whispers against my lips. "Really fucking high."

Relief drops inside me like a bomb, but he doesn't give me time to relish it. He grips my thighs and start ramming into me harder, faster. I throw my head back against the glass and claw at his back. He lowers his mouth to my neck and sucks, trailing to my collarbone and back up.

"I'm gonna—" I don't even have time to finish the sentence before the orgasm crashes into me.

He pulls out, still holding me up as I spasm, and strokes himself, growling my name as he comes all over my stomach. He sets me down gently and we finish washing. When we're lying in bed, he pulls my back against his chest and drops his forehead to my shoulder, wrapping his arms around me. They feel like a cocoon, a place to take refuge in, but when he tightens them they also feel like a jail cell, someplace I can't escape from. For the first time in a long time, I don't want to.

TWENTY-NINE

CATALINA

LOUD NOISES COMING from downstairs wake me. Loren sits up beside me in the bed and reaches for his gun in one swift motion. I push my body higher on the bed, clutching the covers like a shield to my chest, as if bullets couldn't penetrate cloth.

"Stay here," he says, getting out of bed. I scramble in the sheets and get out after him.

"I'm not staying here alone," I whisper.

The stomping downstairs grows louder. It sounds like a battalion is in the house. My heart won't quit hammering and dammit I'm scared. If it's Vinny and he's here to get some kind of vengeance, I'm as good as dead. I know this and I'm sure Loren knows it as well. He turns around and looks me in the eye. It's dark out, and it's dark in here.

I can barely see him, but I can feel the gravity in his voice when he tells me, "Come here."

I follow him into the bathroom. He moves the shelf holding the towels and exposes a large window, opening it.

"Didn't you set the alarm before we came up here?" I whisper.

He nods, reaching outside and grabbing something. Whatever it is rattles. *A ladder? We're supposed to go down a ladder right now?* He leaves the bathroom and brings me my shoes and the dress I was wearing earlier. Before I know what's happening, we're both getting dressed. I'm just moving through the motions quietly because he is, but my heart is trumpeting in my ears the entire time. He grabs my face with both hands and kisses me hard on the lips, pressing his forehead against mine.

"Go down this ladder and get as far away from here as you can, then call your brother."

"What?" I whisper shout, grabbing onto his arm. He can't be serious. "Come with me!"

"I can't." He hands me the gun he's holding, looking me in the eye, pleading with me. "Please trust me, Cat."

"I don't want to leave you." I take the gun, my lip wobbling as I gaze up at him. "I don't want you to die. Promise me you won't die."

"I can't make that kind of promise, baby," he says, a sad smile on his face. "But I'll try."

A sob escapes me. The footsteps grow louder. "Dammit, Loren."

"Go." He pushes me toward the window, leaving no room for argument. "I'll see you later."

I put on my cross-body, tuck the gun beside my phone and climb out the window and grip the stairs, taking a deep breath. I look in the window just as Loren is shutting it. Our eyes meet for a second before he covers it with the shelf again. *God, help him be okay. Help him get out of this alive. Please.* I make myself climb down the stairs even though I'm terrified and my palms are sweaty and I swear I'm going to fall with each step I take, my feet slipping every time I press it onto the next step. When I make it to the ground, I press myself into the side of the house.

I wait.

And wait.

And wait.

I breathe.

And breathe.

And breathe.

I hear noises, banging coming from inside the house and decide to make a run for it. I don't go out to the street. Instead, I run to the neighbor's yard, and to the next, until I reach a fence that stops me. That's when I go to the street and take out the phone to call my brother. I hear a bang as I wait for him to answer. Another bang. I bite down on my lip.

"Where have you been?" I ask. "Loren's house was broken into and he made me go down a ladder—"

"Where are you?" he asks, cutting into my story.

"I don't know." I glance up at the bus stop. "I see a deli." I walk closer to the street. "Halsey Street."

"Is your GPS—"

"Yes, I switched it on like an hour ago hoping you'd come."

"Fuck, you're in Brooklyn?"

"I'm assuming," I say. I couldn't have gone that far from Loren's house.

"I'm on my way. Frankie, take ninth to Prospect Park West."

"Was it you? At Loren's?"

"No."

"Swear to me, Giovanni."

"I swear to God. I had nothing to do with that."

"It sounded like there was an army of men," I whisper.

He doesn't say anything at all. I press my back against the deli behind me. I hold a hand over my heart and clutch the phone with the other, my mind reeling as I replay everything that happened. The shots, the break-in, the stomps. Please let Loren be okay. Please let Loren be okay. It's on repeat inside my head. What if he dies? Oh my God. Please don't let him die.

"Cat," Gio says in my ear.

I blink. I swear I've been here an eternity. "Yeah, I'm here."

"I'm pulling up now. You see me?"

I look down the street at the blinding lights approaching. "Yeah."

He opens the passenger door and gets out to open the back door. He takes one look at me and I must look a lot worse than I thought because he slams the passenger door shut and climbs into the back beside me.

"You walked here from Lorenzo's?"

"Yes." Something grips at my throat. "We need to go over there. We need to help him."

Gio looks at me. "It's too late."

"What?" I scream. "What do you . . . what do you mean it's too late? What does that mean? Frankie, drive to Loren's house."

Frankie doesn't say a word. I don't even know if he'll do what I ask, but he keeps driving.

"Frankie," I plead. "Please, please drive to Loren's. We need to help him. We need—"

"If that many people went into his house and they all had guns, the chances—"

"Don't," I say, my voice raw. "Don't you dare fucking say it."

I can't help the sob that rocks through me or the mournful cry that escapes my lips. I bury my face in my hands, shoulders shaking.

Gio puts a hand on my shoulder. "I'm sorry."

"Just take me to his house." I wipe my face.

"You heard the girl, Frankie."

I breathe a sigh of relief. My knee bounces the entire ride over, which seems to take forever, but according to the clock, it only lasts four minutes. We're almost at the block when a sound cuts through us. I turn to look at Gio just as a bullet flies between us, then another. Frankie screams. The car spins out of control. I scream. Gio reaches for my hand. I reach for his. Another bullet. I don't know how many they've shot, but I feel no pain so I assume none have hit me yet. Gio grabs me by the shoulders and presses me down to the floor of the backseat.

"Don't fucking move," he says.

The car spins again, this time we hit something, the impact makes my entire body jump off the ground and land with a force that rips the air from my lungs. Then there's nothing.

My ears are ringing. I manage to pull myself up into a sitting position. I look up to make sure my brother's okay, but he's not moving. I try to look at Frankie, but from what I can see, he's not moving either. I see blood covering the driver's seat. I grip the seat to bring myself to sit upright just as the door opens beside me. Someone reaches in and uses a fistful of my shirt to pull me out. I grab the arm, screaming, my ears still ringing. I kick at my brother's leg, at the seat, I even kick the street once I'm dragged onto it. I scream for help, and scream again and again, scratching the arm, thrashing against it. He pulls me up and carries me.

"Relax, Kitty Cat. I got you."

I look at his face, my eyes wide. It's like looking at a ghost. I buried this man ten years ago. Buried him, cried for him, mourned him. I dreamed so many nights about what I would do if he could come back, if he hadn't died, if life would have continued, and now that it's a reality, it all feels wrong. He feels all wrong. I start fighting against him, thrashing and clawing and screaming. I am not going with him. I am not. His grip doesn't ease up and I'm finally forced to stop fighting.

"Why?" I ask.

It smells like smoke, like fire. My nose scrunches at the smell. I look around.

"Was your brother taking you back to your boyfriend's house?" Vinny asks, walking nonchalantly, as if we're on a stroll. My head is spinning. "You were almost there. Too bad you were so late."

I follow his eyes and see the house. It's engulfed in fire, the windows blown out, the front of it completely charcoaled. I start to tremble with sobs.

"No." I shake my head. "No!"

"Don't worry, I'm sure my cousin survived," he says as he walks away.

"No," I scream again. "No, no, no, Loren!"

Vinny brings a hand up to cover my mouth. "It's cute that you've taken such a liking to him. You know he's just using you, right?"

I shake my head, blink to clear the tears in my eyes and scream again.

"Shut up," he says, smiling as he stabs me with a syringe, and then I feel nothing.

THIRTY

LORENZO

IF YOU BREATHE fifteen minutes of straight smoke, it'll kill you. Luckily, I had an oxygen mask that I'd been using to work out and decided to get it before I headed downstairs. Luckily, the paramedics and fire rescue got to my house in under five minutes.

"I need to get out of here," I say, ripping the mask off my face.

The paramedic puts it back. "You need to breathe."

I can't fucking breathe. I struggle again, but this time two guys come and strap me down. They start injecting me, pumping things into me that I don't want. Catalina's waiting for me somewhere. Hopefully she stayed by the park. Hopefully she got ahold of Gio. At least I know he'll keep her safe until I get there. They close the doors to the truck and speed off. Over the radio, I hear them mention a car accident—two males in their thirties are hurt. My heart races. Gio and Frankie? No. There are thousands of men in their thirties in Brooklyn. But how many of them drive?

THIRTY-ONE

CATALINA

"I HAVE TO SAY, you're even more beautiful now than you were as a teenager."

I open my eyes slowly. My head feels like it weighs a ton. I try to make my mouth work, but can't. I close my eyes again and pass out. When I come-to again, I'm lying in a bed. The room is white with a floor-to-ceiling window on one side. A condo. A high-rise, from the looks of it. I sit up slowly, my head pounding.

"I brought you clothes," Vinny says.

I look at him now. He looks like the same man I fell in love with as a teenager. He's filled out quite a bit, but it looks good on him. He looks the same, but his brown eyes are cold and distant. I lick my lips.

"I fucking hate you." My voice is a croak.

"I figured as much." He glances away, nodding. "You mourned for me though. I saw you."

"You're sick." My stomach rolls. "You're a sick fuck. Did you think that was cool? Seeing me crying for you when you were alive all along?"

"Not really." He shrugs. "I felt bad."

I don't know if that's supposed to make me feel better or not, but it doesn't. Each word coming from his mouth feels like one slap after another. I continue to stare at him because I just can't believe he's here. He looks the same. He's gained weight, but his face and hair look the same. My heart feels heavy in my chest, painful even.

"Why did you do it?" I ask, finally.

"Fake my death?"

I nod.

"To get out of here. I wanted it to be you," he says. "But Tabby was pregnant—"

"I was pregnant," I whisper, meeting his eyes.

He reacts like I've slapped him. "Where is it?"

I bite my lip, look outside at the dark sky and the pretty New York skyline. I feel him coming closer, but don't expect it when he grabs me by the throat. My eyes fly back to his. I grapple with his hand, struggling to breathe.

"Where is my kid?" he demands.

I shake my head, gasping for air. He finally loosens his hold. "I had an abortion," I gasp out, holding my neck.

"You—"

"My dad made me get one." The words fly out of my mouth as I cower back. I don't want him to hurt me again. "When he found out he made me go."

"Why didn't you tell me you were pregnant?"

"I was going to tell you but then . . ." I shrug, sneaking a glance at him. "You died."

He looks like he could slap me any minute. I'm already bruised up. I can't even imagine how my throat must look. My feet ache so badly I can't even bear to look at them. If I keep this up I won't be able to dance at all this week and that's not an option. He sits down on the edge of the bed, gripping it.

"I'm going to make him pay for this," he seethes.

My dad. He's talking about my dad. I nod in understanding.

He's taken a lot from Vinny. That's the way these men operate —an eye for an eye mentality.

"You have a show soon?"

I blink. Of course he knows I'm still dancing. "Tomorrow night. My last solo of the season."

"You'll be there. I'll make sure of it." He stands up. "I'll get you ice for your feet."

"Vinny," I call out before he disappears into the bowels of the apartment. He stops but doesn't turn around. "I'm sorry about your mom."

HE SEEMS to stand there for an eternity before he nods and walks away. When he comes back, he brings a big glass Tupperware filled with water and ice. He sets it down beside me. I move my legs to dip my feet in.

"Shouldn't you wash first?" he asks.

"I'm sore. I'm tired. Everything hurts."

He looks up at me from where he's crouching in front of me. I swallow. Ten years have passed but it feels like it was just yesterday when he used to do this for me, when I ran my hand down his face and kissed him. Sadness seeps into me, against my own will. I don't know why I replace hatred with empathy so easily, but it's the way I'm built.

"Why her?" I ask. "What was wrong with me?"

"Nothing at all." He brings one of my feet to the water and then the other. "Tabatha and I grew up together. She was Loren's girlfriend but even then I was in love with her. You were fine, you were perfect," he says, and I believe him. I can still see the truth in those hard, cold eyes. "But she was . . . everything."

Tears trickle down my face. I wipe them with the back of my hand. I'm not sure what I was expecting him to say. Confess his love to me? He's been with her for ten years, dammit. Been with a woman he's actually in love with. A woman I was only a stand-in for, apparently. It hurts to hear. It hurts even more because I'm pretty sure I'm in love with Loren and to him I was only a means to an end. Maybe not now, but I was at one point. Obviously I have bad taste in men. I finally dip both feet into the ice, wishing it were my feelings I was shocking and numbing instead. Vinny stands up and walks out of the room again. When he comes back, I tell him I need a shower.

"No funny business," he says.

I nod solemnly and stop when I reach the bathroom door. "My brother . . ."

"I don't know."

It's all he needs to say. I shut the bathroom door behind me and try not to think about it, but it's useless. I cry in the shower and when I crawl into bed and think about my brother, Frankie, and Loren, I cry myself to sleep.

THIRTY-TWO

CATALINA

HE HAS MY PHONE, so I can't get ahold of anyone. When he opens the door again, the light sweeping in from outside is bright and I'm pretty sure it's mid-morning, which means I must have fallen asleep at some point.

"Breakfast," he says.

He didn't bring anything with him, so I assume I have to get up and follow him. I do. He has a small table set for both of us. It's the first time I actually look around and realize how big the condo is.

"Is this yours?"

He shakes his head. "A friend's."

"Oh."

"I still have those, you know."

"I never doubted it." I lick my lips, drink some orange juice and dig into a croissant. "I did mourn you, you know?"

"I know."

"What do you have?" I ask because I can't help myself. The child I didn't have would be the same age. "Girl or boy?"

"Boy."

My lips try to form a smile, but remain flat. "I bet he misses you. Don't you worry about that? That you're here looking for revenge and he just wants his dad home?"

"If I don't do this, he'll die. Maybe not now, but at some point."

Maybe he's right. It saddens me to think that the only outcome here is death.

"Your father will be there tonight."

My heart slams. "No he won't. He never comes. He's never . . . I haven't spoken to him in almost ten years."

He looks surprised. "Because of the abortion or because of your mother?"

"What do you know about my mother?" I whisper. *Please say nothing.*

"I tried to look for her to spare you all of this," he says. "She's impossible to find. He must've paid good money for that."

"He won't come."

"He knows about Gio, and about you, and this is the only way he can get to me. He'll come."

I'm still struggling to understand all of this. I know why Vinny wants his revenge, but it doesn't make any sense for my father to want to kill him. An eye for an eye, yes, but Vinny never took anything from my father. Unless Gio's actually dead. The thought stabs at me. Vinny hasn't told me anything and I can't bear to ask again. I just want this nightmare to be over. I want to go back to regular life. Vinny lets go of my arm and looks at me. There's a menacing warning there: *don't try anything stupid.* I nod. I wouldn't try anything at all. He already told me he has people watching Emma. The last thing I need is for her to be in trouble.

It's only when I get near the dressing rooms that I feel myself breathe. My shoulders relax as I walk over to Marta's station. She hands me my costume and my backup pointe shoes, extras I broke in and left just in case, raising an eyebrow as if she knows I'm in some sort of trouble. Thankfully, she doesn't question anything. A part of me wishes Justin were in this show with me, he always picks up the slack when I slip up and makes it look seamless. Right now, I have no choice but to keep my head in the game. I warm up and idle backstage, practically bouncing from foot to foot until it's time for me to head to the stage. When I hear the music, I switch my thoughts off and let my body take over. I pour myself into each step. My feet haven't healed from yesterday, but I don't ignore the discomfort. The pain fuels me. It gives me something to focus on, so I push. Once I land my final tour jeté, I make my way off the stage. Normally, by the time I'm back here, I can breathe easily. Not tonight. The fear I felt on stage? It hasn't gone away. It's gripping me by the stomach, and the throat, not letting me think clearly.

A small group of dancers are performing when I dare to look out into the crowd. When I'm on the stage, I'm focused on dancing and the lights are pretty blinding anyway, but from my spot in the wings, I can see the audience. I scan the rows for my father, for Vinny, wondering where he's sitting. I see neither. The show comes to an end, but I'm on hyper-drive, the hairs on the back of my neck on alert. One of the other dancers comes by and grabs my hand to take me out to the stage again as the audience applauds and whistles. Normally, I don't mind this. Normally, it's my second favorite part of the show. Today, I feel sick to my stomach. Sick because I shouldn't be smiling. Not when I don't know where Gio or Frankie are. Not when I don't know how Loren is, or where. Not when something really bad is going to happen to my father, even though I hate him, but dammit I can't be the one responsible for what happens to him.

My hands clutch the dancers beside me a little tighter as we bow because I know what's coming, they're going to let go and let me take my own bow and I don't want to. I don't want to be singled out right now. With hesitance, and definitely not because I loosen my grip at all, they let go of my hand and take a step back. The air feels cooler without them. I take a deep curtsy, then another and quickly rush off stage, not even bothering to look anyone in the eye. I head straight to the dressing room and gather my things. I don't even want to shower here. I'm scared and I really need to figure out how to get information on Gio. The door opens behind me and a group of dancers come in. My eyes dart to the phone one of them is holding.

"Hey, Frannie, can I borrow your phone for just one second?"

"Of course." She frowns, but doesn't question me or ask where mine is as she hands it over.

I open up the internet and type in the local news website. The first image I see is of a house on fire. The second is a car accident in Brooklyn with fatalities. My hands start to shake, my knees start to buckle. I lose my vision and I must be falling because suddenly there are hands all around me, voices asking me things like *are you okay? What's going on? She fainted. Have you eaten anything today? Get her soda or something. We don't have soda! Redbull! Something!* And then I'm floating. When I come to again, it's because my stomach feels like it's about to explode and the urge to throw up is overwhelming. I don't have to open my eyes to know I'm in someone's arms. For a split second I trick myself into thinking they belong to Loren and I smile. That is, until I smell the faint scent of Cartier Sport and I know for a fact it's Vinny carrying me and then the sick feeling envelopes me ten-fold. I start to cough first.

"I need to . . . I don't feel good," I whisper.

"Fuck." He sets me down on my feet.

At least he has the decency to do it gently. He also holds my shoulders to make sure I'm standing upright. He was always like that with me. I would hear rumors of the menacing things he did out in the streets, but I never believed them because he was so kind to me. *Because he was cheating on you with another woman.*

His everything, my brain spits at me. I blink and realize he must have carried me a lot further than I thought because I'm standing in a dark alley. Standing in a dark alley, still wearing my costume, what the fuck? I fold over and start puking. He sighs like he's disgusted by my behavior but this is his fault. He drugged me. I'm bending over like that when I hear commotion —tires squealing, people yelling, women screaming. My stomach clenches again. I'm still doubled over, thinking I could throw up at any given moment, when I hear his voice. It's loud and echoes through the alley.

"Let her go and I'll spare you your life."

"Fuck you," Vinny spits.

Only my dad can say something like that and have it sound like he's in a Western and not some fucked up street. I manage to stand upright and side-step Vinny slightly, just enough to see my father. It's too dark to make out his face, but I can see the outline of his body and those of two men on either side of him. I've spent hours thinking about what it would be like to see him again and this scenario never played out in my head. I thought I would be nervous or angry, but what I feel is numb. Maybe it's because my mind is still too wrapped up in the news of a fatal car accident and a house fire in Brooklyn. Maybe it's because despite Vinny being alive and not dead like I presumed all these years, I know that the chances of Gio, Frankie, and Loren being okay are slim and that's the only thing on my mind.

"Dad, Gio," I say because I can't help myself.

That's all I'm able to get out before Vinny swings his arm back, slamming it right into my chest so hard I stumble backwards and fall on my ass, but not before my hand hooks onto the planks of wood on the wall beside me. I bring it all down with me, the force of it enough to knock the wind out of me. Somehow, probably because my heart is racing and adrenaline has taken over my body's senses, I manage to look up between the wooden boards. Vinny reaches behind him again and I watch in horror as he takes out his gun. I open my mouth to shriek, to beg him not to do this, but it's too late. Shots are fired into the night.

Bang. Bang. Bang.

Bang. Bang. Bang.

I can't see the men on the other side. Can't see my father or his henchmen. I can see Vinny, though. His body falls slowly, in a way I've only seen in the movies—first to his knees, then he crumples to the ground.

Police sirens ring out almost immediately. They must have been really close to begin with. I try to scramble out of the wood, but I can't. I'm completely stuck. I try again, pulling myself up with my arms. The wood planks are on my lower body, mostly on my feet. It's then that the pain hits me—raw and hard. More tires squeal. I hear commotion but I can't really make anything out. Did my father leave me here? I shouldn't be surprised, but I am. Or maybe I'm not surprised but it still stings. I make out people running toward me, flashlights on my face, arms pulling me. Pain shoots up from my right foot to my hip. I scream in agony.

I don't know how long I'm there. Maybe a second, maybe an eternity, before the planks are lifted off my foot and I'm carried out.

"Fuck." The groan is Vinny's. I start to cry. *How the hell is he still here? Where's Loren?* He sets me down and drags me to his car, which is in a garage halfway back to Lincoln Center. Once we reach it, he deposits me in the back seat and starts driving. I sit up and see the blood all over myself and shriek.

"My blood," he says. "Not yours."

"Oh my God." My eyes widen. "Oh my God. Oh my God. Oh my God! You're losing too much blood!" I start to panic. He's driving the damn car. He'll kill us both.

"I'll live." He coughs.

"I don't care whether or not you live," I scream. "I care if I live dammit! I don't want to die in a car with you!"

I cross my arms tightly and look out the window. My foot is throbbing, my nerves are shot, and he's driving like he's on a NASCAR speedway. I try to calculate whether or not I'd survive a jump from the moving vehicle and decide it's not worth the risk. He drives and drives, and swerves repeatedly. At one point, he veers out of the lane completely and I think it's the moment of my death. I scream.

"Vinny! Please!"

"Yeah. Yeah." He sounds like he's dozing off.

"Let me drive. Please. I'll take you anywhere I swear," I plead. "Think about your wife. Your son."

I'm crying so hard now, but I mean it. I'll take him anywhere as long as he doesn't kill us both in this car. After a swerving once, twice, three more times, and more coughing and choking on his end, he pulls over. I limp to the front seat. I can't fully step on my right foot. He scoots to the passenger side. The front seat is long and uninterrupted by arm rests.

"Do you even know how to drive?"

I frown. "Yeah. Sort of."

"Oh fuck." He chuckles, a spray of blood spilling all over my right arm and the console.

My eyes widen as I look over. I feel helpless, my heart breaking in two. "You're really hurt, Vin. You'll die if I don't take you to a hospital."

He seems to consider this for a moment and finally nods. He fishes out his phone and types something. It vibrates right away. He chuckles and types again. I can only assume he's talking to Tabitha. Or his son. The thought isn't nearly as sad as it was the first time. I follow the street signs to the hospital and pull up to the front of the ER, waving down the valet, who waves down some nurses. They bring out a gurney and lay him on it, rushing him inside. One nurse stays behind.

"Are you his wife?"

I shake my head. "No."

"Were you in a car accident?"

"He was shot."

"We'll need to ask more questions," she says, then looks at what I'm wearing. Her eyes widen. "Are you hurt?"

"My leg," I whisper. "My foot."

Then, I'm also wheeled inside on a gurney.

THIRTY-THREE

CATALINA

TURNS OUT, we're in Union City. I'm still stuck in a hospital bed unable to leave. They do an X-ray on my foot and discover I have a nondisplaced talus fracture.

"Nondisplaced," I say brightly. "That's good, right?"

"Eh." The doctor nods her head yes and no. "Good because you'll make do with a cast. You're in superior shape, so it shouldn't be too difficult for you to handle, but you'll need to be off your feet for ten weeks—at the bare minimum."

"Ten weeks?" I breathe.

My heart feels like it's going to burst. Not in a good way. I nod anyway because I just want to get out of here. I need to find my brother and Loren and Frankie. My stomach roils every time I think about them. I'm in a room beside Vinny though and I know I won't get far, especially not with a fractured foot. I start to cry again. It's all I've been able to do in here—cry and cry and cry. They feed me morphine, they feed me IV fluid because I won't eat. They try to get ahold of Gio and Emma with the phone numbers I give them, but they can't get through. I don't know Loren's number by heart. Finally, on the second day here it dawns on me that Madam may still have the same number. I reach for the phone in my room and dial her, my heart pounding with each ring.

"Hello?" she says.

"Carmen?" I've never called her by her name, but it seems weird to not call her that right now.

There's a pause. "Yes . . . who am I speaking with?"

"It's Catalina. Álvarez. I'm . . . I'm . . ." I can't talk through my nerves and my tears.

"Where are you?" she asks loudly, then says to someone else. "It's Catalina!"

I freeze. Who did she tell? Her husband? My father? Someone working with Vinny? I hadn't thought this through before calling. With my heart in my throat, I hang up the phone. Three days is all it takes for them to discharge Vinny. He walks into my room looking completely beat up, but alive. His deep brown eyes are focused on me as he closes the door behind him. I swallow, wondering if this will be when he kills me. He can do it easily. They made me walk earlier, but it wasn't very comfortable. I definitely wouldn't be able to run away. He looks at the boot on my foot and flinches.

"That's my fault."

"Yeah," I respond. No use in arguing the truth.

He walks to the chair on the side of my bed and slumps over there, groaning with the movement. "I'm getting old."

"You were *getting old* six years ago," I say. "Now you're just old."

Vinny grins. He's always had such a swoony grin, like an old Hollywood movie star. That's what all of them remind me of, come to think of it. Loren, Gio, Frankie, Vinny, Dean, even Dom—they all have that old Hollywood charm to them in a twisted way. Too good looking for their own good, too smart for everyone else's.

"I'm trying to figure out what I should do," he says. "I never wanted to hurt you. You were just the easiest way for me to get to Joe. I wasn't counting on you not talking to him."

"A lot has changed since you died." I try to keep my voice light, but instead I start crying again. "Is Loren okay?"

"Of course." He shoots me a look like I'm crazy. "That's my cousin. My blood. I'd never . . ." He shakes his head. "It was a means to an end, but my intention wasn't to hurt him." He meets my gaze. "He shot at me. He's done it before, obviously, but this time he wanted to kill me. I saw the rage."

"You snuck into his house in the middle of the night," I whisper.

Vinny smiles, shaking his head. "Nah, Kitty Cat. It's you."

My pulse trips, but I manage to move on. "Is Gio . . ."

"He's recovering."

I breathe a sigh of relief. The minute I get out of here, I'm going to go to church and pray twenty Hail Mary's.

"Frankie?"

Vinny glances away, shaking his head. "I'm sorry."

The sadness hits me like a wave. A monsoon. Sweeping into me all at once. I let out a strangled sob. Not Frankie. *Not Frankie!* My sob is uncontrollable, my shoulders shake. Poor Frankie. He was too good, always willing to help out, always there when anyone needed him. He can't die. He can't just be gone! It's too soon, he's too young. I cover my mouth to keep from screaming, but it's no use, I'm sure the entire wing of the hospital can hear me. Vinny puts his hand on my shoulder. I slap it off, glaring at him through my tears.

"He loved you," I scream. "He fucking loved you! You bastard! You asshole! I should've let you die! I should've let you die! I should've—"

The door of the room crashes open. I bury my face in my hands so the nurses won't witness me crying. Crying is something I don't do in public, though these last few weeks it seems I've done nothing but cry in front of people.

"Get the fuck away from her." The voice is Loren's. I lower my hands with a gasp and look up, blinking my tears away to watch Loren stalk into the room. His eyes are on Vinny but he's walking toward me. He tears his gaze from Vinny and looks at me when he reaches my bed. His expression cracks as he sits beside me and scoops me into his arms.

"Oh, Red," he whispers against my hair. I cry louder, the sobs racking from someplace deep down in my chest.

"Frankie's dead," I say. It's all I can say.

Loren's arms hold me tighter, he rocks me a little, like I'm some rag doll he's holding for comfort. When my tears stop, he pulls away and wipes my tears with his thumbs.

"I got you, baby."

I nod, swallowing down the emotions clogging up my throat. Loren turns his attention to Vinny, who's still sitting there. I look at him too and see the shock on his face. Who knows why. When Loren gets up, Vinny pushes back in the chair, trying to get away from him. He puts his hands up.

"I didn't mean to kill anyone. I only wanted Joe. I swear to God, Lor. You know me."

"You could have gotten her killed," Loren roars, lifting a closed fist to punch him in the face. I clutch the sheets beneath me and watch as he punches him again and again. I've never seen him this angry. He's seething, uncontrollable, his entire muscled body coiled tight. At the first sight of blood and Vinny's eyes rolling, I scream.

"Loren!" I shove the sheets off me and stand upright. I'm not going to cower from him. I'm not going to hide from this side of him. *This is what you're getting into* a part of me screams. *This is what you've always said you wouldn't do.* I tear my gaze from his and look at Vinny, who's slumped against the wall, face all bloody, lips swollen. I feel my bottom lip tremble, then my shoulders, then my chest, then my knees. He killed Frankie. He deserves worse than this. That's the argument Gio would make, and obviously from what I can tell it's the same one Loren would make as well. My anger sides with them. A part of me wants to avenge Frankie's murder too, but that's not me. I remind myself. That's not me. I am not my father. I am not my mother. I am not a product of how I was raised. I make my own decisions.

"Loren!" I grab fistfuls of Loren's black t-shirt and pull. I haven't walked on the boot yet so I'm wobbly, but I have to stop him. I didn't drive and bring Vinny here so he could fucking die. "Loren!"

He looks at me over his shoulder, his eyes narrowed, his expression filled with clouded rage. I let go of his shirt and stumble back, reaching out for the side of the bed to ensure that I won't fall. I've never seen him like this, never this angry, never this mean. He stares at me for a moment and it's as if the shutters in his eyes start clicking back into place. He lets go of Vinny and stands up fully.

"Fuck," Loren says, running a bloodied hand through his hair and turning away from me. "Fuck."

"He didn't hurt me," I say, shaking. I look into his eyes, hard and filled with disbelief. "He didn't."

"He took you," he growls. "He took what's mine."

I bite my lip. I don't know if he means me or his ex-wife. I hope he means me. God, I hope he does, but what if he doesn't? What if he's still caught up in what he lost ten years ago and this is all part of his revenge? He must see it in my eyes, in my expression. Of course he does. Loren sees right through me. He reads me the way you read a favorite book, one you don't even need to open to recite.

"You are mine," he says, punctuating the words as if to prove a point. He brings his hand to my face, his gaze unwavering. "Mine."

I simply nod, because I'm tired of denying it. "I'm calling the nurse."

Loren's jaw twitches. He knows what that means. Instead of arguing, he turns around and walks into the bathroom, shutting the door behind him. I push the button for the nurse and help Vinny stand up. I'm not much help as he weighs twice, maybe three times as much as I do, but he manages to sit back down in the chair.

"Disagreement," he tells the nurse who walks in and turns frantic when she sees his face. She looks at me in horror. Vinny chuckles. "She's a tiny terror."

The nurse cleans his wounds and stitches him up. Loren walks out of the bathroom while she's still there. She looks between the three of us and zones in on me.

"We're fine," I say. "They're cousins. Long story."

"No more fighting," she says, finally settling on *something* to say, then turns and leaves.

Loren walks over to my bed, the side opposite of Vinny. When I look up at him, I notice that he's zoned in on the boot. His gaze flicks to mine, filled with sorrow, remorse. It breaks my heart. He sits down beside me.

"What did they say about dancing?"

"I can't do anything for ten weeks." My shoulders slump as I say it.

I'm supposed to start a new job in three weeks and I won't even be able to do that. They'll probably rip up the contract. I'll probably be forced to do absolutely nothing, no pay, no nothing until my foot heals and even then I'll have to train twice as hard to get back in shape. Another sob bubbles up inside me. Loren sighs heavily, lifting my hand in his. I focus on that, his knuckles are raw, fresh blood forming on the cuts.

"You'll dance again," he says. "I promise you."

I nod. I know I will, but still. He looks up at Vinny.

"We're not done," he says.

"I know." Vinny sighs. "Why don't you kill me and get it

over with? It's either you or Gio or Joe, and I'd rather it be you. At least you're humane about it."

I stiffen, taking my hand back from Loren. He notices.

"We're not talking about that here," he says, putting an end to the conversation.

As if not talking about it will put an end to my ramped thoughts, the ones that keep picturing him going off and killing people in the middle of the night, coming home all bloodied and hurt.

"I'm tired," I say finally, turning to my side. They removed the IV earlier. As long as I keep eating real food, they'll let me go soon. Loren stands up from the bed, leans down to give me a kiss on the head, and walks out. Vinny looks at me one last time.

"I'm sorry for everything, Kitty Cat," he says. He puts his hand on my cheek. "This was never about you. I hope you know that."

I nod against the pillow. He walks out and leaves me there. I cry again. If this was never about me, why bring me into it at all? Because they don't care. That's what they do. They're too blinded by power and status to realize that they're hurting the ones they love.

THIRTY-FOUR

LORENZO

"YOU CARE ABOUT HER," Vinny says as I drive away from the hospital.

I stay quiet. I don't need anyone knowing my business, least of all him. I look at him when we reach a red light. "You're only alive right now because of her. Don't push your luck."

That bothers me. The fact that she drove him to the hospital so he'd live, the fact that even after she knew he was responsible for Frankie's death she stopped me from beating his ass. It's hard for me to think about killing my own cousin but it's harder to think she may still have feelings for him and that's why she's not okay with it. I'm fucked up. I need help. I know this.

"Where are you taking me?"

"Who was working with you that night? Who was shooting at the car Frankie, Gio and Catalina were in?" I grind my teeth together.

He could've killed her. She could have died because of his stupid fucking carelessness. As it is, Frankie died. One of the good guys. One of the best guys. It should've been Vinny. Thinking about it now, it should've been Vinny ten years ago.

"Hired men," he says. "No one you know."

"Gangs?"

He nods once. I shake my head, trying hard not to lose control.

"You're so fucking stupid." I slam a fist on my steering wheel. "So fucking careless."

"They won't snitch. They won't—"

"They're hired guys, Vincent. If someone else hires them for a better price and asks them to talk, they will."

He's quiet for a moment. "I came here to die. I knew going after Joe would be a death wish but I wanted to do it anyway."

"What did Tabatha say about that?"

"What do you think?" he scoffs. "She begged me not to come."

"You have a son. You got a second chance at life. Why the fuck throw it away?"

"I don't know." He exhales. "Revenge blinds people."

I parallel park across the street from the warehouse and look at him. "If they let you live today, I don't want to see your face again. If I even think you're looking for Catalina in any capacity, I'll kill you myself. If you see her in the fucking newspaper, throw it away. I don't want your eyes on her—period. Are we clear?"

He stares at me. I know what he's thinking. I know what he's trying to tell me without saying a word. We used to be thick as thieves, he and I, finishing each other's sentences and shit and that's exactly why he should know how serious I am.

THIRTY-FIVE

CATALINA

I WAKE up in a cold sweat, screaming. *Frankie. Not Frankie! Please not Frankie.*

"You're okay. You're okay. You're in the hospital."

I blink, and sit up even more startled because I don't know that voice. I continue blinking until my eyes adjust to my surroundings. He's sitting in the chair Vinny was sitting in before I fell asleep, wearing all black, his hair slicked back. Last time I saw him, he had a beard, but he must have shaved it, his angular jaw is even more pronounced now.

"Dominic," he says in case I don't remember him. As if I'd forget anyone from the meeting the other night.

"Where's Loren?"

Dom doesn't say a word. No shrug. No comment. Nothing. He's looking at his phone, typing away.

"Did something happen?"

Finally, he looks at me. "Everything's under control."

From my experience, that means shit is going down. I don't like it. I don't like the words and I don't like the feeling that develops in the pit of my stomach.

"Where's Vinny?"

Dom lifts an eyebrow. "I don't know if—"

"Is he dead?"

He shrugs. Shrugs like it's neither here nor there. Either way, it's not an answer. I realize that I want him to be alive despite everything. Frankie didn't die and I didn't go through all of that for a ten-year-old boy to wake up without a father tomorrow. No.

"Take me to the warehouse," I say.

"No women allowed."

"I was there the other night!"

"That was an exception."

My eyes narrow on his. "Take me to the fucking warehouse or I'll take myself there."

"No."

"I'll call the cops."

He blinks. "What?"

"If you don't take me, I'll call the cops. I'm sure they'd love to escort me."

He looks contrite for a second. "Your brother's there."

"I don't give a shit." I shrug, hoping like hell I actually look like I don't. "He deserves to get locked up."

He's quiet. Finally, he says, "Vinny's not there anymore."

"Is he dead?" I wish my voice didn't sound so desperate and shrilly.

"I don't know. You think your dad would kill him?"

"Hand me the phone." Panic slams in my chest but I manage to keep my words steady. He idles. I get the urge to scream, but I keep calm, keep my cool. If that's what gets through to these guys, that's what I'll do. It works for about ten seconds before I lose my shit again. "If you don't want me to scream for the fucking cops, hand me the phone and get out of here."

Dom takes a deep breath and does as he's told. He pierces me with a warning look. "I'm only doing this because I have to

205

go outside to make a call anyway. Don't call the fucking cops. If you do, you'll be arrested for aiding a criminal and you don't want to hear the laundry list of shit he's done these last few weeks."

I grip the phone on my lap, heart pounding. "I won't call the cops."

I dial the last person on earth I want to speak to. Luckily, I learned this number way before cell phones, so it's one of the three phone numbers I know by heart.

"Hello?"

I frown. "Wallace?"

"Yes," he says slowly. "And this is?"

"It's Cat. Catalina. Is my dad around?" I roll my eyes at myself. If Wallace, Dad's right-hand man is there, Dad is there as well.

"Uh . . . yeah. One second." He sets the phone down. I hear movement, noise, and then, "Catalina?"

The sound of my dad's voice instantly makes my eyes water. I blink it away. How can I possibly feel this way about a man I haven't spoken to in so long? A man who I told myself over and over I hated. A man who made me do something unthinkable. I guess the heart simply doesn't care about logic.

"Dad, I know Vinny's with you," I manage. "Please don't kill him."

He's quiet for a moment. "Ten years of not speaking to your old man and this is what you call me for?"

I cringe, but continue, "He has a son. Kids deserve to have their father in their lives."

"Really." It's a dead-pan *really*. He's either calling me a hypocrite or calling my bluff. I can't tell. Maybe he's already killed Vinny and this is all in vain.

"Please, Dad. Please." I wipe my tears. I know he can hear that I'm crying. I know it's a sign of weakness but I don't care.

"He killed Frankie."

The sob I was trying to hold back breaks free. "I know."

"And you still think he deserves to live?"

"Who am I to say who deserves to live or die? I know his son won't understand why his father didn't come home. He won't understand why he has to mourn the loss of his grand-mother," I whisper. "I can't even wrap my head around it. Why kill an innocent lady?"

"Eye for an eye. Your unborn child was an innocent crea-ture. You were an innocent creature when he decided to leave you," he says, disdain clear in his voice.

"He didn't kill me. He didn't . . . " I can't even bring myself to finish my sentence. My throat hurts from crying, from plead-ing, and pointing fingers on something that can't be reversed is a waste of time. I clear my throat and try again. "Please, Dad. I've never asked you for anything."

"Yet when you do, you ask for too much."

I cover my mouth. He already killed him. He's already dead. I'm about to hang up the phone because there's no sense in staying on the line with him any longer when he speaks again.

"You dance beautifully," he says. I hear the pride in his voice. Something I'd been chasing after most of my life. "I'm going to use those family tickets next season."

I laugh, a surprised sound. "I'm not dancing next season. Not there anyway."

"I'll go somewhere else then. I don't care."

I pull the receiver away from my face so that I can cry silently. It's an olive branch. If I take it, I know what I'm opening my life up to. Constant criticism, coddling, unwanted opinions, annoyances, bear hugs, and love. When I wipe my face I decide to try.

"I'll let you know where," I say.

He's quiet another beat. "I'll let Vincent know he has you to thank for his second or third chance at life."

Relief floods through me for the son he has waiting for him. "Thank you, Dad."

"Anything for my girl."

I cry again. This time, I hang up. Dominic comes barging in again. I nod. "Leave it here though."

He sits down on the chair again and looks up at the television. Ellen is on. It's the only show I can bear to watch. She's the only person who can bring light to this somber room right now.

"Loren's not going to be happy," Dom says after a while.

"About Vinny?" I ask. "He wanted him dead?"

"I don't think he wants him dead," he says, "but every time we bring you and Vinny up in the same sentence he looks like a bull seeing red." Dom shrugs. "If you ask me, I think he's scared you're going to go after Vinny again."

I snort. "Right."

"His ex left him for Vinny. It's not that far-fetched."

"His ex is a fucking idiot. Obviously."

Dom grins at me, then looks at the television again. "Your sister's been calling the hospital to check up on you."

"Really?" I haven't been able to get ahold of Emma for days. It's not unusual when she's away on business, but it still worries me.

Dom's phone starts to vibrate in his hand. He stands up and starts toward the door. "I have to get this."

The minute the door shuts, I reach for the phone and call my sister. My relief only lasts two seconds before she tells me the trouble she's in.

"You're so stupid, Emma."

"I know," she says weakly. "But I know where Mom went."

I close my eyes. "If Mom wanted to be found, she would've called."

I don't think I have tears left to cry, but somehow they find their way to my eyes. What kind of mother doesn't even let her children know she's okay after years of being missing all together? It shouldn't be our jobs to find her and make sure she's all right and honestly, it's more than just that. I'm scared that my sister chasing after a maybe will turn into her caught up in a web of something she won't be able to get out of and I can't bear to lose her. Not her. Not now.

"Where are you, Emma?"

"Miami."

"You've got to be kidding me." I take a breath. "I'll try to come as soon as I can."

We hang up and I pick the receiver back up and call the only person on neutral ground, not because she has to be, but because she's not one to be bossed around by anyone. I call Madam Costello. This time, I don't hang up.

THIRTY-SIX

LORENZO

"I DON'T UNDERSTAND how you can just let a patient walk out of here." I look between the head nurse and Dominic.

I don't know which one of them I want to strangle more right now and I'm so fucking worked up that I just might. This is what I get for leaving. My plan was to come right back but then things came up with my contacts at the airport and I had to delay. I should've been here. I should've sent one of the two men I trust to handle the big airport deal, and come right back here.

"She checked herself out in the middle of the night," the nurse says.

"I want to see the papers."

"Are you her husband?"

"No." I scowl.

"Brother?"

"No." My scowl deepens. I'm done playing this game. "Where the fuck did she go? She couldn't even walk."

"She left with a nice older lady."

"Does this nice older lady have a name?"

"I'm now allowed to say."

I glare at her, then at Dominic. "Find her."

I leave the hospital reeling. Where the fuck could she have gone? Who came to pick her up? A nice older lady? Her mom? An aunt? A dancer . . . *my* aunt? I step outside and scan for Dean's truck. When I spot it, I walk toward it and take out my phone to dial my aunt's number. She answers quickly.

"Aunt Carm, have you heard from Catalina by any chance?"

She pauses. "Maybe."

"Did you pick her up from the hospital?"

"It's possible."

"Why are you being short with me?" I ask, heart pounding. "Is she okay? What's going on?"

"She's fine. Relax."

"I can't." I can't relax. I need to see her. I need to *see* that she's okay.

"She's dealing with some things, Lor," she says. "Give her space."

"Space?"

"Yes, space. I know it's a difficult concept for men like you to grasp," she says. "You can't catch a butterfly and expect to keep it in a glass jar forever."

The words weigh heavily on my chest. I wasn't trying to keep her in a glass jar. I was just trying to keep her—period. I'll build a fucking atrium for her if that's what it takes. I get into Dean's truck and shut the door.

"She left."

"Huh."

I look over at him. He looks more pensive than usual. "What's huh? What does that mean?"

"Is she with Emma?"

"I don't know. It's possible. You know where she is?"

Dean nods, driving out of the parking lot. We're not going to wherever it is Emma is. Or wherever it is Cat is. We have business to conduct right now, shipping containers that need picking up. I look in the rearview at the black SUV that's been trailing us for the last five miles. People are funny when they think they're being inconspicuous. Ultimately, it's the way they switch lanes that makes them obvious, the way they throw themselves in front of cars in order to keep ours in sight.

"You see that car?" I ask.

"Yeah."

"You know it?"

"It's one of Joe's."

I glance at him. "Fuck. What does he want now?"

"Same thing you want, I reckon," he says.

"The million dollars in the cargo plane?"

"No, but I bet he'd love to hear about that too." Dean chuckles. "I meant his daughter."

I sigh, throwing my head back on the headrest. I need an encounter with Joe like I need a bullet in my spleen. Dean takes the next exit and pulls over on the side. It's a populated area, with a huge mall across the street. It means nothing to Joe. If he wants to kill us, he'll do it inside of a damn daycare. He's ruthless like that. Dean lowers the window as one of Joe's henchmen, Wallace, walks over.

"What can I do for you, officer?" Dean asks, a hint of amusement in his tone.

Wallace fights a laugh. He glances over at me. "Costello. The boss wants to speak to you."

I look at Dean. We both know there's no saying *no* to Joe. "I'll call Dom and tell him to meet you there."

Dean nods once as I get out of the car and follow Wallace.

"You really should've stayed in the family business," I say to Wallace.

He grins. "Mike's holding it down pretty well."

I extend my arms so he can take a good look at my suit. "I'd say so."

Wallace opens the backseat of the SUV for me. I get in,

sliding to the center. It's a custom, so it's more like a limo with seats that face each other.

"Joe," I say by way of greeting.

"Lorenzo."

The car starts to move and I'm instantly filled with doubt. I don't let it show though. Not in front of Joe. I stare at him, waiting. He stares at me, waiting. I don't answer to him, so I have nothing to say. He's the one who's stalking me, so I wait. He'll have to speak at some point. We're back on the highway. We pass three exits in silence. Finally, after a long moment, Joe chuckles.

"Gio was right about you," he says. "You're a tough nut to crack."

"Hmm. Surprised he had anything nice to say about me at all."

Joe's brow lifts. "Are you really?"

I nod.

"He wants me to convince you to work with us."

"You mean for you," I say. "No one works with you."

Joe grins, a hint of amusement in his eyes. Eyes that are too much like his daughter's for me to kill him. I wonder if he knows my weakness. That's the thing about this line of business. People with families, with wives, with loved ones never remain untouchable. Before Catalina, I was one of those people. I should've stayed like that. I shouldn't have gotten so close to the flame, but here I am, sitting across from the fucking lighter.

"You looking for a lawyer?"

"Not exactly, but now that you mention it, I may be swayed to upgrade. How much would I need to pay to keep you on retainer?"

"Fifty grand a year."

He raises an eyebrow. "Cheaper than mine. All the old guys have you on retainer?"

"Young ones too." Gio included. I don't say that because either he knows it or he doesn't but I don't talk about my clients.

"Why not charge more?"

I shrug. "I'm good with that amount."

Joe chuckles. "I bet you are. I'm curious, what do you do with all your money? You must be raking in at least two million a year."

I mull over my response. I don't talk to anyone about how much money I make. I don't spend lavishly, with the exception of the cars and vacations. "I send a lot of money back home," I say. "I put away a lot of it."

"Why not spend it?"

"Legacy." I shrug. "I want my great-great-great grandchildren to see it. Besides, I'm not flashy like that. I leave that to the Masseria's."

That makes him laugh, a full-out belly laugh. "My wife would like you."

I don't ask, but the question is there: what happened to Evelyn Masseria, the queen of the Masseria empire? She's been missing for at least six years now. Vanished, just like that. No one has seen Joe with a woman on his arm in that long either, which really makes you wonder what's going on. The Masseria's are notorious for their wandering eye.

"I discovered that isolating myself wasn't good for business," Joe says suddenly. "It wasn't good for family either."

"I wouldn't know."

"What do you want with my daughter?" he asks. "Now that Vincent has been taken care of, you have no use for her. You got your revenge. Isn't that what you wanted?"

I stare at him, but my jaw works and stiffens. I try, but I can't hide every emotion. As far as I know, Catalina hates this man. He drove her to an abortion clinic, berated her for her career choice, then wrote her off. He left her in a fucking alley crushed under wooden planks. As far as I'm concerned, has no right to talk about her.

"What do you care?" I ask, unable to keep the bite from my voice.

"She's my daughter."

"That means nothing."

"You care about her," he says. And because I'm sick of people coming to that conclusion, I shrug.

"I do."

"I need you to stop looking for her."

The car slows to a stop. I look outside and see we're at one of his restaurants. Is he going to invite me to one of his family dinners? I don't want to go. I want no part of anything he has to offer, especially if it'll drive a wedge between myself and his daughter. I can't stop thinking about the way she looked at me at the hospital. Like I was a monster. That's probably why she left in the first place. I meet his eyes again.

"I'm not going to stop looking for her."

"I was afraid you'd say that." He sighs, shaking his head.

My heart pounds. He reaches into the pocket of his jacket. I go over the motions quickly in my head. I won't have time to reach for my gun in my waistband before he pulls the trigger. I won't have time to take the first shot, and at this close range, he's not going to miss. He'll shoot me between the eyes point blank. It won't matter than I'm the consigliere's son. It won't matter that my name also carries weight. In the last moment of your life, none of the things you've worked hard for make a difference—not your rank, not your title, not how much money you make in a week, and not your last name. I focus on the only person I seem to really care about. I won't get to say goodbye to Catalina. I won't get to see her dance again. I won't get to hold her hand or look into her eyes. I won't get to fuck her again. But I did. I did all of that, and for a moment, she made me feel whole again.

CLAIRE CONTRERAS

Joe pulls out a phone. My eyes widen. His twinkle. "You thought I was going to shoot you?"

I shrug. I try for nonchalance but my shoulders are too stiff to pretend.

"In the back of my new truck?" He frowns. "This is custom."

I can't help it. I laugh. This is where Gio gets his over-the-top extravagance from.

"She's looking for her mother," Joe says when he speaks again. He looks at his phone and types quickly before looking up at me. "Emma and her. They're on this witch hunt to find their mom. I'm surprised they don't hate her, but then again, I'm surprised they don't hate me considering the things I'm responsible for."

"Catalina hates you," I say. "She should hate you."

Joe smiles. "She doesn't. She doesn't have a hateful bone in her body. Why do you think Vincent survived?"

I blink. *Vincent survived?* "You let him live?"

"I roughed him up. I wasn't going to have mercy on the boy, but then Catalina called me," Joe says, a hint of wonder in his voice. "First time in a decade that I hear her voice and it's because she wants to plead with me not to kill that man." He pauses, brows pulling in. My chest hurts at this admission. She pleaded for his life? Not only that. She called her father, a man she hates, to plead for his life?

Joe types on his phone again and then continues speaking, "That night was the first time in over ten years that I'd seen her dance. My little girl." He sounds proud, his voice full of emotion. It's cleared away when he looks up at me. "She begged me not to kill Vinny. Not for him, she said it wasn't for him, but for his son. She said children need their fathers."

"So you spared him?" My voice is barely audible.

"I killed his mother. It was the least I could do."

I let that settle, think about how I feel about it all—about

216

Cat calling her father in order to save Vinny's life instead of calling me. Of her leaving the hospital with my aunt's help instead of mine. Of her running off with her sister trying to be the savior instead of letting me be one for her. I look out the window, at the establishment that says Masseria, her family name. A name that demands power and respect. One that ensures that she won't have to work a day in her life if she chooses not to. Yet, she does. Yet, she has. Catalina isn't a damsel in distress at all. She's strong and self-assured. She never needed me at all. I feel myself smile. Shaking my head, I look at Joe again.

"What am I doing here?"

"I wanted to speak to you man to man," he says. "I wanted to see if I approve of what my daughter's getting into. She's never wanted this life, you know. She doesn't like the late nights and unknown."

"I know." I swallow.

He's asking me to give her up. To set her free. I don't want to, and what's more, I don't even know if I can.

"The best thing you can do for her is let her go," he says.

"Like you let your wife go?"

He smiles. "You and I are more alike than you think, Costello."

"I don't see how."

"I'd walk through hell to make sure my wife is safe, even if it means hiding her and not seeing her as often as I'd like. Even if it means having our children think she's wiped her hands clean of them." He raises an eyebrow. "And you're going to get out of this car and do whatever it takes to get my daughter."

I say nothing. I don't have to. He reads me like a book.

"When you find her, tell her to call off the search. People are watching all of us."

"You're a king, the boss, can't you call off the dogs?" I can't imagine who would possibly try to fuck with him, aside from Vinny who had a death wish to begin with.

"The Colombians aren't like us," he says. "They're not organized or careful. She's their only claim to a throne that's long been crumbling, but I won't give her up."

"You're not willing to feed her to the wolves," I respond. I get it.

Joe grins. "We are the wolves, Costello."

I feel myself smile back. "We done here?"

"We're done for now," he says. "I still want to talk business. I have an idea that requires stealth and silence and I think you're the man for the job."

"As long as it pays more than two-hundred a week, I'm available to listen." I reach for the door handle and open the door, shooting him one last glance. "Two-hundred thousand."

Joe chuckles. "Try five-hundred."

I pause, the door handle forgotten. "Drugs?"

"No." He shoots me a look like I'm an idiot.

It used to be that no one would touch drugs at all, but times have changed. Money has changed. I don't deal with drugs though. Not ever. Too many problems. We already have the FBI on our backs most of the time. I don't want to add the DEA into the mix. I reach for the door handle again.

"We'll be in touch."

I walk down the street, heading toward the hotel I've been staying at for the last week. After Vinny set my house on fire to try to pin something else on Joe, I had to leave. For that alone, I could kill him, but a house is just a house. I walked away with my life, and more importantly, Catalina walked away with hers. My phone vibrates in my pocket just as I get to the lobby. I take it out and look at the screen. A text from Enrique. Three simple words: *she's with me.* My heart trumpets. If the universe didn't want me to go after her, it wouldn't make it so easy for me to find her, right?

THIRTY-SEVEN

CATALINA

"I CAN'T BELIEVE Carmen set me up for this," Enrique says as we drive away from the airport. "Loren's going to have my fucking balls."

Enrique, who's Loren's friend and the man who actually teaches at Columbia. The man Madam Carmen called to pick me up from the airport in Miami and drive me around as much as I needed. It makes you wonder how deep their connections run.

"I can't believe my professor is this heavily involved with such bad people," I say.

His gaze slides over to me. "Your sister's professor technically."

"Right." I take a deep breath thinking about Emma.

"Loren never had me track down his wife," Enrique says.

"Okay?" I frown, unsure of where this is going.

"His high school sweetheart. His college sweetheart. She left him and he acted like he didn't even care. The minute you left that hospital he started looking for you. Might as well have sent out an AMBER Alert."

My pulse spikes. "Did you tell him where I am?"

"Not yet," he says. "He doesn't need my help to track you down you know. He may not find you today or tomorrow, but it's only a matter of time."

"He wouldn't." I lick my lips. "You just said he didn't go after his wife, a woman he was with for years. Why would he come after me?"

It kills me to think, let alone say the words aloud, but it's true. To Loren I was just another notch on his bedpost. Maybe he cares about me, sure. That doesn't mean he'd come after me. He shouldn't. God, I hope he doesn't. If Emma's right and she has an idea where my mom is, he shouldn't get involved.

"There's this guy who makes people disappear," I say, looking at Enrique. "You know him?"

"I know a lot of people who do that."

"This one is very particular."

"I need more information than that."

My eyes narrow. "Are you sure you're not a narc?"

"A narc?" He laughs, this boisterous laugh that rattles me. It kind of lightens my mood a little. Kind of. His eyes cut to mine. "And this is why Loren is going to come after you."

"Stop saying that," I whisper, but I can't deny the way my heart quickens at the thought. "Do you know the guy I'm talking about or not?"

"Why do you want to know?"

"Because he was helping my sister with her book."

His green eyes widen like saucers. "The one on organized crime?"

"Yeah."

"The guy who makes people disappear was helping your sister." He sounds like he doesn't believe me.

"Yes." I say this with a little more conviction than I really have. What the hell do I know about what Emma's really been up to?

"If it's the person I'm thinking of, I don't know where he is."
He parallel parks in front of three homeless people sitting
outside of what looks like a pink church. "He's the kind of man
who comes and goes as he pleases. It's why he's been able to fly
under the radar for so long."

"Hmm." I get out of the car and follow him toward
the steps.

"Is your foot okay?" He looks at my boot.

"Yeah," I lie.

It's not like he gives a shit, but I lie to myself daily about it.
I *want* it to be okay again, so I figure if I put that out into the
universe maybe it'll grant me the favor. It is getting better. It
would probably heal a lot more quickly if I weren't on it as
much as I am, but I have a show to start soon enough and I
need to get used to being on it. I'm not going to throw away the
contract I signed with Lotus over a fractured foot. I push those
thoughts aside and walk up the stairs of the church.

"Why are we here anyway?"

"So you can repent for your sins, naturally." He grins over
his shoulder as he reaches for the door. I roll my eyes and
follow him in, freezing at the entrance.

"Wow," I breathe. "This wasn't what I was expecting at all."

It's a lovely cathedral. It looks and feels old. I wonder just
how old it is and once again, what we're doing here. Enrique
looks at me.

"It's the oldest Catholic Church in Miami," he says. "They
used to have a record of all of the immigrants. It's kind of like
our own Ellis Island."

I smile, looking around. "Nothing is like Ellis Island."

"In a sense, all cities have their own Ellis." He shrugs,
walking toward the center of the cathedral like he owns
the place.

I'm a little slower, because of my boot and because I don't
want to be disrespectful. I haven't stepped foot in one of these

in forever. We go down a set of stairs on the right side and then walk down another.

"I'm feeling winded already," I say, "which is worrisome considering my usual stamina."

Enrique chuckles. "It's not you, it's the humidity down here. And the travel. You've had a long couple of days."

That makes me feel better. "I'm literally following you into the dungeon of an old church and you still haven't told me what I'm doing here."

"Patience, young Padawan."

God. I'm going to die in a dungeon with a professor who quotes Star Wars. I don't care how hot people think the man is, this isn't exactly the way I envisioned my death. We reach a hallway with a row of wooden doors. He knocks on the second one. It opens slowly and a nun peeks her head out. I gape.

"Emma?"

She smiles, walking out and throwing her arms around me. "Oh my God, you came."

"What the fuck is happening?" I ask, bewildered. I pull back and stare at her. "Why are you wearing a nun's habit? That's like, blasphemous."

She pulls me into the room. I let her and look over my shoulder. Enrique salutes us as if we're part of whatever branch of the military he was in, and turns around and walks away.

"What is happening?" I look around the small room. There's a twin size bed in the center with a crucifix over it and that's basically it. She doesn't even have a television in here. I look at her and sit down on the edge of the bed. "Why are you here?"

"I kind of . . . no, I witnessed something while I was working and Gio pulled some strings to get me out. Of course, that meant skipping town without telling anyone and hiding here. Enrique set that part up."

I look around again. "This is so creepy."

"You kinda get used to it."

"Living in a church basement?" I feel my face scrunch up. "I doubt it."

"It's temporary," she says. "So, apparently at some point, mom was here."

I sit up straighter. "Where is she now?"

"I don't know."

"But you just—"

"I said she was here. I don't know where she is now." Her shoulders cave a little. She looks down. My gaze follows and I realize she's playing with a rosary. I look at my sister's face. She looks serene, which is saying a lot since she's always so uptight.

"What are you doing here then? How'd you even find that out?"

"I came down here to write a story about a woman that became a nun in order to escape a really horrible past and the way that sadly, bad things got ahold of her anyway," she says, meeting my gaze. "Her killer is on trial. The nuns here took a liking to me and asked me to stay."

"And the nun outfit?" I ask, taking in her attire.

"Oh. Well, I'm sort of incognito."

"From who? What the hell did you get into?"

"Nothing," she says, frowning. "Really, but anyway, I got to talking with one of the nuns and she showed me a photo and mom was in it so that's how I know she was here."

"She didn't say where she was going next?"

"No. Apparently some bad people caught up to her."

"Her brothers."

Emma shrugs. "Must be. Either way, I'm sure she's fine."

"I'm sure she is."

"Yeah." She gives me a sad smile. "What about you? What's going on? What happened with Loren?"

My heart feels like an elephant is sitting on it, but I manage to answer, "I fell for him. For *one of them*."

One of our brother's friends. *One of the mobsters*. I'd sworn all of them off and here I was, pathetic and in love with one of them anyway.

I shake my head. "I'm so stupid."

"So stupid," she agrees.

"I'll have to do twelve Hail Mary's and five hundred Our Father's for that," I joke.

"I missed you." Emma laughs, setting down the rosary. "How's your foot?"

"Healing."

"Why don't you stay down here a while? We can catch up."

"Do you want me to?" I look around again. "Would you mind if I stay somewhere else and just come visit?"

"Of course! I even know of a place you can get a temp job. One you'll love," she says, looking entirely too excited about the prospect. "You'd be surprised the stuff you can uncover when people think you're not listening. I should seriously keep this outfit forever."

"Pretty sure that's a sin or something." I raise an eyebrow, standing up. "I'll have to be home in a little over a month, but I'll make some calls to see what I can figure out with Jermaine."

She reaches for my hand and pulls me down to sit beside me, her eyes glossy with unshed tears. "Tell me what happened with Frankie."

So I do. I tell her what I can recall. I tell her about Frankie and Vinny and the car accident and the fire and the way I called Dad to spare his life. Emma listens intently. I swear to God she takes notes at one point. She tells me about the article she's writing for a well-known magazine and how she's hoping to land a full-time job there. We talk until my eyes can't handle staying open any longer. Finally, after my fifth yawn, I stand up.

"If I don't leave now, I'll have to share this twin size bed with you and you're a bed hog, so we know how that'll end."

Emma laughs. "Aw, come on!"

"Nope. I have to leave. I'll be back tomorrow anyway."

And I will. After losing Frankie, Dad's trial, and Mom on the cusp of either being discovered or coming back on her own, the three of us have to stick together.

THIRTY-EIGHT

CATALINA

THE DREAM IS ALWAYS the same. On a desk. My hair being pulled as Loren thrusts into me from behind. I can't see his eyes in the dream, but I feel his lips, soft as they make their way down my spine. I feel his palm, hard and biting as he slaps my ass. I spasm around him as his fingers find my clit and the thrusts get deeper, harder.

I wake up sweating, chest heaving, and open my eyes to the rain. All it does is rain. Not that pretty, light rain that you can enjoy from inside. This is a torrential downpour, with lightning that crackles and thunder that shakes the small apartment I'm renting. I roll out of bed slowly and start stretching. I found a little dance studio not far from here that I've been going to every day. First, just to watch, but the owner asked me if I'd be interested in filling in for her for a few weeks. I took the job because why the hell not? My first class starts in two hours, which means I need to get up. Between the traffic and now the rain, I'm probably already running behind. Showers take me much longer than usual. Getting dressed has gotten easier, but it still takes time. I grab something quick to eat and decide to get coffee at the place next door to the studio.

The little car I'm driving belongs to one of the nuns at the church Emma's staying in. It's a tiny two-door that my brother would never approve of and makes me feel like a hamster every time I get in it, but it gets me from point A to point B. I call Gio every morning on my drive. The loss of Frankie wasn't one he handled very well. He's still mourning. I can hear the despondency in his voice every time he answers the phone. It kills me. Today, he doesn't pick up, but sends a text.

Gio: I'll call you later. I feel good today. Love you.

I smile at it. Maybe he's coming around. I park in the space directly in front of the studio and get out carefully, walking over to get coffee in the window right next door. I push the door to the studio open with my side and hold the coffee up, careful not to spill it.

"I hope one of those is for me," Jermaine says.

He came down here to choreograph with me. We need to come up with a few pieces for the opening in a few weeks. I hand him a Styrofoam cup.

"I think we've been drinking these wrong."

"What do you mean?" His eyes widen as he pops the lid and takes a sip.

"I think these little cups," I show him the tiny cups in my other hand, "are so we share one of these."

"Oh fuck. That's why my heart feels like it's beating out of my chest every night," he says.

I laugh. "I think so."

"Shall we start?" he asks, taking a long sip of the Cuban coffee.

"The students will be arriving soon, so we should get in what we can before they get here." I offer him my hand as I set my own cup down. He stands behind me, taking my right hand and extending it and placing the other on my waist. We tilt our chins up as we walk.

227

"Every time I look in the mirror and see how ridiculous I look dancing in a boot I want to break it," I say.

Jermaine laughs. "It's not that bad. You make it work."

"God, I can't wait to put on pointe shoes again."

He raises his eyebrows. "Well, if anyone can get back on their toes quickly, it's you."

"I'm not twenty anymore," I remind him. He turns my body and catches me in a fish dive, my hand pointing toward the audience, or in this case, the mirror.

"You'll be fine," he says. "When are you heading back up?"

"Two weeks' tops." I sigh, letting him lead me into the turn and let go, walking to where I'm supposed to be doing a *jeté*. I stop after that and look at him. "This is ridiculous."

"You're doing fine," he says, coming over to wrap his arms around me. "I promise you're doing great."

Tears fill my eyes, but I don't let them fall. Through the glass partition, I see the studio doors open and little girls and boys start walking into the foyer with their mothers and fathers, all smiley and excited for class. I lower my arms from Jermaine and take a deep breath.

"Thank you, Jermaine," I say. "For everything. For coming down here when you didn't have to and for being here every day. I don't know how I'll ever repay you for it. Truly."

"That's what friends do, Cat." He smiles and taps my chin. "Besides, it's not such a chore coming down here. Have you seen the men in South Beach?"

Loud laughter bubbles out of me before I can stop it. I shake my head as he walks away.

"See you tonight," he says, "Happy Hour!"

"See you there."

I spend the entire day teaching. First the little girls at nine-thirty, then the eleven-thirty class. I take an hour break and fix up the tiny studio store up front and call Vivienne, the owner to let her know how things are going. She's an angel, I swear.

Then, I teach the one o'clock, a three o'clock and the advanced course at five o'clock. It's not like I'm doing much. Without my pointe shoes, I can only use my left foot to demonstrate, but ballet isn't only feet. It's not just jumps either. It's technique and posture. It's selling grace, so I make do with what I have.

After the last class clears out, I try the choreography for the Lotus company and when I decide I look like an absolute moron, I sit down on the bench and let myself cry. The door opens again. I wipe my tears quickly knowing Jermaine will kick my ass if he sees me crying.

"You still move beautifully. Even wearing a boot." The sound of Loren's voice makes my heart go into a frenzy. I gasp as I glance up. He's standing by the door, wearing jeans and a black t-shirt, looking relaxed with one hand in his pocket, the other by his side. I knew I missed him. I knew I craved him and wanted him despite everything, but I didn't realize how much until I look into those deep golden eyes. I stand up.

"What are you doing here?"

"I think that's pretty obvious," he says, walking into the room.

He's so big, so tall. I'd forgotten. I'd forgotten how every time he inched closer to me I felt like I was dying a little. I'd forgotten the way he looked at me, like I was important—the most important. Oh God. What is he doing here? He stops directly in front of me. Near, but far. I have to tilt my head to look into his eyes.

"I was trying to figure out how we could start over," he says. "I could tell you who I am up front, tell you what it is I do and why I do it, but then I realized that I'm too selfish for that because if I told you all of those things and you turned me away, I'd still go after you."

I blink, my heart sputtering in my chest, the tears I'd been trying to hold back cascading down my cheeks. I wipe them quickly, licking my salty lips. I open my mouth to answer, but he closes the distance between us and brings his hand up to cup my face. I close my eyes and lean into his touch, that large calloused hand, with clear intentions and dirty sins.

"I don't want you to answer me right now. I want you to think about it. I want you to envision your life with me, the sleepless nights and the worry," he says. My eyes pop open. "I can't promise that I'll walk the straight and narrow right now, but I can promise you that I want to in the near future if that's what it'll take to have you in my life."

I lick my lips again. "I have plans tonight, but after . . ."

"After," he says with a nod.

He leans in then, his mouth coming down on mine softly, slowly. His lips moving my heart, his tongue against mine shattering my resolve. I bring my hands up to clutch his muscular arms, to take more, and that's when he breaks the kiss and pulls away. He hands me a hotel key in a little envelope and walks away, closing the front door behind him.

THIRTY-NINE

CATALINA

I MEET Emma and Jermaine at a bar a couple of blocks down from the apartment. It's one of those places where you feel like you're in old Cuba, not that I've ever been to Cuba, but the music and the ambiance are so lively that it feels genuine. A lot of spots around here are like that. You get a sense that these people, who were practically pushed out of their country, came here and planted roots so deep that the ground rattles with their rhythm. It's a beautiful thing to witness. Sad to think of what they probably left behind, but beautiful to know their spirit pushes them to start over. There's something to be said about that kind of relentlessness. It makes me miss my mom ten times more because she was once one of those people. I walk inside the bar and go straight to the back where the band is playing *Guaguanco* tonight. In Barranquilla we have *Cumbia*, in Cuba they have a ton of different sounds, but coming to this bar the last couple of weeks has made me realize that *Guaguanco,* with its clear African roots and Spanish twist, is my favorite.

I spot Emma and Jermaine, the only two people dancing as soon as I walk out. It's early and the sun hasn't completely set, so people are still holding up the pretense of being classy. In a couple of hours, the freaks will come out. They wave me over, Emma looks at my foot and starts clapping and jumping. Jermaine does the same. I laugh at the sight and because I feel as giddy as they look right now. Before I came over here I went to the doctor and he took my boot off and gave me a soft cast, which is much smaller and much more manageable. He also told me to take it easy a million times, so as I near them, I shake my hips to and fro and shimmy my shoulders for show before I kiss each of them.

"This will make it much easier to practice," Jermaine says, grinning like a loon.

"I know!" I smile wide. "I still have to ease into it though. It feels so weird."

"Let's sit down. I'll get you a drink." Emma grabs me by the hand and pulls me over to the table they got. "You hungry?"

"A little." I pick up the menu and start browsing as if I don't have it memorized yet. I order some little fried rice balls and a water.

"You seriously need to eat more," Emma says.

Jermaine chuckles, shaking his head. "She eats just fine."

"Mom wouldn't agree with that statement," she responds, her eyes losing a little bit of the light that was just there. Whenever she talks about her, she gets so sad. I feel the sadness too, but not the way Emmaline does. She was always mom's favorite. I reach over and place my hand over hers. She looks up and gives me a small smile. "So, anything exciting happen today?"

I decide not to talk about Loren yet. Instead, I pick up the drink she ordered for me and take a couple of sips, shivering when I swallow and taste how strong it is.

"I have a date tomorrow night," Jermaine says suddenly. We both look at him, eyebrows raised.

"Do tell," I say.

"I met him at a bar in South Beach last weekend and we've been texting." He shrugs. "We'll see."

"Is he a dancer too?" Emma asks.

"Banker."

"Ohh." I smile. "Good for you."

The band starts playing another song that the three of us can't help but dance in our seats to.

"You think you can handle being on your foot?" Jermaine asks, his intention clear.

Do I think so? I'm not sure, but the alcohol in my system says yes, yes you can, so I take his hand and stand up to follow him. Emma pulls out her phone and starts recording us. I shoot her a look. She's supposed to be inconspicuous. She's living in a convent for God's sake.

"It's not for social media," she says. "I'm sending it to Gio."

Jermaine and I start dancing a sort of salsa, sort of whatever-the-hell it is we're doing. It's mostly us laughing and when we're joined by more people on the little dance floor, we try to mimic them instead. He pulls me to the edge of the dance area and leans in.

"You okay? Your foot okay?"

I nod. "It's fine. I think this will be good for it."

I have no fucking idea if this will be good for it but I'm doing it anyway because I haven't felt this free in weeks. When the song is over, we sit down. Emma claps.

"Your face is so red," I tell her. "You're drunk."

"I'm not drunk. I'm feeling nice."

"Nice equals drunk," Jermaine says, laughing.

"Whatever." She sticks her tongue out and looks at her phone, laughing. "Gio says you better not hurt yourself more or he'll kill you and then Jermaine."

"Oh, fuck that," Jermaine says. "No more dancing for the rest of the night."

I laugh and take a sip of water. I'm eating one of the little rice balls when Emma starts asking about Loren.

"How long has he been in town?" she asks.

I drop a rice ball. "How do you know he's in town?"

"Because he's literally sitting in the corner booth, staring at you."

I turn around, heart pounding. Sure enough, there's Loren, sitting in the corner booth wearing a fedora and a black short sleeve *Guayabera* and jeans looking so very Miami and so very hot.

"He came to the studio today," I blurt out, facing Emma and Jermaine again.

"That fine specimen came to the studio? Where was I?"

I roll my eyes. "He came after classes were over."

"Has he been here long?"

"I don't know how long, but he insinuated that he's been here a while."

Emma frowns over her margarita. "He followed you here?"

"Damn girl. He followed you all the way from New York?" Jermaine asks.

"I'm not sure it's very flattering," I say. "Some would call that stalking."

"If he were ugly, yes, but the man is hot as hell," he says. Emma and I laugh. Jermaine smiles. "So, what's the deal? You with him or what?"

"I don't know." I sigh, shrugging. "I don't know."

"Is he the reason you've been so down these last few weeks?"

"Partly."

Jermaine doesn't know about Frankie or Vinny or anything that happened and I'm not going to sit here and try to explain any of that. It's hard enough living with it inside my own head.

"You love him." Emma's words are a statement. "I can see it in your eyes."

I shrug. No use in denying it.

"If that's the case, why not say fuck it and go over there? Give into it?" Jermaine asks.

Because he's involved in shit I've been trying to escape most of my adult life. Because above all else, I can't stand the thought of losing him. They say time heals all wounds but I've been away from him for a couple of weeks and every single day the hole in my chest deepens. I don't know if being with Loren is the smart choice, but I know it's what I want.

"Because I'm scared of losing him," I whisper.

"Oh honey." Jermaine reaches over and grabs my hand. "We're only here for a moment. Might as well make it a good one."

"Fuck it." I drink more water, stand up, give them each a kiss and a hug. "I'll see you guys tomorrow."

Jermaine whoops excitedly. Emma smiles like she's unsure whether to be happy or worried.

"Be careful," she says.

I nod and wave as I walk over to the booth, but it's empty. I look back at them with a frown. They both frown back and shrug. Where the hell did he go? I look around the bar, but don't see him there either. Finally, I decide on an Uber. My stomach hurts the entire ride over to Loren's hotel. I've never been so thankful for this bumper-to-bumper traffic. My knee is bouncing and my emotions are crisscrossed. When we finally reach the Fontainebleau, I scramble out of the car quicker than I would've with the boot. The physical therapy four times per week and the daily dance classes have been so helpful with recovery. I walk to the elevators beside the hordes of women wearing teeny tiny tight, mini-dresses and press my palm against the spaghetti strap floral slip dress I have on. I hadn't even thought about my outfit. It's not exactly sexy. Not like everyone else here anyway. I take the elevator up to the eighteenth floor and walk down to the last door in the hall, exhaling when I reach it.

I pause as I take the key out. What if he's not alone? What if he's . . . no. I push the thought aside. He wouldn't have given me a key if he were going to be with someone else. What if he's not here though? He was just at the bar. He could've gone to another. I should've called. He could be with Enrique or whatever other friends he may have here. He could be—the door opens suddenly. I freeze. Loren eyes me curiously. My pulse quickens at the sight of him. How long has he been here? It looks like he's had a shower, his hair is damp and he's barefoot, wearing a black t-shirt and jeans. I lick my lips.

"What are the odds of you letting me come in?"

His mouth forms a slow, sexy grin as he holds the door open wider. "I'd have to be crazy to bet against that."

I walk inside, taking in the suite. It's spacious, nice, minimal. It smells like him, the lingering scent of his cologne. I inhale deeply. I missed that scent so much. He lets the door shut as I walk toward the window, where there's a small balcony that overlooks the water. I feel him behind me, his warmth on my back, his fingertips grazing over my shoulder. I shudder, my eyes shutting as my breath quickens from that touch alone.

"I miss you so much," he whispers behind me, letting his hand trail down the side of my arm, he kisses the back of my neck gently, sending shivers down my spine. He wraps an arm around me and pulls me to his chest, burying his nose in my neck, just breathing. "So much."

"Why'd you leave the bar?"

"I wanted to give you space. I didn't realize how hard it would be for me to just watch you from afar."

I never asked him to just watch me from afar, but I'm glad he did. I'm glad he gave me some space and didn't try to just barge right back into my life. I turn around in his arms, bringing a hand up and running my palm over his jaw, the five o'clock shadow there tickles my hand. With his eyes shut, he makes a little groaning sound that seems to vibrate through me. When he opens them again, they look like untamed wild fire.

"I think I'm in love with you," I whisper. "I must be to even consider this so seriously. And I'm scared. I'm scared to be with you, but more than that, I'm scared I'll lose you—lose you for good, the way we lost Frankie. I won't be able to heal if that happens, Lorenzo. My heart won't recuperate if you're not here to share this life with me."

"Oh, Cat." He pulls me close, crashing the side of my face against his hard chest.

His strangled words make me start crying. I didn't know I was such a crier but evidentially, it's all I do these days. When he pulls back, he brings both hands to my face and brushes my tears away with his thumbs.

"I don't think I'm in love with you, Catalina. I know I am," he says. "Stupid in love with you."

I smile, laugh. "Good."

"Good." He brings his lips down to mine and kisses me like a starved man, growling against my mouth, his hands making their way down my body, exploring my breasts, his fingers teasing my nipples. I gasp, my mouth parting against his.

"I want you so bad it hurts," I say. "I've been dreaming about you every night for two weeks."

"Fuck," he breathes, taking my straps off and letting my dress pool at my feet—one sandaled, one soft casted. He pulls back, eyes raking down my body hungrily. "So much better than the fantasy."

He helps me lift my foot and boot out of the dress and walks me toward the bed. I sit in front of him, eye level to his crotch. I hook a hand in his waistband and crane my neck to look up at him, my eyes hazy with lust. I undo his jeans then. He's barefoot, so when I tug them down to his feet, he kicks them off easily. I bring my hands back to his thick thighs, running them up and down, feeling the soft hair on his legs beneath my touch. His cock is hard, I don't need to undress him to know that. It's barely contained by the boxer briefs he's wearing. I pull them down gently to his feet. When I look up again, he's still staring at me, pulling the black t-shirt over his head and tossing it, his muscled abdomen and arms flexing with each movement.

He brings his hand down to my face, pushing his thumb into my mouth. I suck it hard, my tongue lashing against it like a sword. Loren groans, his eyes hooded.

"I won't survive you, Little Red."

I let go of his finger with a pop and focus on what's in front of me, jutted out toward me all long and thick. I bring a hand up and close it over his cock, pumping once, twice before I bring my mouth to him. I lick first, tentatively, before closing my mouth over him. It's so big, my cheeks expand with it.

"Fuck," he breathes, his hips rocking forward.

With his other hand he grabs a fistful of my hair. He fucks my mouth relentlessly and even though it's not comfortable, I'm so turned on by the noises he makes that I would never dream of stopping. He thrusts one more time before pulling out of my mouth completely. I look up to find that wild look in his eyes again. He bends down and gets on his knees in front of me, reaching for my thong and pulling it down my legs, then he kisses the heel of my foot and drags his mouth up my leg, biting and sucking my inner thighs. I fall back on the bed, my fingers threading into his hair and tugging. He hasn't even touched me there yet and I'm already panting, writhing, begging.

"Please." I rotate my hips. "Please." He blows over my clit. Fucking blows. I shimmy again. "Oh my God, Loren please."

He reaches up and fondles my breasts, pinching my nipples. I arch, moaning, giving in to the tingling sensation. He licks me then, a slooooooowwwww lick followed by another, then sticks his tongue inside me, pumping in and out, in and out, until I feel like I'm going to come from that alone. I grip his hair harder, shutting my eyes as I grind against him chasing release.

"That's right, baby," he growls against me.

Every muscle in my body coils up and lets go with that growl. I shriek his name, throw my head back and arch, still grinding even after his mouth is gone. He moves my foot and spreads my legs in a split, settling between them, his thick tip at my entrance. He eases into me, making me feel every single inch of his girth as he stretches me. My eyes pop open, I gasp as he lowers himself onto me, his chest against mine as he thrusts inside deeply. I claw at his shoulders.

"Oh my God."

His lips come down on mine. I expect the kiss to be hard, fast. Instead it's soft, slow, taking my breath away. He fucks me like that too, in a slow tempo that seems to last forever. Each time I think he's going to make me come again, he pulls back and slows down even more, his hands caging my face as if he doesn't want me to look anywhere else but up at him. That's when I realize he's not fucking me. He's making love to me. It makes my heart stomp wildly. He makes me feel alive, this man. The emotion rivaling only what I feel when I'm on stage. Heat builds deep inside me, like a fire that starts in my core and spreads through my veins. I scream out his name as he rocks into me, he's groaning my own name as he explodes inside of me. It's only when I stop shaking and am able to fully breathe again, that I realize that he didn't pull out or use a condom. I'm good, of course. I'm on the pill. He knows this. Still. My eyes widen on his.

"I'm clean," he says. "Kinda lost control there."

He drops a kiss on my forehead and pulls out as slowly as he entered. He goes to the bathroom and comes back with a wet hand towel for me. I clean myself and stand up, walking shakily to the bathroom. Loren helps me and when he's not, he watches me like he may need to jump in at any given moment, as if I haven't been doing it all on my own with the boot for weeks now. It's cute though. We shower together, and when we're done, he wraps a big fluffy white robe around me and gets one for himself. Then, we lie in bed, our heads propped up as we face each other.

"You got a smaller boot," he says. "How do you feel?"

I'm about to just shrug it off when I decide to tell him the truth instead. I'm not going to hide anything from him. I look into his eyes. "Better now that I have this one, but still not great."

"At the risk of sounding like a stalker, I've been watching you and you looked completely at ease with the boot."

I smile. "Jermaine says if you were ugly it would be creepy but since you're hot, it's fine."

"I kinda wanted to kill him for making you dance so much tonight." Loren chuckles. "But I've decided that I like him."

I shake my head, smiling. "I need to start sometime."

"Is it safe?" He frowns.

"The doctor says that everyone is different and because my feet are stronger than the average person, he thinks my recovery will be different too." I smile.

He glances at me, and I swear I'd pay money to see that look in his eyes every day. He licks his lips and asks, "What made you come over here?"

"I decided I'd rather be with you than without you."

He smiles, running his fingers through my hair. "I like that."

"But."

He raises an eyebrow. "But?"

"I have questions. And conditions," I say, sitting up.

"Uh-oh. My little lawyer has conditions." He sits up and I sit up across from him. "Let's discuss."

"Will you have women on the side?" I blurt out, hating that it's the first thing that comes out of my mouth.

"What?" He frowns. "Why would I do that?"

"To fuck, obviously."

His lips twitch. "I kinda love fucking you though."

"Loren, be serious. My dad had mistresses, my brother has never been with just one woman, and by all accounts you were like that when you were married, and Vinny . . ." I lick my lips, letting that hang. I don't have to spell it out to him. He's quiet, his face tilting slightly.

"I made mistakes when I was younger. I won't deny it," he says. "But I've matured. And I know how it feels to be cheated on. I would never do that to you. I swear it."

"How can you be sure?" I whisper.

"I just am."

I nod once and take another deep breath. "I don't like the idea of being with someone who . . . kills people."

"I don't kill people," he says, shooting me a pressing look. "I don't. I just steal from people."

I laugh. "Oh, no big deal at all."

"Trust me, they're not crying themselves to sleep." He tilts his head, thinking. "Let's not say people. I don't steal from individuals. And let's not call it stealing. It's more like . . . redistribution of goods."

I raise an eyebrow. "You like downplaying your criminal activity, professor?"

"I think I fell in love with you then." Loren grins, it's a sight that makes my ovaries quiver.

"One more question. Enrique said when your wife left you, you took it well. Did you ever go after her? Try to convince her to stay?"

"No."

"Why not?"

"I don't know. I was young, I was over it. She left me for my cousin." He shrugs. "I just didn't care enough to chase her."

"But you chased me."

"I did."

"And you'd keep chasing me? If I say no to this? If I turned you away?"

"Probably."

I stare at him. "Why?"

"Because you're mine."

It's a simple answer, a caveman answer, but it does it for me.

FORTY

FIVE WEEKS LATER . . .

I'M WRAPPING MY FOOT, getting ready for the performance
that's about to take place in thirty minutes, when the
door opens.

"It's too soon," Loren says.

My eyes snap up when he shuts the door and walks over to
me. He's dressed impeccably in a dark suit that makes him look
lethally gorgeous. His gaze is fixed intently on me, a small
frown tugging his dark eyebrows, making him look simultane-
ously grumpy and even hotter, if that's possible.

"I'm fine." I smile brightly, hoping I look convincing.

His scowl deepens. He grabs a chair and sets it in front of
me, wrapping his other hand around the back of my neck and
kissing me deeply as he sits down. It's a quick kiss, but it makes
my heartbeat quicken.

"Let me see your foot."

I set it on his lap, watching him as he examines the wrap-
pings. I feel myself smile. "You know how to wrap injuries?"

"Yes." His gaze flicks to mine. "But no amount of wrapping
is going to make me feel comfortable with you going out there
tonight."

My heart constricts with the concern I hear in his voice. The urge to kiss him over and over and over again sweeps through me, but I push it down, knowing what it would lead to. When we got back from Miami, Emma was offered a full-time job in Chicago. While she hasn't even had time to fully move out of our shared apartment, Loren moved in with me the day we got back. It wasn't something we discussed. He kind of came home with me and never left. In his defense, his house is still being renovated and in all honesty, I love spending as much time with him as possible.

"Are you working tonight?" I ask, moving my foot off his leg and purposely brushing against his cock. He bites his lip, shooting a heated look my way.

"Nope. I'm not working tonight or tomorrow night or the night after that," he says. "I have some cases to look over while you're rehearsing tomorrow."

"No work any night this week?" I press my hand on my chest. "What did I do to deserve that?"

"You're a pain in my ass." He chuckles, shaking his head as he stands up. He leans down and kisses me hard on the lips. I wrap my arms around his neck and deepen the kiss, wanting more. He breaks it and pulls away. "Don't tempt me, baby. You have a show in fifteen."

I groan. "I know. I still have to warm up."

"I can warm you up." His eyes dance. I roll my eyes, but can't help my laughter.

"I'll see you after the show."

Once he heads outside, I finish putting on my pointe shoes and hit the floor, stretching as much as possible. The door opens again and this time Jermaine and Madam Costello walk in.

"How's my favorite principal?"

"Excited to get back out there." I mean it.

It feels like everything has fallen into place. I've been in contact with my dad, talking to him a few times a week. Loren and I are going to Chicago on Friday to have dinner with him, and I am definitely a lot more nervous about it than he is. I've never met a man my father didn't intimidate, but it seems that with Loren, he's finally met his match. It makes me feel kinda giddy, if I'm being honest.

Carmen comes over and examines my foot, as does Jermaine. They decide it looks good enough for them.

"As long as you're up for it," Carmen says. "I don't want you getting hurt on my stage."

Her stage. Lotus is owned by a group of investors, Madam Costello and her husband being part of it. Once I found that out, I understood everything—the pay rate and the fact that they asked me to come on board. Loren, of course, knew all along, but didn't want to tell me because he didn't want me to think he had anything to do with it.

On stage, I dance my ass off. My foot could definitely use a little more time off, but I manage to dance as though it's one-hundred-percent healed. After the show, I take a deep curtsey and smile when I see the white hydrangeas coming toward me. I walk up to the edge of the stage, smiling even wider when I see Loren holding them up for me. Our fingers graze, and I swear an electric current pinches its way up my arm. He doesn't let go of the flowers or my hand. Instead, he pulls me closer to him and puts his mouth on mine, giving me a slow, deep kiss. When he pulls back, he gives me a sly smile.

"What are the odds you'd say yes if I asked you to marry me?"

I gasp. "What?"

He chuckles, taking a step back and tucking his hands into his pockets. I'm completely shocked, but manage to step away from the edge and walk back stage with the flowers in my arms. Oh my God. Did he seriously—? Did he just—? I can't even wrap my head around it, but I also can't stop smiling and laughing like a lunatic.

"I LOVE it when you wear heels." Loren slaps my ass.

I set down the champaign flutes in my hand and turn in his arms, looking up at him. "I do too, it means I have no blisters and my ankles are healthy."

"That's my second favorite part about it," he says, "My favorite is ripping your clothes off and leaving the sexy heels on your feet so they dig into my ass when I fuck you."

"Loren." My cheeks blaze as I look around the quiet, opulent store.

He chuckles, bringing a hand up to cup my face and dropping a kiss on my forehead. "Remind me again why we need this shit?"

"Because the house will be ready soon and you have no plates." I reach up to grab his hand and pull it away from my face, threading my fingers through his. "We need plates, glasses, utensils. You know, things we can eat all of the yummy food you're going to be cooking for us."

"Is that so?" He laughs again.

"You said your chicken cacciatore is better than the one at my family's restaurants, so I think it's only right that you make that for our house warming slash dinner party next week." I grin as I reach for a different glass. "This store is so damn expensive. We should've gone to Target."

"Not happening. You already invited your brother to our house. I'm not going to endure his snarky comments about our fucking silverware," he grumbles.

I shake my head. I pray the day comes when Loren and Gio stop bickering but for now I'm just glad they're willing to hang out outside of work, even if it's just for my sake. We pick out what we need and agree to get the rest elsewhere. I just can't fathom paying two-hundred-dollars for place settings and fabric napkins that'll only add to our laundry. I try and fail at not cringing at the amount they ring us up for.

"I can't believe we just spent that much money on things we're not going to use every day," I whisper shout as we walk out of the store.

Loren shrugs, grabbing my hand in his. "We'll use it enough. We can have weekly dinner parties if that's what makes you happy."

"And you can cook for me every night."

"Most nights," he offers.

"That's fine by me." I smile wide.

"Did I tell you my parents are coming in a few weeks?"

I stop dead in my tracks. "What?"

Loren turns slightly and frowns. "They want to meet you."

"But like . . . now? When are they coming? Where do they stay when they come?"

"They have a place in Jersey." His lips twitch like he's trying to hold back a laugh. "Relax. They're going to love you."

"Oh my god," I breathe, bringing a hand to my chest. It never occurred to me that maybe we were moving to fast until this moment. "What if your mom thinks I'm a hussy because we already live together? Are they super conservative about stuff like that?"

"Oh, Little Red." He chuckles, wrapping an arm around me and pressing the side of my face to his chest. "My parents approve of anything that makes me happy. They're going to adore you."

I pull back and look up at him. "Okay, I feel better now."

"Good." He throws an arm around my shoulder and leads me to his car again.

"I was thinking," I say once we're in his truck.

"Uh-oh."

I roll my eyes. "Maybe we should go to my dad's house one of these days."

Now it's his turn to look shocked. "Really?"

"We've been talking and I think I want to."

"You think you want to."

"I want to." I nod firmly.

I do want to. At the risk of sounding weird, being with Loren makes me think a lot about Dad and the kind of man he is – dangerous, caring, and loyal to a fault. Men like them are a dime a dozen and I'm fortunate to have them all around me.

EPILOGUE

CATALINA

"OH MY GOD why am I so nervous and you're cool as a fucking cucumber?" I say, looking up at Loren standing beside me. We're outside my parents' house, waiting for someone to come to the door.

He smiles, shrugging. "What's there to be nervous about?"

"I don't know. The fact that my dad is like the scariest man in Chicago!"

Loren shrugs again. "Not scarier than me."

I don't bother to argue. I've seen the way people cower in Loren's presence. I ask myself if I was one of them before we got to this blissful state we seem to be in, but I can't recall anything about it. Even when Emma brings up how different my relationship with Loren is from my relationship with Vincent, I don't know what to say. I try to think that far back but everything that came before Loren is hazy in my memory. Not worth mentioning. When the door finally opens, I freeze, thinking it'll be my father, but it's Wallace, his right-hand man, on the other side. I practically sag with relief. Wallace's light gray eyes bounce between the two of us in amusement.

"I approve of this thing," he says in that heavy Jamaican accent I love.

"I'm honored," Loren says. "I don't think I could have gone on if you didn't approve."

"Don't think I appreciate that tone though," Wallace says, his eyes twinkling. He pulls me into a hug. "It's good to have you back."

I pull away and smile up at him. "I'm only here because I was promised rice and peas and champagne Kola."

"Don't worry, I got you." He closes the door, locks it and leads the way for us to follow.

My hand instantly finds Loren's. His grip is hard, sure, and it helps ease my nerves. Wallace steps into the dining room first.

"Catalina and Lorenzo are here," he announces.

My grip tightens as we walk in. I instantly spot my dad sitting in the corner seat, his favorite. It's not the one at the head of the table, that one is reserved for my mother and is currently empty, which makes my heart heavy even though I knew it would be. Dad pushes his seat back and stands. Lorenzo leads me over to him, half dragging me. It's one thing to talk to my dad on the phone, but an entirely different one to see him. He still looks the same, thick salt and pepper hair brushed back, no hint of facial hair, that wide jaw and straight nose. His blue eyes such a contrast to his dark lashes and tan skin. Dad is classically good looking, something he passed on to Gio for sure. They're both confident to a fault, and now that I'm older I know their looks have a lot to do with that. The only differences are the lines on his face, the heavy bags under his eyes. He's seemed to have lost some weight, which doesn't make him look bad, but I know would worry the hell out of Mom.

"My girl," Dad says, a smile splitting over his face.

It's a proud smile. A relieved smile. One that makes my

throat clog up with emotion. I force myself to let go of Loren's hand and close the distance between myself and my father. I'm not even fully there before his arms close around me. I close my eyes against his chest and cry. For years, Emma and Gio have been telling me to pick up the phone and call, to visit, to do something to end this stupid feud and my answer was always simple: I don't care to. If he cared to end it he would call. Why should he be allowed to have more pride than me? But now that I'm in his arms, it all feels so stupid, so meaningless and irrelevant. Now that Frankie's gone and Gio's mourning his loss, that we're all mourning his loss. Now that I'm here in this house that feels vacant without my mother's spirit. I can't imagine how my father's been handling any of it.

"I should've come to visit you sooner," Dad says. "I should've been at all of your shows."

I pull back and wipe my face. "You can go now."

"I will go now." He looks over my head and his smile drops, his business mask slips back in place. I don't have to look back to know Loren's standing right there. Dad puts his hand out and Loren shakes it. "I can't thank you enough for bringing my daughter home."

"It was her choice to come. I just came along for the ride," Loren says.

I feel myself smile as we take our seats at the dinner table. Dad looks at me like it's the first time he's seeing me or something, but I don't mind.

"G's in pretty bad shape," I say.

"He'll be okay," Dad responds, grief clear in his eyes. "Francisco was a good kid."

"He was," Loren agrees, his hand finding mine beneath the table. I squeeze it.

"Emma found a convent Mom had gone to," I say after a long, quiet moment.

"I heard." Dad shakes his head. "That girl is going to give me a heart attack. Your mother is fine and she'll stay fine as long as she stays put." He exhales heavily. "I'm amping up security next week and bringing her home."

"Company or private?" Loren asks. "I know some trustworthy guys who do that."

"I appreciate that, but I'd rather keep this close to home."

"She's coming home?" I breathe. "Does Emma know?"

"Not yet. I want to keep this under wraps. Your uncles are fucking psychotic. Who knows what they'll do."

"What do they want?" I whisper.

"Your grandfather died and left her everything. They want her to sign it all over."

"Everything, everything?" My grandfather owned a ton of land and businesses.

"Everything." The way dad says it makes me think he doesn't want to expand on what's so important to my uncles, so I don't push it. His eyes light up again before he asks, "What's this Emma says about you wanting to start your own dancewear line but not having the funds to do so?"

"Oh my God." I groan, covering my face with my free hand.

Loren lets go of the other. "What dancewear line?"

"It's nothing." I meet his serious gaze.

"Tell me anyway."

I sigh, looking back and forth between him and my father as I speak. "It was just an idea I had a few years ago. Another dancer has a line of tights and she wanted me to help promote it, so I thought I'd design a leotard line, but I haven't had time and I didn't have the money."

"I'll give you the money," Loren says.

I look at him. "I don't even know where I'd start."

"I'll help you."

"Listen to the man," Dad says. "They don't call him Midas for nothing."

"They call you Midas?" I laugh, frowning.

"Not to my face," Loren says, a small scowl on his face.

Dad's still smiling when he asks, "Let's get down to business."

"Business? I thought we were here for dinner."

"We are," Loren says. "And because I wanted to find out how much longer until your mother comes home."

"What?" I frown. "Why?"

"To see how soon we can get married," he says.

My jaw drops. "Loren!"

Dad chuckles.

Loren grins at me. "What? Can you blame me for wanting to marry you right now?"

"No."

Truth is, he didn't even ask me like a normal person. He set a box on the table beside my breakfast, sat beside me and told me we were getting married. I'd set it aside without opening it just to piss him off, but all he did was laugh, probably because he knew curiosity would get the best of me—it did. When I pulled it back, he got down on one knee, pulled my hand toward him and kissed it.

"I'll be yours forever whether or not you say yes to this," he'd said. *"But I would really appreciate it if you did—say yes, that is."*

Of course I said yes over and over and over again.

"Why don't you set the date for two months from today?" Dad suggests.

"Really?" My eyes widen. "Things will be cool by then?"

"Not cool, but cool enough."

"We can always get married in Italy," Loren suggests. "You have to go meet my parents anyway. We can kill two birds with one stone."

I'm still gaping when Dad says, "I like that idea."

"What do you think, baby?"

I look at Loren, my mouth still hanging, and nod. He

chuckles as he pulls me toward him and kisses me, the kind of kiss no man in their right mind would ever give me in front of my father, and dammit, I love him for it.

ACKNOWLEDGMENTS

I stopped adding acknowledgements to my books because I always forget people. I decided to add a few to this one because I feel like I need to thank them on more than just the inscription I write in their personalized books. I do want to say that even if I don't mention you here, your support means everything to me. I mean that.

Jen Frederick - This book would not have happened had it not been for you pushing me every day. THANK YOU. Let's do it again soon (like now).

Clarissa - your passion for my books is the reason I write them. "Thank you" seems so small for everything you do for me. I will forever be indebted to you.

Nina Grinstead - thank you for always answering my emails, texts, and not killing me lol.

The rest of Social Butterfly (Jen Watson, Hilary, Chanpreet, Brooke) - you guys are team goals. Thank you for everything.

Kimberly Brower - you are a total badass. Thank you for everything you do!

My FB Crew - THANK YOU for existing. Thank you for your time, excitement, and just being you.

My exclusive review team - Thank you for dropping everything to read my books when I throw them at you.

Mara White - Thank you for squeezing me in with such short notice. Your expertise made this book a lot better than it was when I sent it to you.

Virginia Carey — Thank you for proofreading this. Twice. LOL

Mia Asher, Tarryn Fisher, Willow Aster, J. Sterling, Corinne Michaels, RS Grey, Charleigh Rose, Mara White, Karina Halle, Dina Silva, Beth Ehmann, SL Jennings, Tillie Cole, Calia Read, Penelope Ward, Vi Keeland, Leylah Attar, Mia Asher, J.M. Darhower, Ella James, Staci Hart, AL Jackson, Alessandra Torre, Lauren Blakely, Jessica Hawkins, CD Reiss, Tijan, Penny Reid, Adriana Locke, Meghan Quinn, Melanie Harlow, Kandi Steiner, Amy Daws, Jana Aston, R.K. Lilley, Brittainy B. Cherry, Lucia Franco, Liv Morris, Nana Malone, Kennedy Ryan, Carrie Ann Ryan, Julie Johnson, Rebecca Shea, Sarina Bowen, Kendall Ryan, Meghan March, J. Daniels, Julia Kent, Kayti McGee, Laurelin Paige, Susan Stoker, Rachel Van Dyken, Aly Martinez, LJ Shen, BB Easton, Sara Ney, Tara Sivec, Sierra Simone, Kristen Proby, Rebecca Donovan, Jillian Dodd, Jennifer Probst, Jay Crownover, (I know I missed a TON, which is why I don't do this shit anymore lol) - I'm humbled and honored to be on this ride with you. You inspire me so much.

Abraham & Moses - You're too young to read my books. I'm not sure you'll ever read them at all, but I want to thank you first - for understanding that my work hours aren't the same as your friend's parents, for cheering me on and telling me I'm the best author in the world without having read a word I've written, for loving me in spite of my flaws. I love you more than anything in the entire world.

Christian — I love you. Thank you for always taking care of us and being the hottest personal chef I'll ever have.

ALSO BY CLAIRE CONTRERAS

Also in Kindle Unlimited:

Kaleidoscope Hearts - brother's best friend romance

Paper Hearts - ultimate second-chance romance

Elastic Hearts - forbidden second-chance romance

Complete Hearts Series - all three bundled up in one

———

Prefer a standalone?

The Player - sports romance (Kindle Unlimited)

The Wilde One - music industry romance (Kindle Unlimited)

———

Want a little suspense with your romance?

There is No Light in Darkness - a little mystery, a lot of love.